Geoffrey Peppiatt is a former scientist and physics teacher. Apart from his family, his interests are playing squash, writing, reading and book collecting. With his wife, June, and cat, Marlowe (aka Bear), he splits his time between New York and Pennsylvania.

Geoffrey Peppiatt

PRETTY EYES

An Agnes Trout Mystery

Austin Macauley Publishers™
London • Cambridge • New York • Sharjah

Copyright © Geoffrey Peppiatt (2020)

The right of Geoffrey Peppiatt to be identified as author of this work has been asserted by the author in accordance with section 77 and 78 of the Copyright, Designs and Patents Act 1988.

All rights reserved. No part of this publication may be reproduced, stored in a retrieval system, or transmitted in any form or by any means, electronic, mechanical, photocopying, recording, or otherwise, without the prior permission of the publishers.

Any person who commits any unauthorised act in relation to this publication may be liable to criminal prosecution and civil claims for damages.

This is a work of fiction. Names, characters, businesses, places, events, locales, and incidents are either the products of the author's imagination or used in a fictitious manner. Any resemblance to actual persons, living or dead, or actual events is purely coincidental.

A CIP catalogue record for this title is available from the British Library.

ISBN 9781528915007 (Paperback)
ISBN 9781528915014 (Hardback)
ISBN 9781528961073 (ePub e-book)

www.austinmacauley.com

First Published (2020)
Austin Macauley Publishers Ltd
25 Canada Square
Canary Wharf
London
E14 5LQ

A huge and grateful thanks to my wife, June, and son, Jonah, for their advice, encouragement and boundless technical knowledge.

Chapter 1

Agnes Trout, Aggie to her friends, woke up with a start at 5:03 am. Sweat ran down her neck into the small of her back and she ran her thumb across her forehead to sweep away more moisture. A sound in her modest one-bedroom New York apartment had penetrated her dreams. It was a sound that had legs and caused her body to hit high alert and her brain to focus immediately. Through the semi-darkness she was aware of, rather than saw, a presence by the window to the fire escape. Someone was crouching there. She just had time to catch the faint glint of a knife blade as the figure lunged towards her bed in silent, grim determination. She instinctively threw the bed covers towards the intruder, gaining fractions of a second as she leapt to her feet, and allowed her martial arts training to galvanize her into action. A high kick from her left leg slammed an ankle against the attacker's ear, causing an annoyed grunt, but when her right elbow squelched into an eye, the reward was a satisfying squeal of pain. Almost disdainfully, Aggie chopped sharply downwards with the side of her hand on the back of the exposed neck, causing a faint gasp of air and the rustle of clothing and soft bumping sounds, as the attacker folded down to the carpeting amid the sheets and covers. She blew out two loud puffs of air and reached for the light.

The room took on a rose-colored tint as her custom lighting bathed the scene. Aggie bent over the inert form, taking in the thinning, greasy black hair, stubble, pale features and blood from an eyebrow gash, as well as from a right hand, which had been cut through a rubber glove by a nasty looking blade. She checked the pulse, not really caring about his condition but he was breathing normally, a bubble of mucous hovering at one nostril.

Aggie only took a moment to decide on calling her friend and occasional lover, Detective Jack Coletti of the New York PD.

She dialed but it went straight to message as she realized that it was early morning. She left a short message stating that there was an unconscious man in her bedroom and that she needed help. Aggie turned to the wall and took stock of herself in the mirror. She was around 5'6", had spiky brown hair, and lightly muscled, toned arms, a bit like that Australian tennis player. She wore a tiny stud in the side of her nostril and one in the lobe of her ear. A strong nose, dark brown eyes, full lips and a faint tan completed the picture. She thought that she looked more than a little shocked. There was not much doubt about that.

The intensity and impact of the circumstances were just beginning to settle over her consciousness like an invisible mist. She had, perhaps, been close to death. Was it random?

Did this guy know her? Was the fact that she was a PI, a factor? She turned away and looked down at the inert form, wondering if she would deliver another blow if he stirred. She hoped that it wouldn't come to that. She was beginning to feel real anger now and, on second thoughts, she decided that she would quite easily deliver that blow – maybe two. As thoughts began to buzz through her head, her cell coughed out the first chords of the Stone's 'It's All Over Now'. She grabbed it, saw that it was Jack and, with gasp of relief, answered it.

Jack said, "Hey Ag, who's the lucky guy?"

She said, "This is not funny. Some guy tried to kill me. Broke in and came at me with a knife."

"Ah, not so lucky then. What did you do to him?"

"Took care of him. What do I do now?"

"Is he awake? What's he doing?"

"He's asleep but I don't know for how long."

"OK, I'll be right over with one of my guys and an ambulance. Sit tight. I'll be about ten minutes. If he shows signs of life, tie him up."

"Thanks, see you soon."

They hung up.

Aggie changed out of her shorts and carefully torn tee shirt, putting on a light blue vest and jeans while remaining barefooted. Seven minutes later, the apartment buzzer went off and Aggie left the bedroom and crossed over the living area to buzz the front door. Moments later, Jack was at the door as she opened it. He stepped into the room and hugged her tightly. He was followed by another detective whom she knew vaguely as Moody. His name was uniquely suited to his demeanor.

As they broke apart, Jack said, "What have we got, Ag?"

Aggie said, "In there."

Jack, tall and rangy, walked to the bedroom, followed by Moody and Aggie. He bent over the prostrate form and checked the neck pulse.

He said, "Alive, but not too happy. That's quite a gash. You?"

She said, "Yes. He deserved every bit of it."

Moody said, "That's a Fällkniven hunting knife," indicating the knife lying partially hidden by a hand in a small pool of blood.

Jack looked at Moody with a question in his eyes.

Moody, a large, bulky, impassive presence, said, "I recognize it…plus, it's written on the blade."

He put on some rubber gloves and carefully slipped the knife into a plastic bag. He put the bag into an inside pocket of his jacket. Just then, loud footsteps near the apartment door indicated the arrival of a medical team.

Jack called out from the bedroom doorway, "In here."

Two medical attendants moved into the bedroom and squatted next to the intruder, checking his vitals. One of them cracked a phial and waved it near the man's nose, causing him to make choking and coughing noises as he returned to consciousness. His eyes widened as he took in the situation and his predicament.

Jack addressed the attendants, "Can we put him in a holding cell or does he have to go to the hospital?"

One attendant, who had carefully removed the glove from the cut hand, replied, "Might need stitches for the hand, otherwise he's OK."

Greasy hair spoke for the first time, "I'm not OK, my head's killing me."

Aggie said, "Good."

Jack turned to Moody, "Cuff him and get him to a cell. Do you need help?"

Moody said, "Two's better than one."

He bent down, turned the attacker over and cuffed him rather roughly. After some thought Jack said, "OK, I'm coming with you. Ag, can you come in when you're ready and make a statement. There have been other assaults and we don't know if your—sorry—this guy, is involved. There may be a connection. No way of knowing right now."

Aggie was beginning to feel shaky. Jack noticed and said, "Are you alright? Better sit down."

He led Aggie to a couch and sat with her. Moody hauled greasy hair to his feet where he stood with drooping shoulders. Then he half walked, half dragged him, through to the living area.

Jack watched in silence and then turned to Aggie and said, "Shall I call someone to sit with you for a bit?"

"Thanks, but I'll be OK. It's just dawning on me—what happened."

Jack put an arm around her shoulders and patted her back. He looked up to the medical team and said, "Thanks guys, if you could wrap the hand and do something to the eye, we'll take it from here. Could you drop a brief summary into my office later today?"

"Will do," said the spokesman and they took care of the damage, a little awkwardly because of the cuffs, and left.

Jack stood up and then stooped and kissed Aggie's hair lightly.

He said, "If you want, I'll come and pick you up later to come in and make the statement."

Aggie said, "No, thanks, I need time alone. I'll call when I'm on my way."

Moody was standing near the door with greasy hair, who had been watching, staring intently at Aggie.

"Fuck you," he said, "I'm in a lot of pain."

Moody kicked him on the shin, hard.

"Shut up," he said.

Greasy hair did, wincing in pain.

Jack gently touched Aggie on the shoulder and then headed for the door.

He said, "Let's go," and, while directing a withering stare at greasy hair, said to him, "question time. You're in a pile of shit."

There was no reply as Moody steered him out of the apartment and they set off, tramping loudly down the stairs. Aggie stood up, went over and closed the door, leaned against it and closed her eyes. She felt drained and exhausted. Moments later, she headed for the bathroom and ran a hot bath. Then she went to the kitchen and, in spite of the time of day, poured herself a generous helping of Californian Chardonnay and took it to the bathroom. In seconds, she had stripped off and settled into her bath, occasionally sipping the wine.

Chapter 2

Aggie climbed slowly out of the now cold water in which she had fallen asleep, and hopped into the shower. She washed her hair in very hot water, soaped her body and rinsed off, before stepping out of the shower and onto the few square feet beyond the porcelain that allowed the space to be called a brownstone bathroom. She toweled off and slipped into a white Egyptian cotton robe and began to allow the events of a couple of hours ago seep back into her consciousness. The questions that had originally assailed her mind were still wholly relevant and, she thought, perceptive.

Why had she been attacked? Was it random, just unlucky? Or, had she been targeted? If so, what was the reason? She is a successful licensed PI and had pissed off quite a few people over the last six years. Could this attack be related to a case? People had been killed for less.

Questions continued to bubble up and there were no real answers. She had been threatened before, both verbally and physically but she was tough and the reasons were mostly obvious or known and out in the open. This was different. It had been a malicious and motivated assault with the intent, perhaps, of achieving her demise. This was frightening. It's nature and the lack of warning made it more so. She hoped that Jack was getting some answers. She checked her watch which had been left on the coffee table. She hated clocks in general but, as a concession to her job, she kept a watch, an old Timex. She saw that life in her part of the planet was approaching mid-day which meant that a snack, or, maybe more than a snack because she was hungry, together with a trip to the precinct, seemed a good plan. She found a box of pre-cooked bacon, which she heated in the microwave, toasted some fairly recently bought 12 grain bread and made up a couple of decent sandwiches which she ate reflectively while on a kitchen stool. Bacon, she recalled, was the item that had dragged her back from a two-year foray into vegetarianism in her early twenties. Who can live without bacon? She squeezed half a lemon into a bottle of Fiji water and drank deeply. With a reluctant sigh, she went into the bedroom, now forever sullied; well, perhaps not forever but a long time, anyway. She ignored the mess on the floor, thinking that a clean up could come later and gathered some clothing from the closet which was not too well stocked, fashion not being her thing, and deposited them on the couch in the living room.

She quickly donned black jeans, a black vest, a black fake leather jacket, dark socks and dark grey sneakers. A thin silver chain hung outside of her vest. With a shake of her head and a few finger combs, she felt ready for the rest of the day ahead. It felt as though two days had passed since she went to bed the night before. She grabbed her shoulder bag, keys and phone, slammed the door and headed down the stairs. Her wheels were a recently acquired eight-year-old BMW Z4 Roadster, bought through a friend and which was pushing 100K miles on the clock; but today called for a hassle-free cab ride. She hailed a taxi and headed for the precinct, texting Jack as she went.

The precinct was a four story, minimalist affair of glass and steel with a light blue panel under every window. As Aggie passed through the revolving doors, she caught sight of Jack talking to a guy in uniform who was standing at a desk/high counter structure which was the first point of contact on entering the building. He was surrounded by files and paperwork and they were both peering into a computer. As Aggie walked towards them, they both looked up and Jack detached himself and met her in a step or two. They embraced lightly and quickly before Jack said,

"Hey Ag, how're you managing?"

She said, "Well enough, I'm OK. You got anything?"

Jack said, "Not much. Come with me and we can talk."

Aggie followed Jack through a pair of battered swing doors that squealed alarmingly as they opened and closed, down a short, paint chipped hallway, lined with cork boards and framed anonymous photographs, to a room labeled conference room. Two letters were missing from conference. They entered the room which was empty. It was carpeted which struck Aggie as incongruous, given what she had seen so far, and the windows were draped. It felt stuffy and slightly oppressive. They sat at a long table which was surrounded by many chairs, some mismatched, and facing a screen and two whiteboards.

Jack said, "Would you like some water?" A cooler stood in one corner.

To her surprise she heard herself say, "Yes please."

Jack complied and came over with two paper cups of water.

He said, "OK, the knife and the guy's clothes are at the lab. It'll be a day or two before we get results, and that's pushing it. High priority for us but not upstairs. We are trying to find out where the knife came from, using a photo of your guy but the knife is fairly common and that doesn't look very promising."

Aggie said, "He's not my guy."

Jack said, "Sorry but we don't have a name. Moody has had a shot at him but he's clammed up; won't answer anything. Moody's good but even he can't get him to talk. We're following procedure but the guy hasn't even asked for a lawyer. When we get forensics, we should be able to get him to talk, especially if he is in the database. We'll have a name and all that goes with it."

Aggie said, "What about his possessions? No wallet or anything?"

Jack said, "All he had was a key. A car key. A Toyota car key. We are searching around your block for a radius of three or four blocks in the hopes of finding the car. That's assuming that he did not want to walk far after…after attacking you."

"Killing me you mean."

"Alright, killing you, maybe. It could have been a sexual attack."

Aggie said, "Not if you saw the way he came at me!"

Jack uttered a long, drawn out, "OK."

He continued, "Then, if we find the car, we might get something out of it. It's likely to be a stolen car but you never know. If not, we'll still have a lot of info to go on."

Aggie said nothing. She just stared into her cup, reflectively.

Jack said, "Are you OK?"

Aggie said, "No, I can't say that I am. Someone wants me dead, or out of the way. Or, this guy is a crazy or, someone put him up to it. Any other choices? I don't like those."

"Look, at least we've got him."

"So, end of story? I don't think so! Fuck, maybe someone else will try now, maybe with a bit more subtlety."

"More subtlety?"

"Yes. You know, an accident or something."

Jack said, "Agh, this is getting a little out of hand. We don't know anything yet. This guy could be a one-off and done."

"Or not."

Jack's blue eyes crinkled momentarily before his face took on a serious expression.

He said, "You could stay with me for a couple of days until this gets resolved."

"I could. We could both be attacked then."

"I'm serious. You would be much safer."

Aggie smiled her resistance.

"Nice as that sounds, I'll be OK. I can deal with it."

Jack sighed.

"OK. If that's what you want."

"I'll manage. Besides, I've got a new case."

"When did you get that?"

"Phone message today, a missing person, urgent. That's all I know."

Jack said, "A little odd, don't you think? Coincidence?"

Aggie said, "I think it is. Much too obvious otherwise."

Jack looked concerned and said, "Drop it. You can afford it. Keep a low profile for a week or two."

"No, I'll watch out. It'll keep me busy. Ninety percent of these cases finish quickly."

"OK, text me names and places you are going. I need to know."

"You're worried about me Jack. How nice!"

Jack said, "I am. Indulge me."

Aggie said, "OK I'll think about it. What about this statement?"

Over the next half hour, Aggie wrote out her statement, feeling that there was not much to say. It had been a somewhat traumatic experience but did not seem to amount to much on a sheet of paper. She signed it and gave it to Jack who accompanied her back out to the lobby.

Chapter 3

Aggie left after hugging Jack and thanking him. She headed out into the streaky light indicating, to her surprise, the day was passing quickly. She felt as if she had gone for a week without sleep. She took a cab, telling herself once again that she deserved it, and was soon climbing the stairs to her apartment. She let herself in quietly, tossed her bag and jacket onto the couch and kicked off her shoes. Her lacquered toenails glistened in the half light as she wriggled her toes. The air smelled stuffy, stale and even sweaty and so she opened the only living room window and turned on all the lights. Looking around she felt a strong sense of violation and began a methodical clean up along with occasional spritzing from an old Lysol canister. Soon, the living room began to feel normal or, at least, approaching normal which seemed inversely related to her tiredness. The bedroom looked a mess and needed work; she began by gathering up the duvet and tossing it onto the bed. Next, she picked up a bloodstained sheet, along with a small favorite carpet with the picture of a sleeping polar bear that had been ruined by more bloodstains, and thrust them into a black garbage bag for disposal. She cleaned the wooden parquet floor but resisted using polish because she had once fallen heavily after slipping on a similar polished floor while wearing socks. She put a bottom sheet, duvet cover, pillow cases and mattress pad into the washer and switched it on. It barely managed the load but eventually struggled into life. Aggie checked the window which exhibited scratches and a few scuff marks on the sill, all of which she cleaned meticulously. There was nothing else to see. Nothing on the fire escape. The window had been uncommonly free to movement which had been a blessing but now she had to consider locks and bars which was completely alien to her way of thinking. For the time being the window would just have to be locked in position. She also closed and locked the living room window but left all of the lights on. At last, she started to feel much better.

Next on the agenda will be to call the client and then to take another bath, because it felt good.

Aggie returned the call from her cell and after four rings it went to message.

'Katherine is away from her phone. Leave a message.'

Aggie put in a returning your call shot in a slightly irritated tone, really because she felt irritated, although, as far as she knew, Katherine had nothing to do with her feelings.

She headed for the bath with a glass of Shiraz which was a bit heavy but she felt like it. Thirty minutes later, as she was toweling down, her cell began its

Stones chant. She pulled on her robe and unhurriedly picked up her cell, recognizing the client number as she did so.

She clicked it on, decided to be minimal.

She said, "Agnes Trout."

The caller said, "Katherine Toomey. I called about a job. Finding someone actually. Are you available and can we talk?"

"We are talking."

"Right, well, can we meet?"

"I am available but I need to know more. Who's missing?"

"I'd rather this was face to face. You can always say no. This is urgent, as I think I said before."

Aggie was silent. This felt rushed.

The caller said, "I pay well."

Aggie said, "It's not money. I'm feeling pressure. I'm thinking of saying no."

"OK, I'm sorry. I'm just anxious and need help quickly. Can we meet?" she repeated, "and I'll explain."

"When?"

"Now. If it's too late, early tomorrow."

"Tomorrow at 8 am then."

She took down the address and said, "Goodbye," to Katherine's curt "See you then."

Aggie tossed the cell onto the couch, went back to the bathroom, finished drying off, trimmed her nails, replenished the black nail polish and went back to the bedroom. She put on baggy pyjamas and a sweat top.

Time for Chinese food, some reflection and some research.

She ordered out and soon was gulping hot and sour soup and eating creaky chicken which was tasty, quick and easy.

Satisfied, she thought about what to do next.

More wine, feet up and some Googling on her iPad.

There were three viable Katherine Toomeys.

Katherine Toomey #1 is a breakout American actress, born in 1985, lucky to be 5'10" in height and had appeared in an HBO series. Her father was a more than recognizable soap star…

Katherine Toomey #2 was born in 1954, is a naturopath and sometime guru or teacher with a reputation for promoting alternative medicine. There was no mention of any research or book writing. She came from a wealthy family whose money appeared to come from her father's side. He ran a hedge fund and had become an enthusiastic philanthropist in his eighties retirement years.

Katherine Toomey #3 is a dermatologist with an affiliation to Mt. Sinai hospital who had acquired her medical degree from the Albert Einstein college of medicine. She had eleven years in practice. There was no date of birth.

Aggie sipped her wine in a somewhat mellow mood. She could find no more useful information and was putting her money on KT#2. The only real drawback, an obvious one, was why would a woman of such substantial means choose a PI of her standing when she could probably afford a whole firm of investigators? A sensitive case maybe? Professionals were capable of keeping confidences so that seemed unlikely. Intimidation or manipulation if needed? She hoped that she had some sort of reputation that would knock that one on the head! Well, second guessing is not productive beyond a certain point. She decided to stop and find out tomorrow. She also decided to sleep on the couch with a light on in the kitchen. She was not as ready to adapt as she thought, Lysol or no Lysol.

Although she had been a little restless, Aggie felt as though she had had a reasonable few hours' sleep. She remembered no dreams. After coffee and buttered toast the next morning at 7 am, Aggie contemplated her next moves. She texted Jack, against her better judgement because she felt that she was surrendering some of her independence, with just the name and the address and the fact that she was headed there this morning. She cast aside the idea of being late on purpose and left enough time to make it with five minutes to spare. She wore the same clothes as on the previous day. The address was of a decent building off Park Avenue at 83rd street. It wasn't flashy, did not look unduly extravagant and had a marble floored lobby with a portly, patrician-like doorman who called up to the Toomey habitat.

The elevator was manned by a guy about her age who was dressed in a black and cream tunic with a starched collar and plain red tie.

She wondered idly where all the bow ties had gone.

As it turned out, the Toomey place was the penthouse suite and Aggie stepped out of the elevator into another small marble floored lobby. She noted the tiny camera in one of the top corners of the lobby. She rang the unpretentious doorbell. The door was opened by a tall woman with long grayish hair fashioned into a neat bob at the back of her head. She was wearing a long woolen blue green belted dress down to below her mid-calf and had a fine flimsy scarf tossed around her shoulders, barely covering a natural pearl necklace. She wore soft brown moccasins and no stockings. She had little make-up on because she didn't need it. Her skin was fine, thin and pale. She was probably over 60 years old but did not look it, elegant and assured. Aggie thought that this has to be KT#2.

The woman said in a low, slightly accented voice, "Ah, Ms. Trout." Almost a question but not quite.

Aggie said, "Ah, Ms. Toomey."

Katherine Toomey said, "Come in. I gather now that we are introduced."

Aggie did not respond.

She followed her through a small hallway littered with jardinières, flowerpots and gold framed paintings, into an extensive sitting room, dotted with cream colored armchairs and a large five-seater couch, all of which nestled on a gigantic Persian rug. The surrounding floor was of polished wood. The white marble fireplace flickered with fake flames which, nevertheless, added some atmosphere to the room. The one anomaly in the room, as far as Aggie was concerned, was an antique wooden commode, just sitting by the side of an archway which appeared to lead to another hallway. All Aggie could see was sunlight reflecting off the chrome frames of an array of pictures. One wall in the room was almost entirely glazed and Aggie caught sight of the rooftops of surrounding buildings. She walked over and looked down on city life from the top of the heap.

Katherine Toomey said, "It's a nice view. It gives one perspective."

Aggie thought it could certainly do that.

She said, "Yes, it would be hard not to get perspective from here, wouldn't it?"

Katherine Toomey indicated that Aggie sit on the couch, which she did, while her host settled into an armchair.

She said, "I have money, there's nothing that I need, I live well and I enjoy a certain amount of social clout. I can get things done if I need to. Money is not everything but it does remove a lot of stress from one's daily existence."

Aggie said, "I can imagine. What stress are you thinking of pushing my way?"

Katherine Toomey said, "That's an odd way of looking at it. I'm offering you some business and I'm willing to pay well for your services. Before we get there, would you like some tea or water?"

Aggie said, "No thanks. What is the business? I can tell you then if I am interested."

Katherine Toomey said, "OK, well I hope that you are interested. In fact, I am counting on it." Before Aggie could respond she said, "Hear me out. My immediate family is my father, who lives in North Carolina, my daughter who lives in Vermont and my son, who lives here, in New York. I have two grandchildren through my daughter. My son is not married. He is the one who is missing."

Aggie said, "How do you know he's missing?"

"I call him every two or three weeks. His phone has gone to message the last two times."

Aggie took out her notebook and a pen and jotted down some notes. This was reasonably productive but, more importantly, it gave her time to think.

"Is it a cell?"

"Yes."

"He could have lost it."

"His home phone does not pick up either."

"Any friends that can check on him for you?"

"He isn't the friendly type."

"He lives on his own?"

"Don't many of us?"

"I'm just asking. I need to get a feel for things."

"OK. Yes, he lives on his own. He has a two-bedroom apartment."

"Have you contacted the police?"

"No."

"Why not?"

"They move very slowly and tend not to believe there is a problem. I want action as soon as possible."

Aggie did not respond. As soon as possible seemed a little obsolete at this point.

After a pause, she said, "What does your son do?"

"Not a lot. He works from home. He writes articles for a gaming magazine. He has had a couple of minor games accepted by a gaming company."

"That's his job? He's not really employed?"

"Is something wrong with that?"

"No, but he has no regular employment?"

With an impatient sigh, Katherine Toomey said, "He's freelance." She paused and said, "Well, he doesn't need to work much. He does it because he likes it."

"He has independent means then? I mean, how does he pay for his apartment?"

"My father subsidizes him. The apartment was a gift from my father." Katherine Toomey grimaced in an ugly way with her mouth which turned down at the ends. She glanced towards the windows and drew her eyes back again to Aggie. "He also gives my son an allowance every three months."

Aggie said, "You don't like that?"

"It's not like or dislike. I don't approve. It doesn't help him to stand on his own two feet. That's a nice cliché for you."

Aggie ignored the comment. She said, "When did your father last speak to your son? I take it that the allowances are paid electronically with no real discourse."

"I don't know for certain but about two months ago."

Aggie said, "What was the reason? What did they talk about?"

"I have no idea. I was sort of aware there was a contact but that's all I know."

Katherine Toomey sounded flat, emotionless, matter of fact.

Aggie sucked in some air and said, "Ms. Toomey, you don't seem very concerned."

Katherine Toomey's eyes flickered across Aggie's face in a flash of irritation but without any other expression.

She said, "I'm tired. My feelings are internalized."

"But this is your son. You could have gone to his apartment and checked on him."

"He is an adult. I've never been to his apartment, and, nor do I want to go there. He has his own life to lead. I am very concerned about him because I think he is missing. I can't interfere when I am not wanted but this is different." As an afterthought she said, "When I am wanted it is usually for money."

"Are your calls unwanted?"

"What do you mean?"

"What do you talk about? How long do you talk?"

"That's not important. Family stuff."

"Is there a problem between members of the family? Your son and daughter for instance?"

"That is irrelevant."

"I'm just putting together what I can. I need substance. I need material, background. I need all that I can get."

Katherine Toomey's gray eyes hardened and she said, "I said that is irrelevant. It has no bearing on this case. It's just normal family stuff."

Aggie again let it go and made no comment but she continued to jot down notes in her notebook.

"Does your son go out? I mean, does he leave the apartment, go out for dinner, movies?"

"How do I know? As I believe I have just said or indicated, he is a grown man. He likes auctions, goes to the gym. That sort of thing. He is not a recluse."

"No girlfriends?"

"There have been girlfriends."

"How many?" Aggie was pushing a bit but was curious.

"I don't know. One or two a year perhaps. Nothing serious."

"Just girlfriends?"

Katherine Toomey leaned forward in her chair, uncomfortably tense. Whether it was all of the questions or this one Aggie had no idea.

"What do you mean?"

"Any boyfriends?"

"He is not gay. What difference does it make?"

"None at all. I'm just finding out as much as I can. Anything could help. It really doesn't help if you are defensive or even hostile. Believe me, this is only the beginning."

"I don't like personal questions."

"Most of us don't. But, if you want me to go ahead, it could get very personal."

"I do want you to go ahead. Keep it to a minimum is what I'm asking."

"You said that you have made calls. When was the last time that you actually spoke to your son?"

"About five or six weeks ago."

"That is a very long time in terms of a missing person. I mean, if you have heard nothing for all of that time, he is truly missing or just doesn't want to talk to you. You should have asked the police to check the apartment. He could be ill or even dead."

"I'll do that after we have finished and call you as soon as I know something."

Aggie was getting some distant vibes about all of this. It was beginning to not hang together. She pressed on.

"Have you checked with your daughter, to see if she has heard from him?"

"I called her this week. No contact. My father and my daughter are not regular callers like me."

Aggie returned to an earlier theme. "Does everyone get along in your family?"

"My son and daughter basically keep to themselves."

"What does that mean?"

"It means that they talk when they have to."

Aggie said nothing. She thought that this line of questioning was not going to be fruitful. Change of direction.

"Did your son graduate college?"

"Yes. A degree in Sociology or English, I think. He went no further."

"You don't know what his degree was?"

"Does it matter? It has slipped my mind, that's all."

Aggie let it go. She might need to look at some of this again later.

She said, "Your father, he must have done well financially to be able to help your son all of this time."

Katherine Toomey seemed relieved.

"Yes, he has third generation family money. He also discovered that he had considerable natural financial talent and he made the most of it. He was very successful. He gives a lot away these days. Sometimes, I think that it alleviates some sort of guilt that he labors under. I think he feels guilty that he is wealthy." She paused and said, "I can't see it myself. I certainly don't feel it."

Aggie made no comment.

After a pause, she said, "OK, let's look at what we have. I'm getting the beginnings of a background but, the bottom line is that we have your son, who lives and works alone, who does not seem to go out much, who doesn't need to work but plays around with gaming, while having any financial gaps in his life filled by his grandfather and his mother and who has not been heard from for about two months. You are going to contact the local police as soon as possible. That should have been obvious from the start. We need to know if he is home or hasn't been home for whatever time. That's the first thing to do."

Katherine Toomey said, "I said I would do that. I can get an answer by the end of the day."

"Then we will have a starting point."

Aggie was intrigued, in spite of herself. Somewhere in her head there was a warning floating about, that this case was odd, didn't gel, was perhaps dangerous, although, danger had never stopped her before. She had the feeling that the timing of the phone call to take a case being so proximate to her attack just felt off somewhere. And yet, there was not even a remote connection that she could see. She had, though, learned to trust her gut feelings. She suddenly realized that she was going to take the case. Also, she was ninety-nine percent sure that this woman in front of her was KT#2.

She would confirm this in a few moments but first, she said, "Ms. Toomey, I am interested in taking this case. I have to tell you that there are a few final questions to ask you today. Plus, there are the terms under which I wish to operate. But, before all of that, I have two or three points to raise."

Aggie saw relief in this woman's face and a fleeting shot of what looked like triumph as well. That was a bit disturbing. She hoped that was wrong.

Aggie said, "First, you do, in spite of what you claim, seem to be unconcerned about your son and I wonder why. On the face of it, anyway, you do not seem close to him. Do you realize that in this whole conversation you have not used your son's name? I don't know what it is."

Katherine Toomey looked shocked, surprised and irritated at the same time.

She opened her mouth but Aggie said, "Let me finish."

"Second, you are a well-off family to put it mildly. You could hire a company of investigators. Why choose me? And, what was the real reason for not pulling in the police before now?"

There were a few seconds of silence as the two women looked at each other. Katherine Toomey, with some effort, asked again if Aggie would like a drink of water. The anti-climax felt momentous to Aggie. She knew that the woman across from her was gathering her thoughts.

Aggie said, "No thank you," and waited.

Chapter 4

The eyes that caught Aggie's were hard and cold and she knew instinctively that Katherine Toomey was not an emotional person, probably never had been. Personal warmth, empathy, a caring nature, all of those attributes that add up to a decent person were missing. The husky, almost expressionless voice began.

"You are partially correct in some of what you say. I lost the capacity for love a long time ago. Maybe I never had it, I really don't care anymore. I put up with my family, they are just there, nothing I can do about it. My daughter has reasonable personal qualities and I respect her as a person. She made a poor choice of husband. He's just a sponger with nothing to recommend him. I don't like him. My son has no inclination to do any real work or to do anything that makes his life worthwhile. I could go on but, what's the point? You get the picture and, anyway, it's none of your business and it won't help you."

A few dozen words in a dispassionate voice had washed over Aggie and left her momentarily short of a response. She mustered her thoughts and produced a reasonable sentence.

"That was extraordinarily frank Ms. Toomey. I do appreciate your candor. It leaves me with just a few more questions, if you don't mind, about you and about where I fit in."

"About me?"

Katherine Toomey grimaced again. It really was an unattractive facial expression, Aggie thought.

"I was thinking that we were about done here, so be quick."

Aggie overcame a rush of intellectual abhorrence, tinged with pity for this woman and drew some threads together in her mind. Katherine Toomey had no shred of maternal instinct and clearly didn't like anybody except herself. Aggie opened with, "Do you work? I mean, do you have a job or, perhaps, get involved in philanthropy?"

"What do you mean?"

"I'm looking at connections. Maybe someone you know could be involved in the possible disappearance of your son."

"Possible?"

"Until we have more information, yes."

"Douglas."

"Douglas?"

"That's his name. And it's obvious that he's missing."

Aggie didn't respond. After a pause she repeated herself. "Do you work, charitable or otherwise?"

Katherine Toomey leaned forward in her chair.

"I am a staunch supporter of alternative medicine. People pump themselves full of drugs and chemicals at every opportunity for every silly reason. There are natural solutions to many illnesses which are more than adequate and prevent people from poisoning themselves."

Aggie thought this a little contradictory. Caring about others, albeit from a lofty perspective.

"Is this about drug companies? Could you have upset anyone?"

"Of course not."

"Have you published anything on the subject?"

Katherine Toomey's eyes hardened again. She said, "That's enough about me. My son is the one who is missing."

Aggie said, "I just thought that, say, published works perhaps critical of drug companies might be relevant."

Katherine Toomey said, "There are no critical papers."

Aggie said, "Do you teach or lecture on this?"

"I give occasional talks. Can we move on."

Aggie paused. She wondered how someone gets to pontificate on a subject with authority but no academic background. Contacts, or just plain BS perhaps.

She said, "Why do you want to hire me? As opposed to someone else, that is?"

"I'd heard about you. I didn't want some high-powered company, or the police, poking about in my affairs. I want subtlety and discretion. That's you."

Aggie wondered how she'd been heard of; they moved in entirely different worlds. What were the odds? She refrained from asking.

She said, "OK fair enough. My terms are a flat fee up front plus expenses with further negotiable fees every two weeks, as the investigation progresses, or not."

Katherine Toomey got up without a word and crossed the room to a small Victorian desk in the corner and produced a check book. Within minutes, Aggie had a check and was beginning to wonder what she had got herself into.

For years, Aggie had enjoyed the escapism of watching top tennis players displaying their enviable skills, many of them elegant and graceful. In the end though, she could not avoid the fact that there was a group of people, made up of coaches, trainers, psychologists, who watched over every top player. They were literally watching their present and future as their meal ticket performed. Failure could mean changes, and no meal ticket. Aggie found it difficult to suppress this rampant cynicism and simply enjoy the sport. There were many similar scenarios in other walks of life and, ultimately, it meant that she had to work for herself, had to be independent, had to rely on no one. She didn't advertise. Her work came by word of mouth. She had tried several systems of receiving payment. By the hour didn't seem to work because it was too labor intensive. Basically now, she assessed the job, assessed the client beforehand, if possible, and charged a flat fee plus expenses. Six years in, this still worked.

Aggie said, "Thank you. One last thing. Can you give me your son's address?"

She could not, for some reason, use his name, behaving exactly like the woman before her.

"Why?"

"I'd like to see where it is, talk to a neighbor or two."

"I suppose so. You'd look it up anyway."

Katherine Toomey went back to the small desk, took out a box of notepaper, selected a sheet and scribbled on it. She returned to Aggie and handed over the paper after folding it.

She said, with an unfriendly note in her voice, "I'll see you out. Of course, I need not contact the police if you are going there."

As Aggie reversed her path through the building, she pondered her next moves and when the outside air hit her, she breathed deeply and began to shake off the feelings of oppression and some misgiving that clung to her. It was unlike her to feel anything like intimidated but this experience had been disturbing and had prodded her sense of self preservation. She decided to put off checking in with Jack in favor of a quick trip to the address that she had been given by Katherine Toomey.

She grabbed a cab which smelled strongly of cooked meat and sweat and finally emerged gratefully at the address, which was on Ninth avenue and was in a relatively new, small apartment block squeezed in between a row of walk ups.

She glanced at the buzzers and saw that Douglas Toomey lived on the second floor. The building was so small that each floor looked like a single apartment. She pressed the buzzer marked 'Superintendent' and, to her surprise, was quickly buzzed in. In the hallway, a man in jeans and an Irish Magee Grandfather shirt with iron gray stubble for hair and watery blue eyes approached her from a doorway down the hall. The blue eyes ran briefly over her with an air of slight disapproval and a guttural voice said, "What can I do for you young lady?"

Aggie said, "I am a private investigator hired to determine the whereabouts of Douglas Toomey. He is a tenant here."

"That's right. Second floor."

"Is he in?"

"Don't know. I haven't seen him for a bit."

"Can you let me into his apartment to check if all is OK?"

"I don't know you. I couldn't do that."

"Can you check then? I'll wait outside."

"I can't just go into someone's apartment without a good reason."

"I'm a good reason. He hasn't been seen for some time now."

"Who are you working for?"

"His mother."

"Can't she come and check?"

"She's asked me to do that."

"Where's your ID? And, while you're at it, proof that you have been asked to come here."

Aggie showed her ID and, at the same time, remembered the scribbled address. It was written on Katherine Toomey embossed paper. She handed it over. That had a positive effect on the watery blue eyes.

"OK, just a moment."

The super went back down the hall to his apartment and returned with a bunch of keys. They trudged up the staircase to the second floor. No elevators here. On the second floor, they walked along a narrow landing that was thinly carpeted to a door at the end next to a staircase continuing upwards.

The door was shiny black with a peephole, two large locks and a bell push. The super pressed the bell push and waited as a double note sounded in the apartment. He tried twice more with no response.

He said, "OK, you stay here and I'll go in."

He unlocked the door with some difficulty and some large sighs, opened it, entered and pushed it to from the inside. Aggie glimpsed some dark green furniture—a couch, an armchair and that was all. She waited impatiently and considered pushing the door open but decided not to. Two minutes later, the door opened and the super came out, closed the door and locked both locks, sealing the apartment.

He said, "Nobody home."

Aggie said, "Any lights on, curtains drawn?"

The super began to walk along the landing.

He said, "No."

"You checked all the rooms?"

"Lady, there are two rooms, a living area, a kitchen and a bathroom. All were empty."

As they reached the stairs Aggie said, "What was the bedroom like?"

"What was it like?"

"Yes. Tidy? Clothes out?"

"Normal, I'd say. Bed unmade, clothes all over the place. Pile of stuff on the bedside table and a cup or two. Second bedroom had nothing in it."

"Was there anything out in the bathroom?"

"Like what? I didn't notice. Towels."

They began to descend the stairs.

"What about the kitchen?"

"Look, I don't know – dishes in the sink with water. What you'd expect."

"Any food left out?"

"I think there was a bunch of rotten bananas on the counter."

"Rotten bananas?"

"Yes, rotten bananas. In fact, they smelled a bit, of bananas."

Chapter 5

Aggie decided that she needed to regroup with a coffee. She needed to think and run through her notes. She set off, walking quickly, in a northerly direction and two blocks later, with no surprise, found a Starbucks. With a large cappuccino and a slice of lemon cake, she read through her neat but barely legible jottings from the interview and thought about her visit to Douglas Toomey's apartment. There seemed to be little to add except some minor clarification. He appeared to have been away from his apartment for a few days unless he normally left fruit to rot alongside dirty dishes and, probably, other mess which, of course, was more than likely. Some folks, many folks, lived that way. So, all she had discovered was that he had been away. It was not really possible to say for how long. His mother was indicating weeks but Aggie only had her word for that.

She realized, with some surprise, that it was late afternoon. Time to call Jack and see if anything had developed. She finished her coffee, not noticing that she had wolfed down the lemon cake and dialed up Jack's number. The phone went straight to message. Frustrated, she tried once more before deciding to head out for his office. She felt justified in hailing a cab and was soon on her way. She dialed up his number again and, this time, he answered.

"Ag, where are you?"

"On the way to you. If you are at work."

"I am. We need to talk. How about a bite to eat?"

"Just had something but that would be nice."

"See you soon then."

Aggie put her phone in her bag and sat back with a sigh. Perhaps an evening or a night with Jack was on the cards. She felt that she needed it. Sometimes, they did the friend/sex thing which worked well for both of them. Both had so many work commitments that anything stable in relationships was doomed, not that they hadn't tried. Whatever their time together was—down time, refreshment, renewal, pure sex, it was good. This time Jack was waiting outside the building and they hugged lightly.

Aggie said, "Do you have something?"

Jack said, "Long-ish story. If you've eaten, let's just get a sandwich or a salad."

They went to a familiar salad bar less than a block away, talking little and soon settled in at a quiet table. In fact, it was not at all busy. They ordered quickly as Aggie searched Jack's face which was showing barely hidden concern.

Aggie ventured, "Cheap date then?"

Jack said, "Date?"

Aggie said, "OK, not."

Jack said, "No, date sounds good, let's call it a date."

Aggie said, "Let's," and smiled. It felt good to smile.

Jack returned her smile and said, "Great, OK, down to business first. Well, let me go back a bit and take this slowly. First of all, the car. We found it four blocks from your apartment. Rented for cash under a fake name and address, not stolen. I had a guy check all that out. Fingerprints, of course, but this guy is not in any of our data bases. You'd think he would be because this cannot be his first go at this. But he is not among our twenty million finger friends. The knife is common and mostly clean with no fingerprints."

Aggie said, "But…"

"There are traces of blood on it. We have the type. It could be useful later."

"Is that it?"

"No. Now, here's the thing. We tried his photo in a Biometrics program. Facial recognition and iris scanning. It's really interesting stuff and, in the future, we will be able to…"

Aggie said a long drawn out, "Jack."

"OK, sorry. Well, we got a hit."

His blue eyes were a picture of concern.

"An ID?"

"Yep, he is one Douglas Toomey."

"What? Fuck me."

"Well, if you insist."

Aggie ignored him and said, "But I've only just been to see his mother."

Jack said, "I know. So, what's going on?"

"I don't know. Wait a minute. He attacks me and then his mother hires me before I can clean up his mess."

"Well, it's not a coincidence."

"No. It's not. But what is it? She had to know something was up."

"Yep, she knew that we had her son, and why."

"How?"

"That's a separate in-house issue. It's not good but I'll deal with it."

"Leaks?"

"Bit more than that."

Jack's expression clouded and a flash of annoyance flitted over his features.

"OK." Aggie sensed that she should stop right there with the questions. There was some resistance in her mind but she knew that stepping aside was the way to go.

"OK, she knew. She knew it was me. She hires me. No, she gets me to come over to her place to hire me. She called me. I called her and she pretty much insisted that we met."

Their sandwiches arrived. Tuna for Jack and egg salad for Aggie, together with a pot of coffee. They ate in thoughtful silence for a few minutes as they ruminated. Jack finished quickly and poured their coffee—black. That familiarity was somehow comforting for Aggie who was feeling stressed.

The events and all the possibilities and unknowns were churning in her mind and she was suddenly tired.

Jack said, "Ag? You just went away."

Aggie said, "Oh sorry. I need to sort this out."

"You look a bit worn out. Do you want to relax a bit?" Concern not lust.

"No, I want an answer. I'll go and see the mother. "

She put down her half-eaten sandwich.

Jack said, "Hold off. Let's talk first. Did she give you a retainer or pay you?"

Aggie said, "Yes, quite a lot actually. That's lost money. Not that she'd notice."

"I take it that it was a check. Did you cash it?"

"No. It didn't cross my mind."

"Is it crossing now?"

Aggie said, "I'll scan it."

She delved into her bag and came up with her smartphone and, in a few moments, the check. She scanned the check after putting in her account figures and watched as the money entered her account without a hitch.

She said, "Done. No problem."

Jack said, "OK. So, no subterfuge with that then. That's something."

Aggie said, "It doesn't smell like a payoff. She would have come straight out and told me. She's that sort of person."

Jack said, "Well, she had to know that her son would be identified, – and quickly. Plus, she probably knew that we know each other."

"Your leak?"

"Yes, my leak." He changed the subject.

"You know, she may have just been buying time. She must have done this before. That guy has too low a profile for me."

"What do you mean?"

"She needed time to think, perhaps, or needed to check you out."

Aggie drained her cup and shared out the remainder of the pot between them.

"She didn't need time I don't think. She's too used to getting her own way."

Jack nodded, "Go on."

"She was looking at her options. This episode was probably different, violent, out of control. He might be evolving and you could be right. She may have been shocked and looking for a way out. Maybe she thought that she might pay me off. Make me go away."

Jack smiled, his face creasing along laugh lines as he gave Aggie a warm glance. "No way. Not you"

Aggie responded with a half-smile. "No. That must have been pretty obvious when we met."

Jack said, "So, she still gave you money, and you accepted it."

"Yes, I did. I thought that I was being hired."

She paused a moment.

"Anyway, I found the missing person, if you can call him that, or, you did. I'm really not inclined to give it back."

She sighed deeply.

"I'm tired. Let's go to your place and sort this out tomorrow."

They rose together. Jack paid the check, which had arrived unnoticed during their conversation and he followed Aggie to the door. He lived six blocks away and they decided to walk, arm in arm, enjoying the cool evening air.

Chapter 6

Once in a while, Aggie had tried to analyze their relationship but she had backed off rather quickly each time, concerned that analysis would somehow damage that relationship. She was not, she thought, in love with Jack, although that could happen, but there was a strong, mutual bond between them, the nature of which she had not yet come to understand. Love in itself needed work, she thought. It did not just happen. Love at first sight made no sense to her as a premise. The confusion or the juxtaposition of bonding and loving had not resolved itself in her mind. For now, their relationship prospered and developed comfortably but that, in itself, she found troubling. The bottom line was that things were good so don't mess with them. People and feelings were much too complicated.

Aggie left Jack's neat, organized one-bedroom apartment in the early morning light. Knowing her well, he made a mild effort to stop her leaving but she felt that she had to go. She promised to call him before making any moves on the case and headed for her apartment.

Why did she have to leave? Maybe it was too good, too cozy, even too easy but she also knew that she wanted it to continue. There was an uncomfortable familiarity about her needing to retreat from what appeared to be commitment. However, she did feel refreshed and slightly euphoric. She was ready to take on the world or, at least, the tiny part of it containing Katherine Toomey. Aggie reached her apartment in a reflective mood. In the morning light, it seemed unwelcoming, almost unfamiliar but that feeling soon passed as she went back to remaking her bed with fresh linens and a second duvet. She ran downstairs with the garbage bags and put them in the compactor room for disposal, returned to the apartment and took the old bedclothes out of the dryer and folded them neatly before storing them in a closet. She stripped off, had a long shower and dressed in a Rocky Mountain Park tee shirt with a picture of a moose on the front and black jeans. Things were almost returning to normal although her mind was beginning to be overwhelmed with unanswered questions again.

Why was she attacked? Who was this guy in the general sense? She did not recall having seen him before. Of the four million or so females in New York, why had he chosen her? Was it random?

All this did was to make her angry and irritated. She had to do something. She had to visit Katherine Toomey and have it out with her, just to see if anything at all fell into place. She made herself toast and coffee and tried to visualize the confrontation.

Her phone broke into her thoughts as it pumped out the Stones again. She really would have to change that into something quieter and less intrusive. It had, at one time, seemed cool and independent. Now, it was just noisy. She let the phone go to message without moving or checking the number, sipping her coffee as she listened.

"Hi Ag. This is Maisie. Long time, I know, but I need to talk to you. Please call back soon. Bye."

Maisie Beck, one of her longtime girlfriends whom she had not spoken to for a year or so. The time, she thought had shot by since the two of them had had dinner with two other girlfriends, a quartet that had stayed in touch since their college days. She reached for the phone and then changed her mind. She would call later in the day, after her visit with Katherine Toomey. She left a short message for Jack as promised and because he was not picking up. Once again, she took a cab to the Toomey penthouse building. At the front desk, the doorman called up to Katherine Toomey's apartment and announced Aggie. She clearly heard Katherine Toomey's voice saying that she did not want any visitors at this point. Aggie could feel her irritation rising.

She said, "Tell her I need to talk to her. Something very serious has come up."

The doorman relayed the information and the response was a very curt, "Send her up."

Katherine Toomey was waiting at her door in the small lobby.

She said, "It's early, what do you want? We're done."

Aggie said, "We are not done."

Katherine Toomey said, "You've been paid. Go and play private investigator somewhere else."

Aggie dragged in a quick shot of air and said, "Listen, your prick of a son tried to kill me."

"You're still alive, aren't you?"

"He attacked me in my home."

"So what?" That unpleasant grimace again.

"I see, well, I have little doubt that he's done this before. He's a serial pervert."

"He's not a pervert. He's just had some issues. He's never been in trouble."

Aggie raised her voice in anger and launched an intuitive verbal volley. "He's never in trouble because you, his dear mother, keep covering for him, don't you? He's a danger to women. But, you know that."

They were still standing in the lobby hallway by the apartment door, only two feet apart. Katherine Toomey suddenly backed off a little and said, "Just leave. If you don't, I'll have you thrown out."

Aggie stared into the hard eyes and face, tight with anger. "Why did you hire me? You knew what was going on didn't you? You knew that he'd been arrested."

"Did I?"

Aggie said, "Yes, and you knew that this was worse than usual, didn't you? You didn't know what to do. You were checking me out."

"No."

"You are pathetic and so is your pervert of a son. I can't be bought and, anyway, he's going down this time. I'll do my best to see that happens."

Katherine Toomey's face assumed a menacing expression.

"Get out. Get out of here. We'll see who's pathetic."

Aggie turned and went to the elevator and pressed the button. The apartment door slammed shut as Katherine Toomey disappeared inside. Aggie took the elevator down, feeling emotionally drained. The confrontation had taken more out of her than she had expected. She passed through the lobby and out into the street and became immediately aware that someone had fallen in step alongside her. She turned and saw that he was a fairly tall man wearing a dark overcoat and an open necked white shirt. His head was shaved and his bright blue eyes with bags under them, peered out from an intelligent face. His voice was modulated and quiet. He said, "Ms. Trout I presume."

Aggie said, "Yes, who are you?"

"That's not really important right now. I wish to address a recent event in your life."

"Which one is that?"

"An altercation with a gentleman named Toomey."

She stopped walking abruptly and turned to him.

"Really? An altercation? What about it?"

"Well, in terms of your encounter with him, let's say that you have a couple of options ahead of you."

"Options?"

"Yes. Courses of action, if you like."

"And?"

"I think that, of these courses of action, one stands out as the best way to go."

Aggie stared up into the blue eyes with as much defiance as she could muster.

"Are you threatening me?"

"That's a rather harsh observation Ms. Trout. Let's say that I'm offering you advice, as one who has considerable experience in these matters."

"And what exactly would that advice be Mr....?"

He ignored the prompt.

"My advice is to forget all about our mutual acquaintance, Ms. Trout. We have busy lives, things to do, places to go shall we say. I suggest that you move on." The blue eyes softened marginally.

"Good day Ms. Trout. Enjoy it."

With that he turned and walked away.

Aggie remained standing on the same spot for a moment or two, watching her companion striding down the street. What, exactly, had just happened? She had, in fact, been threatened in a mild way. A sort of light but firm admonition. Whatever it was, it felt uncomfortable and she did not like it.

On impulse, she dialed Jack's number. His phone went to message. She didn't leave one. Apartment time. She caught a crosstown bus and, even though it was a double, there was only standing room. Feeling a little irritated and hassled, she made it back without incident and heated up the remaining cold coffee. She had taken to grinding her own beans several years ago and filtering the coffee into a glass coffee pot. The filter was sagging in the funnel but the coffee in the pot tasted good. Nothing quite like Jamaican Mountain Style Coffee with a pinch of French Italian.

She tried Jack again with the same result. She wanted to talk but, also, she hoped that there was more news, any news, about her attacker. She sipped her coffee, casting her mind over the short but eventful morning so far. Suddenly, Maisie's call drifted into her mind. She put the disturbing trend of her thoughts to one side and decided to call Maisie. Maisie picked up on the third ring.

"Hi Ag. Thanks for calling back."

She sounded weary, guarded.

"Hey Maisie. Are you OK?"

"Depends what you mean by OK."

Her friend's voice remained distant.

"Maisie. What's up?"

There was a pause and an intake of breath.

"Ag, can I ask you to do something for me as an investigator? Pay you and all that".

"You can ask but you're not paying. What's going on?"

"Look, there is a lot of catching up for us to do. Perhaps we should have dinner, a get together. We can talk then."

Aggie paused for a moment. There was obviously a problem.

"Maisie, if you called for my help, then something's wrong. Tell me. We can have dinner any time."

"OK. Well, my life is utterly normal. But, for one thing."

"What's that?"

"I think David is having an affair."

Aggie was shocked. Maisie's marriage had seemed strong to her but, who knows? "Do you know? Is it just in your head? Could it be something… sorry, I'm going off. Bit frazzled today. Look, this sounds serious. We can't go through it on the phone. How about coming to my place and I'll put something together…"

"Oh Ag, that sounds perfect. Thanks. When? I can manage the next couple of days. Even easier for lunch, if you can."

Aggie responded immediately.

"Tomorrow at 12:30 pm, if you can make it."

"Done. Thanks Ag." They rang off.

Aggie paused for a moment. Things were happening fast. For the lunch with Maisie, she thought about a quick shop for salad makings but opted for a takeout from a soup and sandwich place. She would organize that tomorrow. No fuss, quick and a bit expensive. But, expedient. Tomorrow would show up soon enough. She needed to talk to Jack.

She called again. This time Jack picked up.

"Hi Ag. Sorry, saw you'd called, couldn't get back. Two interviews and a meeting already. How did it go?"

"Not well."

Jack's voice radiated concern.

"Not well? Are you OK?"

"Yes, I'm OK. Got screamed at and threatened but I'll get over it."

"She threatened you?"

"No, she didn't. Someone else did. She just screamed at me."

"Who? Who threatened you?"

"Some guy. Maybe her fixer, I don't know. I'll tell you about it later."

"Tell me now."

"Oh Jack. I can't deal with it now."

There was a moment's silence as Jack held off on further comment.

Aggie said, "What about creepy? Anything?"

"Well, that's not good either. He's got a lawyer and will probably make bail today."

"What? How can he possibly walk? He's dangerous. What about me?"

"I know. Ag, you should stay with me until we figure out what's going on and if there is any danger. It's coming down to a he said-she said situation."

"What? That's ridiculous!"

"Well, we'll have to talk about it."

"Jack, there's nothing to talk about. He attacked me."

"Ag, I know he did but there are ways around the truth. That's what lawyers do."

"Oh Jack."

"Ag, can you come in? I can't get away right now. We need to talk about it. You need to talk about it."

"This is BS."

"I know."

"OK, OK. I'll be there in half an hour."

They finished up in the same conference room as the day before. It gave them the privacy that Jack's cubicle could not. Aggie guessed that not many meetings were going on.

Pleasantries over, she said, "How can this dickhead get out on bail or get off?"

Jack said, "Look, his story is a little different from yours. He's admitted to being at your window which was wide open. Not much he can do about that. He says that he was waiting for you to put the light on so that he could watch you doing your thing. Sort of Peeping Tom stuff."

"Waiting to kill me more like."

"Very likely. But he says that you put the light on, saw him and then dragged him in and attacked him."

"That's really stupid."

"Yes, but feasible, that's all that's needed. You are more than capable of it."

"What about the knife?"

"He needed it to protect himself. He's allowed to carry a closed knife."

"So, whether I press charges or not, he's going to get away with it, isn't he?"

"Well, there is the peeper issue, but with the clout that he has, yes, more than likely."

"Shit!"

"That describes it well."

Aggie forced a faint smile.

Jack said, "What was the warning?"

Aggie said, "A guy came up to me and, in a polite way, told me to fuck off. Sorry, he suggested that I had better things to do than go after this guy. I think it was a 'don't bother, you'll get nowhere' warning."

Jack's face tightened.

"What did he look like?"

"Tall, shaved head, worn face, well dressed, fiftyish."

"Don't think I know him. I'll ask around."

He paused, glanced around the room before returning his gaze to Aggie.

"Look, please be careful in all of this…"

As Aggie was on the point of mild protest, he continued, hands in the air.

"Just pause now and again is all I'm asking."

Aggie smiled thinly and nodded imperceptibly.

Jack added, "What's your next move going to be? I imagine you will want to press charges. Is it worth it?"

"Someone else who has been attacked might read about it and come forward."

"Not likely. This will not get much press."

Aggie looked down in thought as she rubbed the stud in her nose. "You know, I think there's more to this. The mother tries to buy me off or, at least, buys time to sus me out. Some kind of fixer gives me a warning and now there's a lawyer playing clean-up. My gut feeling is that something bigger is going on here. What, I don't know."

Jack looked at her quizzically but said nothing.

Aggie said, "I think I want to look into things."

"You mean drop it officially?"

"Well, yes but I want to nose around a bit for my own benefit."

Jack looked relieved and concerned at the same time. "OK. You mean look for other attacks, that sort of thing?"

"Yes, but more than that, take a look at the family as well."

"The family?"

"Yes. Well, I don't know. I just want to poke around in general, see what turns up."

"OK. But you have to be careful. We don't know anything about these people and Toomey is obviously dangerous, possibly a nutcase."

"You know me."

"I do, that's the problem."

"I'll be careful."

"Look, I would like to know what you're up to, you know, peace of mind and all that."

"I know."

Aggie felt touched and slightly miffed at the same time. "I'll keep you in the picture."

"Thanks. There's one other thing. I don't know how you'll feel about this."

"What?"

"Well, Toomey is being interviewed by Moody right now. I wondered if you would like to see some of it. There's a lawyer with him, of course."

"Don't know, could be interesting."

"You can get a quick look, anyway."

"OK, let's do it."

Jack stood up and Aggie followed him down the familiar hallway and up three steps at the end of it followed by a left turn to a door with one word on it amid the chipped paint. 'Silence.'

Jack opened the door and they passed through a small dark space to a second door, Jack closing the first door. Once through the second door, they entered a low-lit room which was dominated by a large window used for viewing a brightly lit interview room. Around a cheap plastic and steel table, sat three men. A fourth man stood off to one side by the entrance to the room. Aggie saw the blinking red lights of two cameras; one over the door to the room and one to her right on a bare wall. There could have been more but she did not see any. Moody sat with his back to her but her gaze centered on the two men facing her. One of them, the lawyer, was speaking. He was dressed in an immaculate blue pinstripe suit with a white shirt and pale blue tie. His hair was a wavy iron grey and his features smooth and a little ruddy. Toomey was on his right, staring down at the table where his hands were lying flat on the plastic surface. Aggie could not control the disdain she felt as she looked at the puffy, unhealthy looking, jowly face topped with floppy, greasy hair, now in some disarray with white scalp showing through. She took in the tufts of hair growing out of his ears but noted none in the nostril area.

Curious to even notice something like that.

She found herself fascinated by the scene which was not new in her experience but had extra significance in this case. Toomey raised his eyes in response to a Moody question. His sloppy lips above a weak chin moving to express a "Yes" response before reforming into their former position over his even, but yellowish teeth.

She felt a surge of anger and revulsion racking her body as she stared unblinkingly at her attacker. She thought that he was a pathetic piece of human garbage but a malevolent one, and she resented the inevitable fact that she would always carry some kind of image of him with her, like an unwanted birthmark.

She said, "OK Jack, that's enough. I need to go."

Jack said, "OK, my office or out?"

"Out. I need time to think, regroup. I feel like a shower."

"I know what you mean."

"Perhaps. Let's go."

They left the viewing room and headed for the lobby, which was quiet, except for a different cop rattling a keyboard and shuffling papers.

They embraced and Jack said, "Let me know how you're doing."

Aggie did not reply but stepped out into a drizzly day. The tops of the surrounding buildings were wrapped in a mist of low cloud, small fingers of weak light pushing through the moisture. She did not mind being in rain. She found it comforting and a little invigorating. She didn't care for umbrellas and walked purposefully into the rain, disconnected thoughts tumbling through her head like ping pong balls.

Chapter 7

As her thoughts coalesced and settled down, Aggie realized that she was heading for her apartment. Large drops of rain, amid the drizzle, had fallen from the flowering apple trees at the roadside and run down through her hair to her scalp. The drizzle had formed droplets on her nose and chin and her clothing was beginning to cling wetly to her arms and legs. She was feeling more and more relaxed and approaching some level of mental equilibrium. It was just after lunch and so she picked up some strawberry yoghurt and some bananas from her local Korean market. Once in her apartment, she slipped out of her clothing, put on her robe and toweled her hair and feet. She hung her wet clothing in the bathroom. The memories of the attack were still flooding her thoughts but she found that they were manageable if she stayed in the living area and the kitchen. With a bowl of cut banana and yoghurt, she sat on the couch and fired up her iPad. First, she Googled Douglas Toomey and basically drew a blank. Of the only five prospects, two were clearly identified with photographs, one was dead and the other two were a stamp collector and an architect, neither of whom fitted the unsavory image that she had stored in a corner of her mind.

She thought it sad that stamps, like books, were heading towards oblivion one day.

The pool of each would be finitely limited. They were both beautifully tactile and visually attractive but were nearly obsolete. The research on Toomey was interesting, if only because Jack, with all his resources, had drawn a blank also.

Over the next four hours of research and note taking, she came up with some fairly satisfying information about the family, which filled in some background even if there was no direct relationship to her attack. She wrote down the family members from the top to establish some order in her thoughts.

Father of Katherine Toomey: Ardal Toomey. Investment banker, entrepreneur, philanthropist. Lived in North Carolina in a sizable house with seven acres, a live-in housekeeper and a chef. He seemed in robust health, traveling to St John's in the Virgin Islands twice a year and he played golf on a local country club course. He was almost 84 years old. Nothing yet on his marriage.

Daughter of Katherine Toomey: Ana Toomey – aged 30 years, trained to be a botanist before her marriage and kids. Married to John Plunkett, history teacher at a local private school, who seemed very successful and popular according to student ratings, agreeing not at all with Katherine Toomey's view. Parents: Katherine Toomey and Floyd Pearson.

Brother of Ana: Dougal P. Toomey, aged 28 years. Here was the reward for her efforts.

There it was, a slightly different name in a family with Irish heritage. Suddenly, life had become a little more exciting and she felt a buzz. She had once dated an Irishman who spent most of his waking hours singing quite well and loudly. Before she had tired of this, she had learnt a bit about Irish names. Dougal, she thought was to do with being a 'Dark Stranger'. She could look it up later.

His mother had referred to him as Douglas. Was that to mislead her or did she always use Douglas? Did it really matter? She decided that it didn't. Aggie Googled her new find and began to put some details together. The big deal would be to get Jack to run the new name. There was not a great deal in the public arena. What did she expect? Rapist? Predator? No, but that might soon surface through other channels. Meantime, yes, he was 28 years old, and a purveyor and designer of video games. The ones that Aggie saw all seemed to be of a violent nature. Gang wars with heavy weaponry, murderous aliens, the undead or zombies, etc.

There were no addresses or telephone numbers. All in all, though, this was a breakthrough of sorts. In her new realm of enthusiasm, she almost forgot to finish the research.

Katherine Toomey was next. There was not much personal life but her parents were Ardal and Margaret Toomey. Ardal, she thought, had German origins. Katherine Toomey was 60 years old and there was no mention of her marriage. She seemed to be a naturopath who dabbled in Chinese medicine, faith healing, herbal and magnetic remedies and biofields. Aggie had little knowledge of alternative medicine, believing that much of it was doubtful, although, she had friends who had good experiences with acupuncture and the use of magnets. There was no mention of Katherine Toomey's qualifications, validation for expertise or any published work but she had given quite a few talks to various groups with no mention of fees or any advertising. There seemed to be no intellectual center of learning. None of this had a direct bearing on her attack as far as she could see but a character structure was beginning to emerge, none of it attractive.

Floyd Pearson turned out to be a rather accomplished orthopedist affiliated with Mount Sinai hospital. There was no mention of his marriage to Katherine Toomey, although, he was currently married to one May Bassett. He was 67 years old and still in full professional flight.

In her two meetings with Katherine Toomey, there had been no mention of a husband or an ex-husband, let alone one who was, by all accounts, a successful professional. She probably had no feelings for him either. Aggie paused briefly in her research and called Jack. His phone went to message and so she gave him the new name of their quarry and asked to have him checked in Jack's data base. Once again, she went through the information on the family members, lingering on Floyd Pearson who had worked on athletes, ballet dancers and regular folk, specializing in various surgeries and knee replacements. He was well thought of, occasionally travelled a small lecture circuit and was heavily involved in training interns. All in all, he was an intelligent, caring and warm person and the antithesis of Katherine Toomey. Aggie found no mention of a divorce but supposed there must have been one as he seemed to have remarried. She suddenly felt tired and close to exhaustion. She decided to watch a couple of movies along with a bottle of Australian wine called Boxer. Midway through the second movie, her phone rang and announced that Jack was calling.

"Jack!"
"What you up to?"
"Watching a movie with some vine-o. Any news?"
"I've got something for you."
"What?"
"Our friend has been in trouble before. Three assaults and a flash job. None came to anything."
"What happened?"
"All four women brought charges but then backed off."
"You mean that they didn't follow through?"
"Looks like it. The flashing was standard wave it around. Two of the assaults were physical and involved attempted rape. The third was nasty, rape and a beating. All four women filed charges and then refused to testify."
"Not difficult to figure out why."
"The mother? Or that guy?"
"Yep. Bought off or frightened off, I would think. Doesn't matter which. Do you have names and addresses?"
"I do, well, three of them anyway. What are you thinking?"
"I'd like to talk to them. See what happened."
"If they want to talk."
"Worth a try anyway."
"Is it? Where are you going with this?"
"See if I can get one of them to change her mind. Add mine to it and we've got a case."
"It's a bit thin but it might work."
"Can you give me the names and addresses?"
She heard Jack shuffling some papers.
"OK. The names are Pauline Smith, Adele Morris, Trudy Scofield and Georgia Kaplan. The first was the flasher and the last was the bad one. No address for her." Jack then reeled off the addresses. Two were in Manhattan and one in Westbury.
"Thanks Jack. I'll get on it tomorrow. I need phone numbers. I'm seeing a friend for lunch first."
"Good for you. Take it easy. Keep me posted."
"I will."

Aggie put the phone down. She felt some relief and some exhilaration. This was going somewhere. She checked all four names and got two phone numbers. Pauline Smith and Trudy Scofield. She put her notes aside and settled in for the second half of the movie, drinking more than half of the Boxer.

Chapter 8

Next morning after coffee and toast, and no hangover for a change, Aggie read through her notes and decided to call Pauline Smith. That looked the easiest. At least, there was no physical assault. First, she called for Tuna sandwiches and chicken and tomato soups, to be delivered later in the morning. She planned to have some dry white wine and coffee ready also. She picked up her phone and dialed.

"Hello."

"Hi, my name is Agnes Trout. I am a private investigator. I'm looking into a case that you might be able to help me with. Are you Pauline Smith?"

"Who did you say you were?"

Aggie repeated herself.

"What case?"

"I'm sorry but are you Pauline Smith?"

"I am. What case?"

"Have you heard of Dougal Toomey?"

There was a long silence and then,

"I've heard of the name, yes."

"Great. Were you involved in some kind of legal action against him?"

"Legal action?"

"Yes."

"Well, he flashed me is all. A couple of years ago."

"Ah. Could you tell me the circumstances please?"

"Where is this going?"

"I need to find out as much as possible about his background. He is a person of interest in another case."

"What's he done?"

Aggie took a deep breath.

"Nothing proven yet. We are looking for a pattern."

"OK. I was sitting on a bench in Central Park, having a coffee and a sandwich. He sat down next to me and produced an erection."

"What happened next?"

"Not much. I've seen plenty of them. His was not special. In fact, I laughed. He just got up and left."

"What did you do?"

"I was going to do nothing, but then I thought of all the kids playing in the park. It wouldn't have been nice for them to see it."

"What did you do?"

"I called the cops."

"And?"

"They showed up pretty quickly. Two of them. They talked to me. I described the guy and off they went."

"They must have found him."

"He'd done it again, and not far away. I didn't find out until someone contacted me and asked for an interview. After that I said I would testify against him."

"But…?"

"But what?"

"You didn't?"

"That's right. I didn't."

"Why not?"

"I didn't want to go to court. Nobody knew about it. I felt embarrassed."

"OK. Was that the only reason?"

"What do you mean?"

"Were you threatened?"

"No, of course not."

"Look, this is between us only. What you are telling me really matters."

"OK."

"Were you persuaded or invited not to testify?"

There was a long silence. "I don't want to answer that."

"You don't have to. Look, he has done a lot more than wave his dick around. He has evolved, shall we say."

"Evolved?"

"Yes. Done some bad things. Alleged to have done some bad things."

"Are you recording this?"

"No, this is a one off between you and me."

Another silence. "A man came to see me."

"Fiftyish, shaven head, well spoken?"

"Yes. How did you know?"

"I've come across him. What did he do? Threaten you?"

"No. He was very pleasant."

Aggie was beginning to feel frustrated. She felt that she was close but her patience was running out.

"Pauline, what did happen?"

"He offered me money."

Immediately, Aggie thought that, at last, here it was. A payoff.

"And?"

"I accepted it. What would you have done?"

Aggie dismissed the question.

"So that was the end of it?"

"Yes. It was worth it. No trouble, a decent amount of cash. No contest."

"I can see that. It was cash then?"

"Yes, on the spot."

"How much?"

"A lot."

"Pauline, thanks. You have been very helpful and I really appreciate your candor."

"And you won't bother me again?"

"No, I won't. Thanks again."

Next Aggie thought that her remaining call could see her on a roll. She dialed the number. Two rings again, somebody home. She was in luck.

She said, "Can I speak to Trudy Scofield please?"

"This is she."

"My name is Agnes Trout and I am a private investigator. I'm hoping that you can help me with a current case."

"What case?"

"Do you know the name Dougal Toomey?"

"Of course, I do. He attacked me a year or so ago. I hate that name."

"Right. Were you asked to testify against him?"

"Yes."

"But, you didn't."

"Who are you again?"

Aggie repeated herself.

"So, you have no official capacity for asking questions?"

"Not official, no. I'm working on a case involving this guy, Toomey."

"OK, well, forget it. I'm not answering your questions."

"Why?"

"Goodbye. And don't call me again."

With that the line went dead.

Aggie felt irritated. She couldn't avoid the thought that she had blown it. She told herself that you win one and you lose one. It didn't seem to help at all. She had about one and a half hours left before Maisie showed up. She tried several avenues of research to find information on Georgia Kaplan but came up with nothing. Eventually, she got hold of a number for Adele Morris. Question was, should she ask questions on the phone or try to meet up with her? All in all, she thought that face to face was the way to go. She dialed the number.

"Hi."

"Hi, my name is Agnes Trout. I'm looking to speak to Adele Morris."

"I'm Adele Morris. What do you want?"

"I'm a private investigator. I'm working on a case that you might be able to help me with."

"What case is that?"

"It involves a character by the name of Dougal Toomey."

There was a sharp intake of breath.

"Oh. Really? What's that about?"

"Listen, it might be easier if we met so that I could tell you about the case."

"Where do I fit in?"

"You might have some knowledge that would be helpful to me."

"I don't know if I can do this. I'm trying to forget that name. This is very unpleasant."

"I'm sure that it is. A meeting could help us both, though."

"Just the two of us?"

"Yes."

"To talk about your case and that prick?"

"Yes."

"Stop if I want to?"

"Of course."

"I'm home on my lunch break now. Tomorrow at this time?"

"Yes. I'll buy lunch." Aggie named a diner. "12:30 pm then?"

"OK. How will I know you?"

"Short brown hair, dressed in black mostly, about five-six."

"OK. See you then."

Aggie put down the phone. She hadn't asked for a description. It would work out. She reflected on the conversation. Tomorrow could be productive if she handled it properly. She couldn't afford to scare off another victim. The Scofield reaction had taken her by surprise. A few minutes later, she took delivery of the food, laid it out on the coffee table and began to make some coffee.

Maisie hit the apartment buzzer right on time. They embraced warmly and settled next to the coffee table. Maisie had a heart shaped face, long curly brown hair, a small mouth and large expressive eyes.

She said, "You look good. How's things?"

"Guy tried to murder me a couple of days ago, otherwise I'm good!"

"What?"

"Long story. It's over now."

"What happened?"

Aggie gave a broad outline of the attack and told Maisie that she was still looking into some aspects of it. Maisie listened in some shock and great concern for Aggie's safety.

She said, "Are you going to be OK? I had no idea. You didn't say anything on the phone."

"I'm good, hateful man, a real jerk. I'll be fine. Now what about you? What makes you think something's up? I thought that you guys were solid."

Maisie paused a moment, her eyes clouding up. "I thought that we were in a good place. Now, I'm not sure. In fact, I know we're not."

"How do you know?"

"Oh, you know, little things."

"Like what?"

"Let's start with sex."

Aggie knew the Maisie was a private person and so she was a little surprised at her frankness.

"Ah! Do you really want to do this?"

"Yes. What better place to start? You know that your sex life tells you a lot!"

"OK."

"We have always had a decent sex life. You know, regular without much variation but good, I think, for both of us."

This was a little more than Aggie wanted to know.

She said, "OK."

"Well, suddenly David wanted to try different things. You know, a little tweak here and there, without really asking me. It is sort of expected of me."

"Well, isn't that good? I like variety. Perhaps he's thinking of you. Trying to spice things up."

"It really is not David's nature to just do something new. He doesn't like change."

"Well, maybe he got a few ideas from the Internet. That wouldn't be unusual. Again, it could be that he is being very thoughtful."

"Could be but I don't think so. We've had our routine for six years now. I just can't see changes in what we do happening without some discussion, at least. That's always been our way of doing things."

Aggie was silent, waiting. Masie continued.

"I don't know. There's something different about him in bed. A sort of familiarity that's hard to explain and makes me uncomfortable. Images that I don't need cross my mind and prod me into thinking that he is cheating. I'm worried."

Aggie paused a few beats to make sure the Maisie was done.

"OK. I'm sorry, Maisie. Do you want to go on? Was there anything else?"

Maisie gathered herself, swallowing twice before continuing.

"We're suddenly having wine with dinner."

Aggie suppressed the urge to laugh. "Well, that's good too, isn't it?"

"Same thing, no discussion or preamble. Bottles just started appearing. And he chinked glasses with me—he's never done that. Usually, sex has to follow our wine."

Aggie was silent for a moment.

So he has a bottle of wine and wants to go to bed. Sounds normal. She asked, "Anything else?"

"A few things. He's started using men's cologne. He's started working out. He's never been concerned about his figure. In fact, he's let it go a bit. Plus, he's switched from boxers to briefs."

This time Aggie had to smile. "Sorry, it has its funny side."

"Not for me. He came home recently with a scratch on his cheek. Said that he walked into a tree branch."

"OK. OK. Let's suppose there's something in it. There probably isn't. Men, and women, go through some kind of self-assessment when they see that time is going by quickly. David is probably no different. But, we're friends. I don't like seeing you like this. What do you want me to do?"

Maisie paused for a few moments, her large eyes blinking back a tear.

She said, "Find out what you can. Is David cheating? I need to know."

Aggie said, "OK. Let's have a bite to eat before we go any further."

She microwaved the soups and Maisie chose the chicken.

After they had eaten the sandwiches, she made some coffee but neither drank any wine. Then they talked about their friends and some of the past year.

Finally, Aggie said, "Let me take a few notes. OK, first question. What does David do for a living now? Is he still in finance?"

"No. About a year and a half or so ago, he got out of finance and started a company supplying medical equipment to hospitals. Everything, it seems, from MRI's to scalpels. It turned out to be very lucrative but he has to spend time in his Delaware office, as well as the one he has in Queens."

Aggie couldn't help thinking that the opportunity was there but immediately felt guilty for that thought. "Are his trips away regular?"

"Fairly regular. Three or four days at a time."

"But, is that always the same three or four days of the week or every other week for example?"

"Pretty much the same three or four days, yes. I'm not sure that I've really noticed."

"OK. Any weekends away?" Aggie knew that weekends are important. Family time. Even though David and Maisie had no kids.

"Once in a while, yes."

"Does David call when he is away?"

"Yes, almost every day."

"So, do you have an office address and phone number?"

"Yes."

"Does he stay in a hotel?"

"Sometimes. Other times he uses the company apartment."

"Where's that?"

"In Wilmington."

"You have that address and phone number too?"

"Address yes. Phone number no. But I have his cell."

"So, he's been open with all of this information?"

"Yes. I suppose he has."

"Have you been to the company apartment?"

"No. I've never traveled with him or to him."

"Do you still write from home?"

"Yes. It's going quite well. I'm enjoying it. My next book will be published in a few weeks."

"Good. OK. So, what you want is for me to check everything out. See if David's absences are above board."

"Can you do that?"

"Yes. It's not difficult. It does feel odd though, because you are a friend and I know David."

"Aggie, I just have to know. I need peace of mind. I feel badly about doubting David but I can't help it. I'll pay you."

"No, you won't. You're a friend. I'm not taking anything."

Maisie was silent.

Aggie said, "Give me the address and phone number information that you do have."

"OK. I've got them all written down." Maisie handed over a typewritten sheet.

She said, "What's the next step?"

"Well, when is the next trip?"

"I think he's going next Monday. Yes, I'm certain that he is."

"OK. Where's he staying."

"I don't know."

As they finished up the coffee, Aggie said, "I'll do a bit of checking and then I'll see what happens next week. I hope that it comes to nothing."

"Thanks Aggie."

They talked for another half hour before Maisie finally left. Aggie promised to keep in touch.

She cleared up and sat down on the couch, looking at her notes, which were minimal. If David was cheating, it was easy to accomplish. Regular trips away, access to an apartment and little in the way of expenses. Opportunity certainly, inclination or motivation unknown. How well does one really know someone? She found the regularity of the trips a little disconcerting.

Business trips tended to be as required, dictated by circumstances rather than a calendar, unless the two offices operated on designated days, which would be unusual. Plus, who did David work for? Was he freelance? She should have asked. She thought that a little Googling was in order. She had to prepare for the meeting tomorrow, but, other than that, she had time to nose around a bit. Maisie, she didn't need but she checked her anyway. She was listed as a writer of children's books, had a modest website and a Facebook page.

She had kept her own name of Beck, although Aggie had seen it written in the form Beck Hamilton, after David's name. What little there was on David Hamilton was out of date. He was listed as a financial consultant with Turner and Bowden, Inc., a midtown company with a midtown address. Aggie wondered why the change. Weren't financial consultants well off? Why become what she saw as a glorified salesman? Lucrative or not, it seemed odd. He certainly had freedom of movement now compared with previously. In the end, though, it didn't matter. He had a new job based in two cities and she had to check on both places. After another half hour, Aggie came up with some information. There was a firm named Moreland Associates, Medical Suppliers with one David Hamilton listed as Director of Sales. The address and phone number were those supplied by Maisie and the company was based on Continental Avenue in Queens. No other names were listed in connection with Moreland Associates. She called the number, which went straight to message with the name of the company and a request for the caller's name number and message. She didn't leave any information. She looked for a Moreland Associates in Wilmington and came up empty. She then tried the address given by Maisie, looking for reverse information on the company but nothing of substance emerged. She thought, with some resignation, that a visit was needed to both places. Plus, she thought that something was off with the job change. A word with the folks at Turner and Bowden seemed in order too. The good part about looking into both places was that she could give the BMW an airing, shake out the cobwebs and give it a run. That, at least, sounded good.

Aggie sat down on the couch and, as she laid back, the phone performed its Stones duty and she saw that it was Jack. She picked up.

"Hi Ag."

"Hi Jack. What's up?"

"Bad news, I'm afraid. He's out. No way of stopping him."

"Shit. To be expected, I suppose."

"Yes, sorry. I don't think that you are in danger, at least not for the time being."

"OK. You know, I'll kill him next time, if there is a next time."

"There won't be. He'll move on."

"That's the problem. He'll move on. Doesn't anybody care?"

"Of course they do but there are limits to what can be done. Did you find out anything?"

"Yes. Two down, one to go. One was definitely paid off. Probably all of them. I'll find out more tomorrow."

"Well, that's progress isn't it. Will any of them testify?"

"Don't know. Unlikely, I suppose. Tomorrow's might work. It's Adele Morris."

"OK. Well, look, take care."

"I will. I'll be running down a friend's problem too."

"Your lunchtime friend? What's the problem?"

"Wayward husband, I think."

"Well, good luck with that."

"Thanks."

"Not up for anything are you?"

"Not now Jack. Too much to deal with."

"Rain check?"

"Rain check. Bye."

The phone went dead.

Aggie spent the next two hours trying to locate Georgia Kaplan. Three possibilities came to light but all petered out for one reason or another. She didn't seem to exist. Aggie thought that she could have got married or changed her name, which made it difficult to trace her. It was a long time since that attack and she was apparently now off the radar. Even Jack couldn't find her. Aggie decided that she would have to track down some relatives to see if she could locate her that way. Very time consuming. Meeting Adele Morris began to assume much more importance. Feeling tired, she decided to call it a day after one more futile shot at Wilmington and David Hamilton. She began to experience misgivings about this guy; familiar investigative rumblings began to stir in her mind.

Chapter 9

The next morning Aggie made herself a toasted bacon sandwich with coffee and looked at her day. She thought that she could squeeze in a trip to Queens or midtown during the morning and then meet up with Adele Morris for lunch. She decided on Queens which should be simple and expedient. It would take most of a day to get to Wilmington and back so that would come later, maybe tomorrow or at the weekend. She showered, finger combed her hair, dressed in black jeans, a grey tee and a new faux black leather jacket and headed for the subway. Continental Avenue had changed since her last visit three years ago. It was a very busy thoroughfare full of aggressive traffic and bustling pedestrians. She found the address that Maisie had given her with no difficulty. The street address turned out to be a glass and metal doorway adjacent to a small bakery. Aggie entered the small space behind the door, which was about twelve square feet of cheap marble floor, and looked at a second substantial dark green wooden door with small grimy windows in the top half. She glanced at the three small brass plaques with buzzers on the side wall and saw that they included Moreland Associates in suite 2F. She suddenly realized that she had not thought this through. She liked to think that she planned well and was organized so this bothered her. She couldn't buzz Maisie's husband and go up. What would she say? They knew each other and he would figure out immediately that something was up. She looked through the windows and could see only a narrow flight of plastic covered stairs, leading to somewhere above the bakery. She could wait to see if someone came in or out. Same thing, she might run into David. All she really wanted was to be sure that he was based in an office here, a sort of ground zero. She needed to see it for herself. After a moment's thought she turned and headed into the bakery. It was warm, smelled gloriously of baked bread and muffins and was empty except for a cheery, small Asian woman who greeted her with a smile.

She bought two corn muffins and said, "Do you ever see any of the folks upstairs?"

The woman said, "One lady comes in every day for muffins. The others I don't know. One place is an apartment. I don't see them."

Aggie said, "What about a tallish man with curly, dark hair, mid-thirties?"

The woman said, "There is a man up there but he never comes in here. He is big, yes."

Aggie thought that a photograph would have been useful but, too late for that. She didn't have a photograph of David, anyway.

She said, "OK, thanks."

She walked out and stood on the street for a while, wondering what to do next. She glanced up at the second-floor windows and saw the Moreland Associates sign in gold letters on two of the windows. There were no lights on. She spotted a convenient Starbucks across the other side of Continental and decided that she could spare half an hour or so to watch the office. She made it across and, although it was a long way off, she thought that she could see enough from the Starbucks window seat. With a Grande Latte between her palms, she began her vigil. She ate a corn muffin and had drunk most of the Latte when she thought that she saw David. Dark suit, open necked blue shirt, a briefcase and a vaguely affluent air about him. He entered the double door vestibule, disappeared and, after a couple of minutes, the office lights came on and his large frame appeared in the window. He seemed to be looking directly at her, which was a very uncomfortable feeling and gave a hint of menace. He couldn't possibly see her but it didn't feel good. He moved away from the window and disappeared somewhere inside the office. Aggie realized that she was holding her breath and her mouth had gone dry. She downed the Latte, headed for the door and walked quickly down Continental, feeling a little awkward and exposed. She hoped that David wasn't watching.

There was enough of the morning left to go to her apartment and prepare for her lunchtime meeting. She climbed the stairs of her walk up, entered her apartment and tossed her jacket and bag onto the couch. Full of Latte and corn muffin, plus a bacon sandwich and with lunch looming, she just splashed her face and cleaned her teeth. She felt that she had to cut back on carbs and food, in general. Water would be her dinner tonight and a glass of Riesling. She had just enough time to make the diner comfortably. It was on Broadway in the eighties and had been there for years; the black vested waiters with grey hair, or no hair, had been there for years too. She was shown to a booth in the middle aisle and was soon joined by a tall woman with a long pale face, beneath chestnut hair and devoid of makeup. She wore a pink sweater and a black skirt above black knee length boots and carried a dark coat over her arm.

Aggie said, "Adele?"
The woman said, "Yes," and slipped into the opposite side of the booth.
"I'm Agnes Trout."
"Yes."
"Shall we order something before we talk?"
"Yes."
They both checked the menu. Aggie ordered OJ and scrambled egg and Adele ordered an omelet and coffee.
Aggie said, "Look, I can understand that you might be worried about this."
"I am. I'm having second thoughts."
"OK. But, let me explain what I'm doing."
The OJ and coffee arrived and Aggie continued.
"There is a guy out there who is dangerous to women. He has attacked you, and others, and has always gotten away with it. No consequences."
"How many others?"

"Well, three that I know of, and me."
"You?"
"Yes."
"I thought that you were a private investigator."
"I am. But he attacked me a few days ago."
"Did he hurt you?"
"No. I avoided most of it."
"How?"
"I put him to sleep."
"Oh. So, what's all this about then?"
"I want him in jail where he belongs."
"How will you do that?"

The food arrived and they paused a few moments. Aggie picked disinterestedly at her eggs while Adele worked on her omelet enthusiastically.

Aggie said, "To do that I need a case."
"Well, you have one, your case."
"That's not enough. I need more than one case to get any traction."
"More than one?" Adele stopped eating. "You mean me?"
"Well, yes. That would be two of us."
"You mean that I would go to court?"
"You would have to. Yes."
"I can't."
"Why not?"

Adele ignored the question.

She said, "What about the other three women?"
"One of them I can't find."

Aggie paused but saw no way of softening the response.

"The other two don't want to be involved."
"Nor do I."

Aggie sucked in a breath and stabbed the table with her forefinger as she spoke.

"You mean that you don't want him to pay for attempting to rape you?"
"It's not that. Of course, I do. I hope that one day he will pay."

She looked down at the table for a few moments and then dabbed away a sudden tear.

"I'd like to see him dead or incarcerated in a bad place for a long time. I just can't get into making it happen."

Aggie said, "OK. I have to say this. I've spoken to two of the other women and one told me that she'd been paid off."

Adele raised her eyes. "Paid off?"
"Well, given money not to testify."
"A sort of settlement out of court kind of thing?"

Light reflected from the tears on her cheek.

"If you prefer that term, yes. Were you paid off? Or, did you reach some kind of settlement?"

Adele did not respond. Aggie felt mean and sympathetic at the same time. She thought, sadly, that there was little difference between bullying and cajoling.

She said, "At one time, I thought that you had all been threatened at some point. You know, warned off."

"I was never threatened."

"But, you were paid off?"

Adele said, "Look, thanks for lunch but I think that I am done here. I shouldn't have come."

Aggie said, "So that's a yes?"

Adele said, "I'm sorry but I have to go."

Aggie said, "Just a moment."

She took out a pen and wrote her cell number on a napkin and gave it to Adele. "Please call me if you change your mind. This is a serious business, you know. This guy is a monster."

Adele stood up, picked up her coat, took the napkin and left without a word. Aggie pushed her eggs aside, drank the OJ and paid the check.

She was convinced that her interview technique had been flawed. What had been achieved, though?

Well, in a somewhat clumsy way, she felt that it was reasonable to suppose that these women had all been bought off. An assumption but a justified one. Probably done by the fixer or whatever he was. The cash coming from mother dear. She felt drained. Time to go back to the apartment, relax and figure out what was next.

Chapter 10

At her apartment she decided on the spur of the moment to tackle one of her least favorite jobs. She cleaned her kitchen. It helped her to turn things over in her mind. She cleaned the sink, the counters, the dish drainer, cooker and even the microwave. She balked at the inside of the fridge. That could wait! When she had finished, she felt replenished and slipped into a late afternoon hot bath which felt really good. She toweled off, donned a large Terry cloth light blue robe and sank into the couch with a glass of Hungarian Riesling.

Life on her own with no real commitments had its pluses. Pretty much anything that she wanted she could get. She could also do what she wanted when she wanted to; sleeping, eating, drinking, having sex, all when she was ready for them. Aggie hadn't thought much about children, hadn't felt a biological clock at any time. She had had vague thoughts about the future. Would she suddenly wish that she had a family and a doting husband and all that went with it? But that seemed so far away right now and didn't really have any appeal. Life came in the door and she took it as it came. Could she, or would she, ever change? She didn't know. The sudden, harsh sound of her buzzer broke into Aggie's comfortable reverie. No visitors expected, early evening was sliding into being. Aggie went to the intercom with some annoyance and mild curiosity.

"Yes. Who is it?"
"Jonathan, ma'am."
"And who is Jonathan may I ask?" Although, she knew full well who it was.
"We met a couple of days ago. I'd like a word please."
"You just had it."
"Hmm. Can I come up; we need to talk."
"Really? Well, I don't feel any need at all."
"It would be helpful for us both. I am quite harmless."
"I don't believe that for a moment."
"OK. I am not completely harmless perhaps, but we do need to talk."
"I don't think so."
"I could wait here as long as necessary until you come out. I wouldn't do that; you could have me removed. You probably would."
"I would. All true."
"Or I could find you anywhere, anytime with no effort on my part."
"True also. What then? You'll force me to have a chat?"
"Ms. Trout, this is not helpful."
"It's not meant to be."

"Somewhere, somehow and soon, we are going to talk. Look, why don't you call your friend in the PD? Tell him that I've dropped by for a chat."

Aggie thought that he knows about us as well as knowing where I live. A little disconcerting, to say the least. "He'd tell me not to."

"What I'm saying is that you can tell anyone that I am here to talk. I'm being open about it."

"I don't know you."

"True. OK. What about meeting in a bar or restaurant of your choice? It would be public and I could meet up with you."

"OK. Look, that won't be necessary. Give me ten minutes and you can come up. I need to change and make a call."

"Ah. Thank you. Most appreciated Ms. Trout. I'll be waiting."

As she went to the closet, Aggie wondered if she should call Jack. She put on a sweat suit and a pair of sneakers. She then slipped a kitchen knife under the corner of the sofa. She decided not to call Jack; the mention of a call should be enough, she hoped. She glanced around quickly and then buzzed the front door. With a wave of mild trepidation, Aggie opened the apartment door and waited. Jonathan, shaved head gleaming in the landing light, clumped into view with a measured tread.

"Good evening Ms. Trout."

Aggie looked him over. The long black coat over a lean frame, was hanging open over an open neck white shirt and black slacks, no weapons in sight, at least. She stepped aside and he eased into the apartment. Aggie asked to take his coat but he declined. She offered him an armchair seat next to the couch. He sat with a long sigh and eased back into the cushions.

Jonathan said, "Nice place, ma'am."

Aggie said, "It was nice until three days ago. Would you like a coffee or a glass of wine? I have both ready."

"A coffee would be most enjoyable. Black, please. May I call you something else? Agnes, perhaps?"

"Agnes will do. What is your something else?"

"Black. I am Jonathan Black."

"Good. That's over then."

She went to the kitchen, keeping him in sight out of the corner of her eye and switched on the coffee pot that she usually kept primed. As it heated up, she brought two mugs to the coffee table and placed them on coasters. Black's eyes followed her lazily as she brought the coffee pot to the table. She poured the two mugs and added a French Vanilla creamer to her own.

Black said, "That stuff's not good for you, you know."

Aggie said, "I know but, when I feel like it, it tastes good."

Jonathan Black picked up his mug, sipped the coffee and sat back with a sigh.

"Very nice," he said. "By the way, you have an interesting name; many piscine jokes in your life?"

Aggie said, "Of course. Too many. Heard them all. You? Any gray areas?"

Black smiled.

Aggie thought it a pleasant sight.

He said, "Touché."

A few moments of silence passed as they looked at each other.

Jonathan Black cleared his throat and said, "Let me ask you a question. Are recent events, or imagined interludes, important to you?"

"What? What kind of question is that? Imagined interludes? I was viciously attacked, or has that slipped your mind?"

"Ah. But our malcontent was also viciously attacked."

Aggie's eyes flashed her anger. "As you well know, I was defending myself against a perverted prick."

Black sipped his coffee, his eyes on Aggie over the rim of his cup. "Ah. A magnificent use of language! Let's look at this another way. In the general scheme of things, in the world we live in, all of this is insignificant. You and I are insignificant."

Aggie rolled her eyes. "What the hell are you talking about? This is ridiculous."

"No ma'am, it's not. We are a bunch of folks living on a rock, hurtling through space, probably along with billions of other rocks with something on them. In infinite space, we amount to nothing and yet we think we are important and need to settle silly squabbles."

Aggie glared at him. "How many times have you made that stupid, little speech?"

"Hmm. Some version of it, several times. It often works."

"So, are you trying to threaten me? In my world."

"I am not threatening you. I am advising you, or trying to."

Aggie said, "Have you killed anyone?"

"That is irrelevant Ms. Trout, er, Agnes."

"Have you hurt anyone?"

"That is not part of my agenda."

"You have an agenda then?"

"We all have agendas, Agnes."

"Look, let's cut all of this crap. Why are you really here?"

"Nothing if not direct, Agnes. Well, we have a problem."

"So, it would seem. You wouldn't be here otherwise. So, what's our problem?"

"You have been talking to people that you shouldn't be talking to."

"And who would they be?"

Jonathan Black took another gulp of coffee and sighed again.

"As far as I know, three women so far."

"That's true. And there will be a fourth when I find her. It's what I do."

"Yes, it is what you do, perhaps very well by all accounts. But, I must ask you, advise you, not to pursue this line of inquiry any further."

"Advise all you want. I am going to get somewhere with this."

"What have you got so far? Almost nothing I would think. What's the point of going further down this road?"

Aggie was feeling a little irritated.

She said, "These women were all paid off not to testify against a rapist and potential murderer. At least two of them have, anyway. Presumably, you did the paying off."

Black leaned forward and gazed around the room before turning his blue eyes on her.

He said, "All true. That's life. They preferred the money, not insignificant funds, I might add. Their choice."

"I'll turn one of them. I have to. That prick will kill someone. He tried to kill me. How do you do this? Do you have any morals at all?"

Jonathan Black was silent for a moment and then said, "I do."

"Then, why do it?"

"We all make compromises um, Agnes. Lines are there to be crossed—"

"Or not crossed. We do make compromises, but this? You are protecting a monster."

"Almost true. I am a go between. That's what I do."

Aggie said nothing.

Black said, "Look, you have already spoken to three women. The fourth seems to have vanished, who knows where. What's left?"

"I can find her. Did you pay her off too?"

"Not in your purview Agnes. And, I don't think that you will find her. Thanks for the coffee. Got to be off."

Aggie was shaken.

What did he mean? As he rose, so did she. They stood awkwardly staring at one another for a few moments and then, in unison, turned to the door. Aggie opened the door and Black passed through, pausing in the hallway.

He said, "You know, it's been a pleasure to talk to you. Different time, different place, who knows?"

His blue eyes flashed for a moment as his features verged on a smile and then he turned and made his way noisily down the stairs.

Aggie heard the front door shut and then all was silent.

Chapter 11

Deep in thought, Aggie washed up the mugs and her wine glass and tidied up in general. This rather urgent conversation had gleaned a couple of things. It was not liked by someone, presumably Katherine Toomey, that she was poking around in her son's affairs. None of the women, for that matter, were too pleased either. They had come to a place where a substantial monetary payment had alleviated their distress to a point where they would no longer take part in any kind of prosecution of their attacker. The fourth victim, the most egregiously affected, was not available at this time. It would make sense that she would be the one who might be the most forthcoming. Finding her was vital to Aggie's personal crusade, her only chance, unless someone else emerged, to bring about some justice. The throwaway comment by Jonathan Black about not being able to find her echoed in Aggie's mind. Where was she? More worryingly, was she alive? That thought had finally expressed itself. Still mid-evening, she decided to call Jack. For once, he answered on the first ring.

"Hi Ag. What's new?"

"Hi Jack. I spent some of the day in Queens on the husband case, met with Adele Morris and just said goodbye to one Jonathan Black. Busy day."

There was a moment's silence and Jack said, "Who is Jonathan Black?"

"You remember the guy who warned me off?"

"Him? What did he want?"

"He came over to talk to me."

"Over? You mean your apartment?"

"Yes, he was OK."

"Are you crazy? Why didn't you call me first?"

"I was going to but, in the end, decided that he was alright. I kept a knife handy."

"That means that you thought he was dangerous. It was a huge risk. You have to be more careful."

"I knew what I was doing."

"Still risky, you should have let me know. Please do that next time."

"OK."

Aggie was once again conflicted between being independent and having someone care about her.

"What did he want?"

"He was basically warning me off talking to any women connected to the case."

"Did he threaten you?"

"No. Not really. Just gave me a bottom line of it wouldn't go anywhere. I got the impression that I was a nuisance more than anything. He did a bit of cease and desist but not in a bad way."

Jack was silent.

Aggie said, "He was super polite."

"And probably dangerous. I wish that you hadn't done this."

"I know. One thing though."

"What?"

He said, "That I wouldn't find the fourth woman. You know, Georgia Kaplan."

"Yes."

"He seemed definite. That was the only time I felt a bit anxious…"

"OK. Look, I'm in the office. I'm tied up in a fraud case at the moment."

"Fraud? Unusual for you isn't it?"

"Not when witnesses are beaten up!"

"Oh. Tell me more when you have time."

"OK. I'll have another go at tracing this Kaplan woman. I'll see what I can dig up on your guy as well. His name is Black?"

"Yes. Jonathan Black."

"Don't know the name but somebody will."

He paused.

"How's the rain check situation?"

Aggie paused for a moment. She was very tempted but, adding another human being to her day seemed just too much, even though it was Jack. There would be the before and after conversations which, normally welcome and satisfying, would, she knew, not be so tonight. A slam bang quickie wasn't Jack's style, she thought, not always hers either, really.

She said, with total honesty, "Not quite there, Jack. Soon though, I do need to see you."

Jack took a breath and said, "OK, I understand." But he wasn't sure that he did.

"What are you up to over the weekend?"

"I'm ready for a bit of down time and then, I think, it's Delaware on Monday with that husband thing."

"Well, keep in touch, then. Be safe."

"And you. I will."

Aggie put the phone down, rested her head on the back of the couch, looked up at the ceiling and closed her eyes.

About two hours later, she awoke with a start and had no idea where she was for a moment or two. She looked absently around her and a rush of thoughts and images flooded into her mind. She rubbed her face with both hands, fluffed her hair where it had bunched at the back of her head and climbed to her feet. She flexed her joints, doubled over and stretched her legs and headed to the kitchen for some iced water. After a couple of gulps, she went back to the couch and sat down. Soon, her equilibrium and thought processes clicked into place and she began to get her mind around the idea of a trip to Delaware. It was a long time since she had been there. She remembered vaguely that there were crowded beaches, something to do with horse racing and quite a lot of residential building construction going on. She picked up her iPad and idly checked ways of getting to Wilmington, although she had every intention of driving her Beamer there. There was a cut rate bus trip, a flight at three times the cost of the bus or a train, which would have been her choice but a car was needed to find the office of Maisie's husband, or, indeed, the company apartment. It seemed that the journey could take a little under three hours or better; not too bad but should she plan for a round trip in a day or stop over? That would depend on her success, or lack of it, she supposed. With a sigh, she figured that it would be a 'play it by ear' scenario, like much of her life. She would wait and see what Wilmington had to offer after the weekend. She didn't fancy her bedroom so she grabbed a blanket and her robe and covered herself on the couch and went to sleep.

The next morning, Aggie found herself reflecting on the events of the past few days and wondered how she had managed to pack so much in since she had been attacked. Just thinking about it, made her feel tired and so she decided to do other things, ordinary things like shopping for some basics and a new bedroom rug and visiting her gym, which she hadn't done for over two weeks. She also had a small pile of books that she wanted to get to, the first of which were The Life of Pi and The Girl on a Train. By Sunday, she had fish, crab cakes, an array of salad vegetables, olives and cheese in her refrigerator, along with a pack of Troegenators as an experiment. She had spent an uneventful, strenuous hour at her gym and was totally unsure of her new rug which was a brightly colored mishmash of abstract shapes. She had remained on the couch for sleeping and reading the first seventy pages of Pi.

By evening, she had consumed most of the cheese and olives and two of the Troegenators, which she found that she liked for their richness. Finally, before sleeping, she ran through her notes and felt more than ready for Delaware. Aggie awoke early the next morning after a dreamless night and, following a lengthy hot shower, felt refreshed and ready to take on the day. Wrapped in her warm, wooly robe, she decided that she could be ready to roll in about an hour and called her parking garage to have her car ready. The good news was that there was no return call and so she could assume that her Beamer must have started with no trouble. While consuming two cups of black coffee and a single slice of dry toasted country white bread, she checked her notes and the addresses that Maisie had given her. In the absence of further information on Dougal Toomey, and not feeling like doing more research on the Toomey family at all, Aggie began to look forward to a spin in her roadster, some fresh air and some investigative work, albeit at her own expense. Since her car must have been persuaded to start, her only worry would be that there was enough gas in it to get her out of the city to a comfortable gas station en route. There just seemed to be less hassle getting gas away from urban areas. She washed up her cup and coffee pot, recalling that she once dated a guy who insisted that the pot should not be washed but should keep the coffee stains to maintain flavor. She wiped away the bread crumbs with a damp paper towel and began to dress in black jeans, a cream tank top and her black denim jacket. She liked sneakers for driving and slipped them on over a pair of black cotton socks. She grabbed her bag and an old thin leather briefcase, stuffed her notes into it, found her car keys in the bedside table, shook her wet hair a couple of times and headed for the door. The walk to her parking garage was only three blocks and she welcomed the cool air and exercise as she walked towards it. Aggie's car was ready for her, as it always was, the guys there being punctual, helpful and efficient. With a cheery wave she slid into the bucket seat of her roadster and started the engine. All was well, except for a faintly musty odor and a windshield filmed over from garage fumes, but the engine purred quietly as she rolled out of the garage, sprayed and washed the windshield and headed for the George Washington Bridge, her preferred route out of the westside of Manhattan.

Even though it was overcast, it was bright and so Aggie slipped on her sunglasses which were supposed to cut out all of the ultraviolet light. They gave a comforting yellowish-brown image, which she liked for driving. Aggie was not a high-tech person by nature but she had invested in a GPS app for her smart phone which did away with map reading and the frustrations of misdirection. Besides her iPad, which was mostly for her notes and writing, she had an iPod which was still adequately useable at five years of age, when she played it through her car radio at the correct frequency. She had over four thousand songs of eclectic taste and for her playlist, she preferred voice and guitar like John Moreland or small groups like Civil Wars, The Low Anthem and The Lone Bellow, as well as seventies rock and a smattering of the Punch Brothers and the Carolina Chocolate Drops. She gassed up early on and the journey was uneventful, if intimidating at times, due to the massive trucks that now inhabited the highways, taking two rotations of her playlist. Even though a little stiff, she felt refreshed and alert as she pulled into a motorway stop, used the bathroom and had a coffee with two bananas, finishing the journey to her first address, the office of Maisie's husband.

The address turned out to be a three-story block of offices with an entrance at each end of the block. It was set back from the road behind a grassy bank and a two-aisle car park. Aggie parked towards one end of the block facing the grassy bank. She switched off the ignition and sat quietly for a few moments, taking in her surroundings and marshaling her thoughts before climbing out of the car. She stretched her legs, grabbed her bag and locked the car. She glanced at the office block and noted that lights indicated occupancy in every one of the offices. Feeling rather exposed she headed for the entrance at her end of the block, opened one of the double glass doors and entered a small, carpeted lobby with a shiny marble counter to her left, shielding a dapper, young, suited, blond man. There was a staircase ahead, next to which was a rather ostentatious brass plaque listing, presumably, the office businesses. There was no elevator and Aggie wondered how that played out with the laws on assisting disabled workers. Perhaps the other entrance compensated for that. She decided to ignore the blond man and walked over to the brass plaque, clearly feeling his gaze as she did so.

Her eyes expertly scanned the list of company names looking for Moreland Associates, without any success. She took a step back feeling puzzled, wondering if the address was correct or if there were other plaques somewhere.

A modulated, somewhat cheery voice asked from behind the counter, "Can I help you?"

Aggie, turned, smiled and said, "Oh, yes. I'm looking for a company called Moreland Associates. It works out of this address but I must have missed it on the board. Perhaps it's new and hasn't been listed yet?"

"Just a moment please, I'll check."

Aggie heard the rattle of computer keys as the blond guy scanned his computer screen.

"No," he said, "doesn't seem to be here."

Aggie had already been thinking of what to say next and what her next move would be but now she was more than curious and felt a little stymied.

"Are you sure," she said, "it's spelled M-O-R-E-L-A-N-D."

"Yes ma'am, I am aware of that. I will check again."

He went through a similar ritual and said, "No ma'am, there is no company of that name here."

Aggie paused for a moment and then said, "Do you have individuals in this building listed separately, as opposed to companies? If the company isn't listed, then perhaps the guy I'm looking for could be working for someone else now."

"We do have individual listings which are mostly up to date. Who are you looking for?"

"His name is David Hamilton."

The blonde man repeated his computer exercise and then looked up cheerfully.

"There is someone of that name listed. He is down under the Frobisher Talent Agency."

"Really? A talent agency? Are you sure?"

"Yes ma'am. It is not an uncommon name, of course."

"No, I know but this was an address I was given for him." Aggie was more than shaken at this turn of events.

"Would you like me to call up for you?"

"Call up?"

"Well, yes. I can't let you go up to visit without a notification. The office is on the third floor."

Aggie needed time to think.

"Not just now thanks. It may not be the right guy. I'd feel a bit foolish. I was thinking of working for him so I'll double check my information. Thanks for your help."

As Aggie turned for the door the blonde man said, "You're welcome."

She pushed through the door and out into the open and walked quickly to her car, without glancing up to the third floor. Once inside, she drew a deep breath and rested her head on the headrest with her eyes closed. At first, she could not decide what to do next. This had to be the correct address and the David

Hamilton had to be Maisie's husband, one fact really confirming the other. Was he in an office this afternoon? What did he do there? A talent agency had nothing to do with medical supplies, so what was the story? Why not tell Maisie what he did, whatever that was? Aggie knew that she could not go and pay him a visit. What would she say? Hi David. How's things? What are you doing here? All she could come up with was to sit and wait to see if he came into the car park to leave. She could then, at least, follow him. She realized that she did not know what car he drove but did not want to call Maisie yet because an explanation would be needed. After a few minutes, she decided to move her car nearer to the center of the office block and facing towards it. She found a suitable space and settled down to watch. After an hour and a half of excruciating boredom, even with the iPod, people began to drift out of both entrances of the building and she was reasonably certain that she could recognize David because of his size. As the car park emptied with no sign of him, she began to doubt her methodology. After another hour, she was convinced that it was a ludicrous approach to the problem. When three cars were left after yet another hour, she was ready to give up. Ten minutes later, with a huge sigh of frustration, she decided to call it a day. There was a Ford F-150 truck, a Ford Focus and Toyota Camry left in the car park, all by the entrance that she had not entered.

Aggie decided to update Jack and to see if he had any news. She called but his phone went to message and she left a brief 'no real progress in Delaware' report and that she would be pressing on tomorrow.

She fired up the Beamer and eased onto the adjacent freeway. She thumped the steering wheel a couple of times and screamed loudly, telling herself that this was what investigators did, although, she hadn't had the patience to see it through to the bitter end. Aggie had driven three miles when she found a Best Western next to a diner and so she checked in with only a briefcase and not even a toothbrush for the night. She thought ruefully, that she hadn't planned this too well. She washed up in her room which had a standard view of another car park, used her finger to clean her teeth with the complimentary toothpaste and headed for the diner which, thankfully, also boasted a liquor license.

The dining area was fairly busy but Aggie managed to get a booth and after a brief look at the menu, ordered a well-done burger with blue cheese and a Portobello mushroom cap, along with fries and a Sam Adams. To hell with the diet. She was very hungry and more than a little fed up. There was a small bar in the corner of the dining area with two or three young suited men propping it up and drinking earnestly and quietly. Her meal arrived in a very short time and looked and smelt thoroughly appetizing. The fries turned out to be curly and spiced. Aggie ate slowly and reflectively, occasionally sipping her beer and trying to find something positive out of her trip so far. To make any progress, she had to know that Maisie's husband was in an office in that building and the only way to do that was to actually see him there. She had to know what kind of car he drove and so, reluctantly, she called Maisie while waiting for her check. The phone was answered after one ring.

"Hi. Maisie Beck."

"Hi Maisie. It's me. I'm calling because I don't know what kind of car David drives."

"Oh! Aggie. Where are you?"

Clearly, she hadn't checked the caller ID.

"I'm in Delaware having a bite to eat."

"Have you found out anything yet?"

"Not really. I'm going to put in some time tomorrow."

"OK, well, keep me posted. David has a Toyota Camry. Dark blue."

"Fuck," said Aggie, thinking that the one she saw was his.

"What?"

"Oh, nothing. Food on my clothes. Sorry Maisie."

"OK. Well, good luck tomorrow. I really don't know what I mean by that."

"Thanks Maisie. Try not to worry. Bye."

That done, Aggie swore again. Patience, patience, patience. She thought that she should have seen it through. Plus, now she was irritable, full of food that she shouldn't have eaten and a whole night to waste.

As she stared at the table and the check, a voice next to her said, "Hi, can I buy you a drink? I'm Ross."

Aggie looked up into the clear blue eyes and clean shaven, young face of one of the guys from the bar. "Hi Ross. Yes, I expect that you could but I am OK thanks."

"You are more than OK. I just thought that you might have a drink with me, you know."

Aggie laughed, which felt good.

"Oh dear. Nice of you but I am in the middle of something. Thanks anyway."

"OK. Worth a try though."

"Yes, it was," Aggie said smiling and just a trifle flattered.

The young man smiled back and said, "If you change your mind, I'll be here for a bit," and he moved off back to the bar.

Aggie had thought that those days were over. Interesting! She sat there turning the check over and over in her hand for several minutes. The guy called Ross glanced over a few times and, eventually, Aggie signaled to him. After all, she could do with a bit of fun and pass an hour or two.

He came over, smiling broadly, and said, "I hope you have changed your mind."

"As a matter of fact, I have. I don't want to drink at the bar. Shall we have a drink here at the table?"

"Great, great! What can I get you?"

"A Bombay Sapphire and tonic please, with olives."

"Olives?"

"Yes, I like olives."

"Coming up, be with you in a bit."

At the bar, she thought that his drinking friends were looking wistful or, at least, that's how she interpreted their glances.

Ross came back to the booth with Aggie's drink and a beer for himself and slid into the seat opposite her. He raised his glass, muttered cheers and they both drank. Aggie was surprised at how well the first slug went down. She followed it with an olive.

Ross said, "Visiting this godforsaken town?"

Aggie said, "Yes, a little administrative work to do, nothing special."

"Funny, I could have sworn that I saw you this afternoon at Greenbanks."

"Greenbanks?"

"Office block up the road."

"Oh. Yes, I was there trying to locate someone."

"Small world. I probably know the person you are looking for. Been there for almost four years."

Aggie sipped her drink. "So, this would be your local. What do you do there?"

"I'm an architect. Well, a budding architect. I'm the lowest on the totem pole in my office."

"Ah. Interesting though or, at least, it can be, I suppose."

"It's not bad really. I can't somehow see me spending my whole working life at it. Prospects are dim, people seem to have to die for any kind of promotion to happen. Who were you looking for?"

"A guy. His name is David Hamilton."

"I know the name. I think he is a big, good-looking guy up on the third floor."

"That's him. What floor is your company on?"

"First floor. It's convenient. No stairs or elevator to worry about."

Aggie sipped her drink and Ross gulped almost all of his beer.

Aggie said, "There's an elevator?"

"Yes, but only at one end of the building. I work near the other end. More space too."

Aggie leaned back on her seat. Ross had both hands around his near empty glass.

"More space?"

"Yes. Upstairs has smaller offices. Look, why all the questions?"

Aggie smiled.

"Oh. Sorry. I hadn't realized. It's my nature. Just conversation."

"Ah."

The earnest blue eyes looked into hers.

"This isn't going anywhere is it?"

"What isn't? Our relationship?" Aggie said with a light chuckle.

"Um, well, yes. I thought that you know…" Ross' voice trailed off.

"I know. I do know. Let me buy you a drink."

Ross looked crestfallen. "It's OK. You don't have to."

Aggie leaned forward.

"I would like to."

She delved into her bag and put some money on the table.

She said, "But you have to get the drinks."

Ross paused, looked down and looked back up.

"OK. What would you like?"

"Same again."

Ross stood up, gave Aggie a long look and headed to the bar. His companions had left unnoticed by Aggie. He returned with the drinks and popped some change on the table. He said, "It's just dawned on me. I don't know your name. I'm just no good at this."

Aggie said, "That's right. I didn't give it. I'm not going to give it. Drink up."

The both drank deeply.

Aggie said, "What kind of day have you had?"

Ross drained some more beer and said, "That's easy. Boring, what about you?"

"Mine was frustrating, fruitless and… Ha, alliterative, let's stop this silly stuff!"

They looked at each other for a few moments, both now wondering where this was going.

Aggie said, "What do you want from me?"

Ross smiled nervously. "You know, I was hoping we could get together."

Aggie said, "The older woman kind of thing?"

"No, of course not. You look great. I just had to try."

"I think you said that before. OK. Ground rules. Let's get this straight. No strings or soppy stuff."

Ross positively beamed as realization dawned.

"Are you sure? I mean, I agree."

Aggie flashed him a hard look.

"I wouldn't say so otherwise. Fifteen minutes, room 34 next door. I'll tell the desk."

Exactly fifteen minutes later Aggie heard a gentle knock at her door and let Ross in, complete with freshly combed hair and two paper cups of gins and tonic.

Aggie said, with a wide smile, "We won't need those." She found Ross an inexperienced, vigorous and thoughtful lover. All in all, she was pleased with her decision to capture some excitement. It felt really good, even exhilarating and primal.

Finally, at 3am she said, "I need some sleep. You'd better go."

Ross rolled slowly off the bed, stood up and, with sleepy eyes said, "OK. You are amazing. Tomorrow?"

Aggie said, "Sorry, no seconds."

Ross looked disappointed, dressed quickly and quietly and leaned over, kissed Aggie's hair lightly and touched her on the shoulder before turning to the door and softly closing it on the way out.

Aggie stared at the closed door for a few seconds and then turned over and went to sleep.

Chapter 12

Aggie drifted into wakefulness at about 8 am wondering, at first, where she was. She slowly allowed her mind to dwell on the events of the previous evening and, with some amusement and a tinge of frustration, observed that she had learnt almost nothing but had had a decent and entertaining evening and night, which was not out of character but did not happen too often these days. She glanced around the room, taking in the minimal pile of clothing scattered over two chairs with her briefcase, bag and shoes lying beneath one of them and nothing else. No change of clothing or underwear then.

Aggie viewed the day ahead as a brand new one. There were new ideas and thoughts waiting to be expressed and new plans to be made. In fact, new ideas did not spring easily to mind. As she showered and slid into the same clothes, she wondered what to do next. She contemplated another day, or part of one, hanging around Greenbanks to see if David Hamilton showed up. That seemed very unproductive. If he did show, it would just confirm that he worked or had an office there or, at least, had some kind of business there. If he didn't, then the whole journey to Delaware was virtually a waste of time and money. What she needed to know, she decided, was where Maisie's husband stayed overnight and what he did at those times. If anything useful was to be learned, she would have to go to Greenbanks late in the afternoon and, if he was there, follow him to his destination. Aggie checked out of the motel and headed for the diner. It looked different in the light of day, unwelcoming and imbued with a faint odor of cleaning fluid, percolating through the bacon and coffee dominated atmosphere.

Over coffee, toasted, buttered English muffin and a banana, she scanned her brief notes and decided to check out the address that Maisie had given her for the company apartment. Back in her car, she called Jack but his phone went to message. She said nothing and hung up. She plugged the address into her GPS, using the voice facility for the journey. She wondered if she could learn Spanish by using that language on her GPS but thought not.

Almost twenty minutes later, she was coasting down the address street which seemed upscale and boasted several apartment blocks, each blessed with the name of a tree. Almost every town seemed to have tree names for streets and now, it seemed, the idea worked for buildings too. The one she wanted was called simply Hemlock Apartments.

It hadn't really crossed her mind before but now she thought the name was bizarre, even intimidating, although she had seen enough Gallows Roads and Cemetery Roads. The GPS told her that her destination was six hundred feet away on her side of the street, which corresponded to the fourth block. She cruised on, past well-established trees set in the grass verges on both sides of the street, their roots pushing up through the nearby paving. She turned into a wide entrance which was essentially a gap in the low wall that ran along the front of the property and which led to a small car park at the side and rear of the block. In front of the block was a gravel yard covered in rhododendrons, which had been allowed to spread and intermingle with each other. The block was built of red brick and each apartment had a brick terrace with a cream cement surface to the terrace walls. The car park was half full and she found a space labeled visitor in large yellow letters. Aggie climbed out of her car, grabbed her bag, locked up and headed for the only entrance to the building, which had an ornate, dark brown canopy, supported by two poles, above two glass double doors. Hemlock Apartments was printed across the canopy in white letters. She pulled open one of the doors and found herself standing on a thick coconut mat, emblazoned with the building name, and facing another set of glass doors. Adjacent to the inner doors, was a large metal frame, housing the building buzzer system, each buzzer with a name next to it. The center of the opposite wall was covered with mail boxes, let into the wall itself. Aggie guessed that there were about forty or fifty. She ran her finger down the buzzers, scanning the names. Some were single second names, some were first and second names and some were pairs of names. All appeared to be residential. As far as Aggie could tell, there were no company names.

That probably meant nothing because David's company could have used any second name for the buzzer. There was no Hamilton name either. She made a mental note to check on David's company, annoyed that she had not done so already. Perhaps, he was the only person in it. Anyone could start a company. She was relieved to see the magic word 'Supt' next to someone named Frank Guthrie. She pressed the buzzer but there was no reply. She glanced around, looking for a camera but saw none and pressed the buzzer again and, after a loud click, a deep voice said, "Yes?"

Aggie said, "Hi, I'm trying to locate an apartment. All I have is this address but no apartment number."

Guthrie coughed and said, "You don't have the name of the tenant?"

Aggie immediately registered the word tenant. Rented property then, not owned.

"I have the name Moreland Associates."

"Sounds like a business. There are no businesses here."

"Well, it could be rented by someone in the business for employee stopovers. I think that's how it works."

"Well, all the names are on the buzzers. Look there."

"Yes. I looked at them. It's not there."

"Any other names?"

"Hamilton. That's not there either."

Guthrie coughed again. "So, you have the names and they are not listed. What do you want me to do?"

"Um. Perhaps you could come out and I could describe the tenant to you. It would be easier than like this."

There was silence that seemed to punctuate the fact that she did not seem to be getting anywhere. Then Guthrie said, "OK, I'll be out."

A very tall, thin figure showed up in less than a minute. His head was completely shaven and he carried a mustache and goatee beard rather well. He wore sweats and a grubby tee-shirt and his brown eyes peered at Aggie from an angular face. He opened one of the inner doors and indicated that she enter the lobby, which was marbled and airy; it also had two elevators and two green armchairs next to a coffee table set up on a nondescript beige carpet. He pointed to one of the chairs, sat in the other and, as Aggie sat down, said, "You are Ms.?"

"Trout."

"Well, Ms. Trout, describe your tenant."

"The renter I am looking for is a tall, dark-haired man, mid-thirties, drives a blue Toyota and would be here twice or so per month."

"Don't think I know him. Does he come on his own?"

"Yes or, at least, I think so."

"Ah. That sounds a bit vague. What are you trying to find this guy for?"

Aggie thought that question a bit cheeky.

She said, "He gave me this address and told me to look him up."

She thought how easy it was to lie, if need be.

Guthrie said, "I see. Well, can't you just call him or something? That should be an easy way to track him down."

"I can't. This is all I have."

"You know, this sounds a bit weird, if you don't mind me saying so. Did he pick you up or something?"

Aggie laughed and said, "No, of course not. This is about a job proposition. I do legal work."

"Oh well, sorry, I can't help you."

Aggie looked disappointed.

Guthrie said, "Look, I don't recall the guy or the car and I've been here eight years."

Aggie sighed. "OK, thanks anyway."

She stood up, smiled at Guthrie and headed for the door. He didn't rise, just watched her pass through the doors and into the midday air.

Aggie reached her car, unlocked it and popped in. After a few minutes' reflection, she climbed out again and headed to the building entrance. Once inside, she used her phone to photograph all of the buzzer names and then scanned all the mailbox names for her quarry, with no luck, before heading back to her car and settling into the driver's seat. After a few minutes of allowing her frustration to calm down, Aggie decided to go back to Greenbanks. It was that or New York. She fired up the engine, reversed out and as she turned towards the exit, she scanned all the visible windows. Nothing unusual stood out. She pulled out into the street and, twenty minutes later, was in the Greenbanks car park. She could not see the Toyota at first glance, so she drove slowly back and forth past all the cars in the car park and, reluctantly, concluded that David's car was not there. She thought that a bit odd; a very short trip perhaps, but there could be any number of explanations for David not being there. She parked her roadster to think.

No David, no following and no progress.

She could wait until the end of the day but could not bear the thought. Not enough possibility of a reward for all of those hours.

Then she recalled Frobisher Talent Agency. She Googled the company and got a telephone number. Moments later the Agency telephone was ringing.

It picked up after two rings and a woman's voice said, "Frobisher Talent Agency. Maria speaking, how can I help you."

Aggie said, "Hi, can I speak to David Hamilton of Moreland Associates, please."

She was sure that he wasn't there and had no idea what she would say if he was. Caller ID would mean that there would be no point in hanging up.

She thought that a good reason to invest in throwaways.

Maria paused a beat and said, "He's not been in today so far and I don't know when he's coming in. I'm not sure that I've heard of Moreland Associates."

Aggie said, "Oh."

Maria said, "You know, he has his own number," and then, rather robotically, "this is Frobisher Talent Agency and he is not with us."

"Oh. OK. Do you have his number please? I'll call him."

Maria was silent for a few seconds and said, "Are you a friend or a client?"

Realizing that a friend would have the number, Aggie said, "I am a prospective client."

With some reluctance, Maria gave her the number.

Aggie said, "Thank you. I'm calling because he gave me your address and number."

"That's strange. He just shares an office and has no real connection to us."

Aggie said, "There you go." and hung up.

At last, something. David Hamilton had an office here and came here occasionally. He didn't use his company name and he didn't list himself in the lobby, which meant that he just rented space from the Agency in a private deal. Sort of incognito. He needed a base here for some reason.

Now that she had something, Aggie's thoughts shifted to New York. She saw no point in wasting more time in Delaware.

She decided to call Jack and, while doing so noticed that her telephone was almost dead. As she plugged it in, she heard Jack's line go to message and said that she was leaving Delaware and would be back early evening.

She turned on the ignition and pulled out for the return journey, switching on her iPod and Nathaniel Rateliffe and the Night Sweats as she went.

Chapter 13

Traffic was heavy because of the time of day or, perhaps, it was always heavy on this route. Aggie arrived back at her garage at about 6:30 pm, dropped off the car and was soon inside her apartment, having picked up her mail which was mostly bills and catalogs. She went straight to the bathroom and began to run a hot bath. She went to the fridge and hauled out a bottle of Riesling, taking a full glass to the bathroom. She tossed all of her clothes into the laundry basket in her bedroom and climbed gratefully into the hot water to think and sip the wine. Half an hour later, glass empty, she showered, washed her hair and slipped into her robe. Next, was some toasted bread which was past its best, stuffed with cucumber and tomato slices with another glass of wine. As she ate, she made some notes, summarizing the last two days of information. She then decided that it was time to put it all into her iPad, which she usually did after initial longhand notes.

That done, she took her glass and plate to the kitchen to wash up when she noticed the message light winking on her landline telephone. She stood by it as she played the message. It was a long message from Jack. He must have called when she was in the shower. He was still at work and had had no time to do her research because the fraud case had been all consuming due to the violence involved. He'd fill her in later. If he had time tonight or tomorrow morning, he would call her and they could talk over lunch. Aggie plopped onto her couch as all of the Toomey affair coursed through her mind again. Maisie's problems had pushed it aside and now she immediately thought of Toomey lurking somewhere, anywhere. She suddenly jumped up and went into her bedroom, checking the window and the empty fire escape.

She stared at her reflection in the window, thinking that she had to get this guy off the streets and out of her life.

Aggie went back to her couch where she intended to spend another night. She poured another glass of wine and switched on her newish flat screen television, not recalling the last time she had done so. After some Antiques Roadshow and Jimmy Kimmel, she fell asleep.

The next morning, full of coffee by 8 am and with no call from Jack, she began to review her options. She proposed to find out about Georgia Kaplan's past as best she could and use it to try to predict the present, in case Georgia had changed her name but followed old habits.

Sounded vague but, if she was alive, it felt like doing something useful. She thought about calling Maisie but decided to wait for Maisie to call her. She spent two and a half hours going back and forth through various websites and social media outlets and began to piece something together. Georgia was born in 1982 in Brick, New Jersey and had probably gone to school in that area. No information on parents or college but she had worked for several years as some kind of assistant in a dental practice in Ortley, New Jersey. Aggie would have to call them to find out more. The next bit of useful information was that she appeared in New York linked to a guy who might have been her boyfriend. Anyway, he was a musician of sorts and they lived on Broadway in the low hundreds about three years ago. Then there was nothing.

Aggie was taken out of her research mode by her cell phone ringing. She checked the screen and saw that it was Maisie.

Aggie said, "Hi, Maisie, how's things?"

"Hi Aggie. About the same, I suppose. David is around. He's out shopping now."

"He's back already?"

Maisie said, "Yes, he showed up suddenly yesterday. I mean, it wasn't that unexpected. I never really know when he's coming home. It's usually more than one night though. He said that all his meetings had been cancelled due to illness and he had no reason to stay."

"Did he say who was ill?"

"No, just no meetings. I don't know much about what he does."

Aggie said, "Was everything OK when he got back?"

"I don't know. He's different."

"How's he different? Unless it's personal."

"No, it's not. He stares at me when I'm not looking and…he's more affectionate than usual."

Aggie suspected that he had something on his mind and was, perhaps, assessing his domestic situation.

She said, "Are you worried?"

"No, not really. It just feels odd. Things are quite definitely not the same now. Did you find out anything?"

Aggie took a deep breath. Her intuition told her that David was up to something but there was no evidence to suggest anything amiss, although the missing company apartment was just hanging there.

She said, "Made some progress but nothing definitive. I've been to the Queens office and seen David show up and spend time there. All perfectly normal. In a way, you'd expect that because it's the usual day to day thing from home."

Maisie said, "Right."

Aggie went on. "I also found the Wilmington building and confirmed that he has an office there. I did not see him but I did see his car. I haven't located the company apartment."

"But you do have the address."

"Yes, of course, but I have only seen the building. That's about where I am."

"OK."

"Sorry Maisie, but it's taking time."

"I know." Maisie sounded down. "What's next."

"I have a couple of things to check and, when you know that David is making his next trip, let me know. I'll keep in touch."

They hung up and Aggie immediately wished she had asked Maisie whether David was solo or had help in his company. She would double check that and call his previous company to find out why he left. She looked up Turner and Bowden and idly ran through a swath of analysts, a small group of in-house lawyers and some lesser lights. Upper echelons were blessed with photographs which were not that interesting she thought but there were a lot of nice, clean, white teeth, though.

No call from Jack yet and it was approaching mid-afternoon. She began to feel that time was slipping by and decided to pay a visit to Turner and Bowden. She called Jack and got the inevitable message. She said briefly that she was off to mid-town and would be back later. She quickly slipped on a cream shirt, brown jacket, black jeans and sneakers. As she was lacing up the sneakers, her cell rang. She saw that it was Jack.

She said, "Jack. Hi." She sounded more excited than she intended to.

Jack said, "Hi Ag. How're you doing?"

"Good. A bit of progress on the hubby thing."

She mentioned her checking out David's two business addresses and the lack of anything concrete in his overnight accommodation.

After a pause, Jack said, "Well, that shouldn't be difficult."

"I know but it turned out to be more difficult than I thought."

At that she steered the conversation away and said, "Enough about me, I can tell you later. Are you OK?"

"Yes. Haven't had much sleep. I need down time. I'm caught up in a pyramid case that's turned nasty. I'm on it though. It'll be a few days yet. Look Ag, I've got some info for you but not on the phone."

Aggie said, "Ears around?"

"Yes. In spades."

"OK. Call me when you can and we'll meet, or you can come over."

"Sounds good. Well, more than good. I'll look for some time. Take care."

"And you."

Aggie put the phone down, stared at it and thought it a good time to fix The Stones. She would do it soon.

She finished lacing her sneakers, fluffed her hair and set off for the subway, which took her close to the offices of Turner and Bowden. They were on Lexington in mid-town. There was an innate satisfaction in subway riding as if in so doing one was a part of the city, a true city dweller. On tramping up the steps with their shiny metal edges, she emerged from the subway and pulled out her telephone and saw that Jack had texted. He would drop by at about 7:30 pm with a Chinese takeout, unless she messaged otherwise. She smiled at that and rather looked forward to it plus she was desperate for some good news on the Toomey front.

Lobby reception at the building directed her to the fourth floor where, on leaving the elevator bank, she was faced with a substantial counter with 'reception' emblazoned on the wall behind it. Three women and a man were behind the counter fronted by computers, only one woman appearing free for visitors. Young, blonde haired and blue eyed, she scanned Aggie as she approached. Aggie, glancing sideways, took in a floor of cubicles with a line of office doors down one side of the floor. A rather large, heavy man, who looked to be in his fifties, was making his way through the wood, glass and people, settling down in one of the cubicles. Aggie turned her gaze back to reception as she reached the counter, looking into the expectant eyes of the blonde woman.

"Hi. I am looking for David Hamilton, who is a financial analyst here."

The woman said, "Do you have an appointment?"

"No. I'm dropping by just to say hello."

The woman looked askance at that and said, "And you don't have an appointment?"

"No."

"Did you, at least, call first or indicate that you were coming?"

"No. It was really a spur-of-the-moment thing."

The woman paused and said, "Just a moment."

She tapped away on the computer and then, with some relief evident, she said, "There is no one of that name in these offices. You did say David Hamilton?"

"Yes. Well, that's odd. You're sure?"

"Yes. Look, I've only been here for nine months. Give me a sec."

She rose from her chair and walked over to speak to a tall, suited woman standing next to an office doorway. They conferred briefly, both turned to look at Aggie and then the woman returned to her seat, sat down and looked up, her blue eyes now surrounded by a slightly flushed face and said, "I'm sorry but Mr. Hamilton left over a year ago. That is all I can tell you."

Aggie said, "Oh, I didn't know," and then, into a protracted silence said, "do you know where he went or why he left? I don't know how to find him."

The woman paused and responded, "We do not give out personal information."

Aggie said, "It's not really personal is it? I just want a general idea."

Aggie was aware of the suited woman hovering a step nearer than before.

Firmly, the woman said, "I do apologize but that is all I can do. You could make an appointment with the office manager if you wish."

Aggie said, "And who is that?"

The woman produced a card and handed it to Aggie who put it in her bag without looking at it. "I might do that. Thanks for your time."

"You're welcome."

Back in the lobby, Aggie took a seat in a small waiting area. It was now late afternoon. She took out her phone and tried to look busy in case her presence was challenged but there was no suggestion of that.

An hour later, people began to emerge from the elevators and from two first floor hallways, hurrying through the lobby to the revolving doors, or a single side door, onto the street. Aggie kept an eye on the elevators, wondering how she would approach her quarry. After about twenty more minutes of humanity flowing through the lobby, Aggie spotted the heavy guy from the fourth-floor office space. He was moving slowly, carrying an expensive looking leather briefcase and sporting a dark, lightweight coat. His full florid face was topped by a head of neat, grey, sleek hair.

Aggie let him pass and then rose and followed him through the single door onto the street.

She drew alongside him and said, "Excuse me."

He missed a step and turned towards her, a puzzled look on his face and when he didn't recognize her, one of annoyance and caution. "What? I'm busy."

He resumed his slow progress along Lexington.

Aggie went for an earnest expression and said, "I saw you on the fourth floor this afternoon."

He paused slightly and looked at her. "So what?"

"I was there looking for a friend."

"Aren't we all. Just leave me alone."

He began his forward motion again.

Aggie could see this going sideways quickly. She moved slightly ahead so that the man could see her face and said, "Do you know David Hamilton?"

He stopped and stared at her.

"Who?"

"David Hamilton."

"He's your friend?"

"Yes. I'm trying to find him."

"Good luck with that."

"Why? You do know him then?"

"I did. Still do."

He resumed walking.

Aggie persisted. "Do you know where he is?"

The heavy guy paused again and with thinly disguised irritation said, "Look, young lady, whatever this is really about, forget it."

"Forget what?"

"Just leave me alone. I'm already late."

Aggie tried a parting shot as he pulled away with some effort. "Why did he leave Turner and Bowden?"

"You don't want to know. Goodbye."

And with that he began an awkward descent into the subway. Aggie stood and watched him go as people jostled past her. He didn't look back.

Chapter 14

Back home Aggie washed up and sat on her couch to look through her notes. She had a couple of spurious bits of information which did not seem to have current significance but might become useful; David's office telephone number in Wilmington and her photograph of the buzzer names at Hemlock apartments. Both snippets pertained to the investigation of Maisie's husband. In the past she had, several times, found this kind of attention to odd, unconnected detail very helpful and, sometimes, crucial to a case.

She had, she thought, confirmed that David had left Turner and Bowden about a year or so ago and that there had been some effort by company employees to protect the circumstances of that parting beyond the realms of confidentiality. That could mean nothing but Aggie felt that there was something there beneath the surface. Financial analyst to self-employed salesman had no ring of truth unless David fancied himself as a rising entrepreneur. The late afternoon had morphed into early evening when Aggie was startled by her buzzer. Jack called up and a few minutes later he was at the door, armed with Chinese food and a couple of bottles of wine. He looked tired but also had a wide smile. He kissed her briefly and she took the wine and followed him into the kitchen where she had put out paper plates and napkins in the hope that he would show up as planned. They opted for forks and spoons and carried the meal, wine and two wine glasses to the couch and coffee table, saying little. Jack washed up in the bathroom and they sank onto the couch. He heaved a giant sigh, shrugged off his jacket and shoes and they tucked into the hot and sour soup before another word was spoken. As they finished the soup, Jack reached out and, with a flourish, opened vegetable fried rice, sweet and sour meatballs, some white rice and fried asparagus. It looked and smelled delicious.

As Aggie opened a Chardonnay she said, "This is great, Jack. Do you want to finish up before we talk?"

Jack said, "No, that's OK."

Aggie thought that it would do Jack good to talk a little as he relaxed.

She asked, "How's the case going? You look tired."

Jack speared a meatball with his fork, rolled it in the sauce and took a languid bite before replying. "Nothing special really. We have a guy who has run a very obvious pyramid scheme, purporting to invest money for mostly friends and guys he met through college reunions. It fell apart quickly because he is not the sharpest knife and four of his ex-buddies beat the shit out of him. Broken ribs, a possible skull fracture near an eye and a load of bruising, quite colorful if you like that sort of thing. I don't see how people fall for scams like that. It happens all the time. Anyway, I picked it up at the hospital because it looked serious and he was unconscious for a time. I got the story from him yesterday. His condition is still not good, his internal bleeding was extensive."

Jack paused, his eyes distant and Aggie said, "Let's eat some more. You look stressed."

She poured two generous glasses of wine and handed him one. They chinked glasses and both drank deeply before finishing up the meal in silence. Aggie put on one of her iPod playlists as quiet background music as they cleared away the empty boxes and plates to the kitchen, returning to settle in on the couch with the second bottle of wine, this one a Sauternes. Jack delved into his jacket and took out a Cadbury's fruit and nut chocolate bar.

He smiled and said, "I'm cheap but it's good."

Aggie laughed and said, "Great," as she opened it and spread some pieces on the foil.

They munched on a couple of pieces and sipped the wine. Finally, Aggie said, "What's next?"

"Oh. We'll pick up the four guys and charge them. There's a lot of interviewing and paperwork to be done. They were screwed but this was a nasty way of dealing with it. We have fraud guys looking into it. There's quite a few people who have lost money and are very unhappy."

Aggie said, "It's their own fault but fancy screwing friends."

"Yes. It takes all sorts."

Jack flopped back on the couch, sipped his wine and said, "OK, news time."

Aggie sat back too and half turned towards him.

"I did the easy bit first. Your guy Jonathan Black?"

Aggie nodded, thinking that he was not her guy but she remained silent.

Jack said, "He's a fixer of sorts, with no violence. At least, none on record that I know of. He's done a bit of boxing and mixed martial arts, mostly around 155 lbs. or less. He has taught at a military training academy—mostly historical context and politics. He's not short of a buck or two, lives in a high rise on Amsterdam in the hundreds. No family it seems, parents died a long time ago and he's light on connections to anyone significant, the Toomey family notwithstanding. That's about it on him."

They both finished their wine and Aggie refilled.

She said, "I wonder what the connection is then."

"No idea. Maybe just a financial arrangement. It wouldn't be unusual."

"No, it wouldn't."

Jack sighed again and said, "I ran through Moody's interview and had a chat with him. You remember, you left early? Plus, I spoke to Larry Dooley. He's the guy you saw on the desk when you came in. A couple of things came out of that."

"What's he got to do with it?" Aggie paused as she figured out what had happened.

"Ah. Your leaks!"

"Yes. We don't know what he got out of it. There was no obvious financial gain but there had to be a quid pro quo somewhere."

"Maybe other favors?"

Aggie paused for a moment. "No, can't see that. They are not far off in age but, no. What happened to him?"

"Transferred."

"That's all?"

"Yes. Not easy to prove, long service, all of that."

"Wow. I expect there will be an early retirement. With full pension?"

"Yes, or whatever is due."

Jack shrugged,

"That's the way it goes."

He shook his head minimally and continued.

"So, it seems that Toomey is a serial pervert who is protected by his mother. She has no feelings for him. I think that she just doesn't want any blowback on the family or, more specifically, on her."

"That figures. He's probably a waste of space as far as she is concerned."

Jack said, "So, she knows exactly what's going on and just clears up the mess each time. That is until you came along. Or, rather, his behavior escalated in your case."

"Lucky me."

"Yes. Rotten business. Who knows what would have happened if you hadn't been handy with your bits."

"Right."

"It would seem that he will plead guilty to a peeping tom or voyeur charge. There is nothing bad in his official record until this escapade."

"Escapade?"

"Sorry. I'm tired. Attack on you. Or, alleged attack on you."

"Wow. So, I dragged him into my apartment just so that I could beat him up."

"That's about the size of it."

Aggie checked but there was no hint of a smile at that. They both sipped some more wine.

She said, "Anything about the knife yet?"

"Oh, yes, I forgot about that. The blood type was Toomey's. There were signs of chemical cleaning where the blade goes into the handle but that's all. No help really."

Aggie was disappointed. "Not much to go on then."

"No. Haven't connected him to any further assaults yet, either. It's possible and I'm still looking. Moody picked up something else about Toomey, though."

Aggie took a deep draft of wine which was going down rather well she thought.

"Like what?"

"Well, he's followed you around quite a bit, or so it seems. No real crime there, just creepy."

"Stalker?"

"Close anyway. He did admit to seeing you in the back of a car with someone."

Jack looked a little sheepish, awkward, even.

Aggie said, "What? When?"

"He didn't say. Could have been lying. Clammed up and refused to say more."

Aggie remembered the occasion quite clearly. It was in a pub car park after a somewhat riotous get together with some college friends. One thing led to another, the another being a passionate and entirely memorable twenty minutes in a very confined space.

"He wasn't lying but it is really scary creepy. This guy is sick."

Jack finished up his wine.

He said, "I'm tired, it's been a long one."

"It has. You too tired? What do you think?"

Jack smiled, a small white scar on his jaw bone, gleaming in the soft light.

"Not at all. Just what I need."

Aggie took the glasses to the kitchen, tidied quickly while Jack washed up again in the bathroom. Then they headed to the bedroom and Aggie felt comfortable in there for the first time in days.

Chapter 15

Early the next morning, after they made love again, Jack got up and made coffee and toasted the heel of a French baguette. They munched on the toast and sipped the coffee in bed in a comfortable silence. Jack spoke first.

"What are you up to today?"

Aggie thought for a moment and then offered, "I think I'll go back to Delaware. My friend texted me that her husband has gone there for a day or two."

"Why? Do you really have to push on with this stuff?"

"I just think that I owe it to Maisie to come up with something, good or bad. She needs peace of mind and she is my friend."

"It's a lot of time and effort, and money."

"I know. You're right. I'll try to resolve the whole thing in the next day or so. But for my conscience check from Katherine Toomey, I'd be a bit strapped. I'd like to follow up on the Kaplan woman as soon as I can."

They finished up the toast and coffee.

"Well, I hope it works out, and quickly."

"Thanks. What are you doing?"

"Interviewing and follow up. I'll do what I can on Kaplan but Mort is on my case about my extracurriculars for you."

"Ah. He really doesn't like me, does he?"

Jack began dressing. "It's not like or dislike. He's the captain and he hates amateurs. PI's."

"No, I think it's me. A woman."

"Well, either way he's not happy."

"He never is."

Aggie got up and headed for the bathroom while Jack finished dressing.

He called out, "Last night was great."

Aggie called back, "So was this morning."

"See you soon. Take care." And he left.

Aggie showered, slipped on her robe and headed for the couch with her iPad. She spent the next forty minutes looking for Georgia Kaplan's relatives. Finally, she came up with an older brother and his family living in Ocean Beach, New Jersey. She knew that it was only a mile or two from Ortley, where Georgia Kaplan had worked as a dental assistant. This was promising news she thought and warranted a trip to the New Jersey shore.

Today was Thursday so she thought that she could manage a quick trip to Delaware today and hit the shore at the weekend. It all felt neat and tidy. She called the garage for her car to be ready and began dressing. Cooler day so she opted for a thin white cotton polo and a fake leather vest, black jeans and boots. She fluffed up her hair, grabbed her bag, iPad and keys and headed for the door.

The journey to Delaware was uneventful, in fact, boring. She listened to music most of the way but needed quiet as she approached Greenbanks. She reached the car park and cruised the lines of cars but did not find David's Toyota. She tried once more and then parked over to one side of the car park near the entrance that she had not used the last time. Feeling frustrated, she sat in thought for a few minutes. It was just after lunch so perhaps David had gone somewhere for some eats. Finally, she decided to go to the lobby entrance closest to her. The inside was a mirror image of the other lobby but for an elevator. A middle-aged woman sat behind the obligatory counter.

She said, "Can I help you."

Aggie walked over to the counter, smiled briefly and said, "I'm looking for David Hamilton. He has an office in the Frobisher Talent Agency."

"Just a moment please." She tapped away on her computer. "I don't know if he is in. People that work here are supposed to check out if they leave, just to know if they are in or out but many of them do not bother."

Aggie looked as perplexed as she could. "Do they go out for lunch?"

"Most here get delivery for lunch so I don't really know what to say. I'm sorry, not very helpful."

Aggie said, "That's OK. I'll try again later."

She left the building, walked back to her car, opened the door and slid into the driver's seat. Almost immediately, a hand appeared on her shoulder and gripped it tightly. She gasped in shock and tried to turn but couldn't, a thought that she somehow forgot to lock her car, flashing through her mind. Too late now.

David's voice breathed into her ear.

"What the fuck do you think you are doing?"

Aggie sucked air into her lungs before finally saying, "None of your business."

He tightened his grip which was beginning to feel painful. "First of all, my Queens office, then my old company and now this."

"What?"

"I saw you outside the bakery. I knew that you were watching me. You poked around at Turner and Bowden and now you are here."

Aggie thought the fat guy told him and then David said. "I'll ask you again. What the fuck do you think you are doing?"

"And I say it's none of your business."

David leaned a couple of inches closer and caught Aggie's eyes in the mirror, his dark features looking menacing. "It is my business. Keep your shitty little nose out of my affairs."

Aggie muttered, "Or?"

"There will be consequences. Serious consequences."

"That sounds like a threat."

"More than a threat. I'm telling you to keep away from me. If Maisie hears the faintest squeak from you, there will be the worst possible outcome."

David's eyes glistened with fury. The pain in Aggie's shoulder was intense. She said nothing.

David continued. "So, keep that foul PI mouth of yours shut and keep away from me and Maisie. Does that seem clear to you?"

Again, Aggie said nothing.

David's hand released her shoulder. He pushed the passenger seat forwards and, with some difficulty, clambered from the car and turned to her.

He said, "Don't fuck with me," and then suddenly smacked her sharply across the cheek.

Aggie recoiled in shock and put her hand up to her face and, in that moment, he was gone, striding away in a burgeoning drizzle, his menace hanging over her as she began to shake with shock.

There could be little doubt of his intent. There was no suggestion of a bluff. Aggie sat back in the seat with her eyes closed. That was nasty, nasty, nasty.

Her cheek stung from the blow and she had the faint taste of blood in her mouth. She swallowed and licked her lips and immediately felt that she would not be intimidated. David had turned out to be a mean, bullying prick but she knew that he meant what he said. She spent a few minutes recovering and thinking things through, an idea forming in her mind. She used her iPad and set her GPS and fired up the Beamer and drove out of the car park into a drizzly mist and headed past the motel and diner and on to an Avis car rental spread.

She parked and entered the rental office, which was deserted. A young guy with a straggly beard and a ball cap waited expectantly behind the counter. She wanted the cheapest available rental car which turned out to be a Honda Civic. Black in color. She thought there was a time when almost no cars were black and now many limos and rentals were. Most of Uber vehicles certainly seemed to be.

When asked, she said that she wanted the rental for half a day, in fact, just for the afternoon.

The guy said, "We don't do that. The shortest period is one day."

Aggie said, "I only need it for a couple of hours."

The guy said, "What, like a motel room?"

Aggie glared at him. "What did you say?"

"Oh. Nothing. Just a joke."

"Well, it's not funny."

"Sorry. Anyway, you have to pay for the day, up until two tomorrow."

Aggie sighed and said, "OK that'll have to do."

She filled out the paperwork, gave her credit card.

The guy took her out back and showed her the Honda in a perfunctory way and gave her the keys.

"Can I leave my car here in the car park?"

"You've got a car?"

"Yes. I've got a car."

Aggie ran a hard look at him.

"OK. Yes, sure."

"Right. See you later."

He wandered back into the office and Aggie climbed into the Honda. She called into a deli and picked up a cheese sandwich and a coffee and headed back to Greenbanks. She turned into the car park, spotted David's car almost immediately and parked as far away as possible while still being able to see it.

She munched on her sandwich and sipped her coffee, hardly aware that she was doing so. Occasionally, cars pulled out of the parking lot as the end of the afternoon approached and the drizzle lifted to be replaced by grayish light. Aggie began to worry that she would gradually be exposed as the car park emptied; but, so far so good. After an hour and a half, David suddenly appeared at the entrance to the building and began to make his way towards his car. He glanced around carefully as he moved through the cars and Aggie automatically sank down into her driving seat.

David suddenly felt very menacing. During the few times that she had met him previously, he had seemed affable and friendly but he now projected this aura of intense threat. He hopped into his Toyota and after a few moments, he pulled out of the car park and set off in the direction of the diner. Aggie started up and pulled into the traffic about ten cars back, being careful to keep him in sight but remaining as far back as possible. It was not as easy as most people think and she did not regard herself as that competent in tracking cars but after twelve miles she saw David turn off on a suburban road followed by one other car. She came up to the turn slowly and saw both cars turn into a small residential development of modest detached homes. David was about two hundred yards ahead when he slowed and entered the driveway of one of the homes. Aggie pulled over and watched as he climbed out of the Toyota and closed the door. At that moment, she saw the arms of a woman, barely visible in the doorway, ushering out a young female toddler who ran to David and clung to one leg. David picked her up and started towards the front door where he reached out an arm and leaned into the doorway for a kiss. Then he stopped, turned and stared down the street directly at Aggie's car for fully ten seconds before entering the house. Aggie, realizing that she had been holding her breath, let out a gasp and began breathing normally. As she processed what she had just seen, she made a three-point turn, checked the name of the street and the number of the house next to her on the same side as the house that David had entered. During her maneuvering, she noted that that house was 10 homes down on the even side of the street. The turn completed, she headed back to the highway.

What did it mean?

On the face of it David had a nuclear family in Delaware. Hemlock apartments now made sense because David had a home or, at least, appeared to have one so he just needed to have a cover address. That being the case, the names in the apartment block lobby had no significance nor did anyone living in the apartments. After a few minutes of driving, she realized that she was heading back towards Greenbanks. There was no point in going there or to Hemlock apartments and so she pointed the Honda towards the Avis franchise. She returned the rental, picked up her Beamer and turned for home in New York. Of course, another possibility was that the woman was a friend or sister, something like that. It came down to that kiss, perhaps.

What kind of kiss was it? Just a welcome kiss?

Hard to see at that distance. Then there was the kid who obviously knew him really well.

That looked like a family hug and was more conclusive. She had a mental note of the address but David probably would not have the home under his own name. It wouldn't take a minute or two to find out who owned the home, that could come later. Sharing an office with Frobisher Talent Agency now also made perfect sense. He was maintaining two homes with the associated costs. Aggie cautioned herself not to jump to conclusions but found it difficult not to. That kid displayed a convincing 'daddy' thing. She reached her garage in darkness without recalling almost any of the journey. Soon, she was in her apartment, sipping a glass of Chardonnay and leaning back on her couch with a sigh. She suddenly felt very tired. With some reluctance she texted Jack to say that she was back, having had some success in Delaware. She drank another glass of wine and headed for bed, feeling that her bedroom had returned to normal again. Friday turned out to be an almost nothing day. Perhaps, the David episode had a deeper effect than Aggie appreciated but, in any event, she could not face any part of her cases and spent time reading a newspaper from end to end and part of a book about hiking in Peru. She took the hint that her mind was giving her, no case work today. Lunch was bottled Mandarin oranges with yogurt. She chastised herself for watching some dreadful television but, nevertheless, the sheer artlessness of it was satisfying in its own way. Aggie had not cooked in some time and as the evening approached, she could not decide on what to take a run at. Nothing fancy, just something quick and tasty. That meant no curries, stews or soups.

Then she remembered. An English friend, named Archie, had once made her a dish called Welsh Rarebit which he had ceremoniously placed in front of her, calling it his filler dish when all else had fallen by the wayside. It was very tasty and quick he had said. And it was. It came on a thin slice of buttered toast, burnt around the edges, and topped with a bubbling, grilled mixture of cheeses, beer, mustard, Worcestershire Sauce, salt and pepper. Aggie made it in under half an hour on two slices of toast. It was perfect, if a little strong on the cheese front and went down well with a cup of coffee. More reading, better television, in fact, Wire in the Blood, made up the evening before bed at a reasonable hour and acceptable, harmless dreams.

Chapter 16

Aggie awoke feeling refreshed. The weekend had arrived and so, maybe, there would be a shore trip.

That was a nice thought. She needed to put Maisie's problems with David on hold at the back of her mind where it could percolate productively. She showered, dressed in a light blue sweat suit and sneakers, made coffee and ate an old Braeburn apple that she cut into slices. She checked her notes for the address of Georgia Kaplan's brother and the dental practice which was still in operation. It all looked good so she called for her car to be ready, washed up the coffee bits and was soon at her garage. She reacquainted herself with Langhorne Slim and Greg Laswell on the two-hour trip and began passing through the Point Pleasant environs just before midday. Minutes later, she was in Ocean Beach, which was actually three Ocean Beaches. Her GPS helped her to find the address without too much trouble. It turned out to be on the bay side of route 9 in a very narrow, unmade sandy street. There were puddles of rainwater scattered liberally across the street and the house, like most others on the street, was a small detached cottage style building, painted in bright blue and yellow colors.

There was a large, expensive looking barbecue in the front garden, which was all sand, and a set of dining chairs around a table with a cream and red umbrella in its center. The only other item on view was a child's paddle pool, containing murky water. The front property line was delineated by four small white posts from each section of which hung a chain made up of large white links. The drive was at capacity with two cars parked in it so Aggie parked in the street as close as she could to the chain fence. She climbed out of her car, walked up the drive and tapped on the screen door as loudly as she could. Sounds of a TV and young children filtered into the afternoon air. Some movement in the hallway occurred and the screen door opened to reveal a tallish guy topped by a New York Yankees baseball cap. He had a long, thin face with a thin nose and small dark eyes. Tufts of straggly sandy hair protruded from the baseball cap half covering his ears. Beneath this unattractive sight was a stained, orange tee shirt emblazoned with the words 'get lost' across the chest. Below this there were acceptable khaki shorts, hairy bronzed legs and brown leather sandals. The thin-lipped mouth offered an irritated, "Yes?"

Aggie said pleasantly, "My name is Agnes Trout. I am trying to locate a woman by the name of Georgia Kaplan."

The man's face clouded at her statement, producing an ugly expression.

She continued, "I understand that her brother Bernard lives here. Would that be you?"

"It would. What do you want her for?"

Aggie decided to go for direct. "I am a private investigator and I am looking for her in connection with a physical assault case. She may be able to help me."

"Oh yes. Well, haven't seen her in ages. Two or three years maybe."

"Oh. Have you heard from her, letters, phone calls—that sort of thing?"

"No. Nothing. Nobody writes letters these days. Thought you would have known that."

Aggie held back any comment. She felt frustrated. This guy was neither bright nor helpful.

She said, "Do you have any idea where she might be?"

"No."

Aggie continued, "If you don't mind me saying so, you do not seem very concerned."

The guy blinked twice, stared at Aggie more intently and said, "We were never close. Didn't like each other much."

"I see. Look, do you mind if I ask you a couple of questions?"

"That's all you've been doing since you've been here."

"Sorry, just a couple more then?"

"OK. Shoot."

Aggie paused and swallowed. She had hoped to be invited in but there was no sign of that. Things were coming to a close and she needed to learn what she could. She said, "Do you remember your sister being attacked? Physically, I mean."

"Er, yes, I do. We got a call from the cops at the hospital."

"How bad were her injuries?"

"Don't know. Serious, I gather."

Aggie couldn't hold back. "You didn't go and see her?"

"No. She was in good hands."

Aggie bit her lip. "Did you know who attacked her?"

"Some guy. The cops got him."

"Yes, they did but your sister did not testify against the guy."

"No, that's right. She didn't cooperate as you people call it."

"Any idea why? Why she didn't cooperate?"

"Not really. Could have been anything."

"She was living in New York at the time. Do you know where she went after New York?"

"I heard that she had moved back to this area somewhere. We didn't get in touch. You done now?"

"Yes, OK. Thank you for your cooperation Mr. Kaplan," she said with a faint smile. "It was very helpful."

"Right. Goodbye."

With that he closed the screen door and Aggie made her way back to her car.

She fired up the engine and drove out to the narrow highway and turned south. Eventually, she found a fish market with a car park and pulled in to gather her thoughts. The only new information that she had gleaned was that Georgia

Kaplan had, perhaps, returned to this area. That was something. She checked the address of the dental practice on her GPS. It was only minutes away. She doubted that it would be open on a Saturday afternoon at the shore but she had to take a look. She backed out of her parking slot and headed down the highway to Ortley and was soon parked outside a small dental business just off Main Street. It was a single story detached cottage style building with a red shingle tile roof, walls covered in white painted shells and a large window with a single glass doorway set to one side. The sign on the window declared 'Parker Dental' and there were various posters in the window with information on procedures conducted by Dr. Samuel Parker with, surprisingly, prominence given to dental implants. Aggie went to the door and saw that there had been '9:00 am to 12:00 pm' hours that day but the practice was now closed. She could see a counter and a small waiting room behind the front window. Looking at the door, she was relieved and excited to see a notice concerning emergencies with a contact telephone number.

Fortunate indeed, but it may not be the dentist himself.

Anyways, a start. She made a note of the telephone number, returned to the Beamer, flopped into the driver's seat and took out her phone, pausing for a moment or two to gather her thoughts. Then she called the number.

To her amazement a voice said, "Dr. Parker."

Aggie said, "Hi, my name is Agnes Trout. This is not an emergency. I got your number from your office door. I've been trying to locate a woman whose name is Georgia Kaplan. I understand that she used to work for you."

"Who are you? A friend or a relative or something?"

"No. I'm a private investigator and I think that Georgia can help me with a case."

"A case?"

"Yes. It is about a series of physical assaults."

"How is she involved in this?"

"Well, I can't go into that. I just need to speak with her. I thought perhaps that she was in touch with you or that you knew where I could find her."

"I'm uncomfortable about giving out information like that."

"Look, I could meet with you and show you my license if you like."

"No. I guess it's OK. She worked for me some time ago. She went to New York at some point."

"Did she just leave?"

"Yes. She was very competent and happy here as far as I could tell. She met someone who lived in New York and went to be with him. Artist I think."

"Musician. Have you heard of her since?"

"Actually, I have. She came back to this area looking for work."

"How long ago was that?"

"Oh, I don't know. Could have been three years ago now."

"You didn't have a job for her?"

"No. We were full. I said that I would contact her as soon as something came up. She said that she needed work."

"Did she give you a contact telephone number?"

"Yes."

"Do you mind giving it to me?"

He paused. "No, I suppose not."

He gave Aggie the number.

"Thank you. Do you have any idea where she lives?"

"All I know is that she bought a house near the beach in Seaside Heights. A terrace house, or a cottage, I think. I don't have an address."

Aggie said, "Thanks Dr. Parker. You've been very helpful and, I assure you, it is for a good cause."

He said, "You're welcome."

Aggie added, "So nothing came up in the way of job vacancies then?"

"No."

"Have you called her recently?"

"No." There was a pause and then he said, "She has called me once or twice. To check."

"To check on vacancies?"

"Yes."

"Well, thanks again Dr. Parker."

There were a few moments of silence and then he said, "There is one thing."

Aggie said, "What's that?"

"She had changed her name to Sandra Taylor."

Chapter 17

Aggie switched off her telephone and sat in a mildly triumphant silence. At last she felt as if she was getting somewhere. A name change which meant, perhaps, the home stretch. Georgia Kaplan, alias Sandra Taylor, was close by. Seaside Heights was the next stop down the Jersey shore. It took her less than ten minutes to get an address thanks to prolific media access. She plugged it into her GPS, started the Beamer and pointed it towards Seaside Heights. Twenty minutes later, she was cruising a narrow-paved street just behind the boardwalk. She came to the end of the paving which changed into a rutted sandy stretch of ground, dotted with muddy puddles of water. She came upon the remains of three beach cottages, in various stages of serious damage and parked in front of the nearest end one, which had once housed Sandra Taylor. Her heart sank as she surveyed the wreckage and recalled Sandy, the hurricane which damaged so much of the Jersey shore. She got out of her car and walked up and down the three foundations with crumpled wood, tile and sheetrock scattered over them. Nothing personal remained, not even the odd chair, cushion or book. It was all gone. Back in the car, Aggie turned around and moved back up the paved part of the street and parked outside a block of six pre-war three-story terraced houses. She picked the second door along and walked up the short drive and knocked on the front door. It was opened by a tiny elderly woman wearing a thin floral dress, topped by a curious, intelligent face crowned with straight white hair. She smiled and said, "Hello."

Aggie said, "Hi, my name is Agnes Trout and I was paying a visit to an old friend along the street there but the houses are gone."

In a surprisingly strong voice the woman responded, "Oh yes, Sandy cleaned them all out. They were not as solid as these places. It was a frightening time for all of us."

"Did you all stay here during the storm?"

"I didn't but I think that some of those folks did."

"Any idea where they are?"

"No. But two of them died. I know that."

Aggie said, "Oh no, that's bad. Do you know which ones?"

"I think a man in the middle house and a woman in the end one. That's all I know."

"OK. Thanks so much for your time."

Aggie returned to her car and contemplated what to do next. It seemed likely that her quarry could have died in the Sandy hurricane. Who would know more about that? Local press and local police were the obvious choices. There turned out to be a small local police station two or three minutes away, so she decided to try there for more information. She parked in front of the station in one of the many empty slots and headed inside. An affable, heavily built cop smiled at her from behind the front desk and asked how he could be of assistance.

Cops tend to not like private investigators and so Aggie usually left that information until later in any conversations. She said, "My name is Agnes Trout. I am down here to visit a friend who lived over near the beach." She gave the address.

The cop immediately looked concerned and said, "Oh dear, we lost a lot of property over there during Sandy. That address is one of them isn't it?"

"Yes. That's why I am here. I trying to find out what happened to my friend and, if possible, where she is now."

"OK. Look, take a seat and give me a few minutes and I'll see what I can find out. What was your name again?"

"Agnes Trout."

"And you are from?"

"New York. Just visiting."

"OK. There's a comfortable seat over there." He indicated three padded chairs in a small space across the lobby. Agnes went over and sat down, reviewing her thoughts. It seemed very peaceful and quiet in this clean, bright space. After about ten minutes the cop said, "OK ma'am, I've got a couple of things."

He looked very concerned and Agnes knew that the news was not good. He said, "What was the name of your friend?"

"Sandra Taylor."

"Oh. I'm sorry, but that person is deceased."

Agnes looked upset. Sandra Taylor having died was very sad and bad enough but now her quest was crumbling fast.

"Oh no. That is bad news. How sad and random. Wrong place at the wrong time."

The cop looked at her for a long time before speaking.

"It is sad but actually, it is not so random."

"What do you mean?"

"Well, Ms. Taylor was a homicide victim."

"Homicide?"

"Yes, she was found stabbed after the storm. She had no relatives or friends that were known to us. She was identified through papers found in what was left of her house."

"Wasn't there an investigation?"

"There was, of course, but no assailant was found and it came to nothing. The case is still open. In fact, no one was found who knew her."

Aggie made a non-committal sound.

The cop said, "I'm going to have to take down your information. Anything could be helpful."

Aggie gave her name, address and birth date. "Occupation," said the cop.

"Private Investigator."

"Ah!" The cop stared at her quizzically.

"Yes, I was trying to locate her in connection with a physical assault case."

The cop sighed heavily and said, "I see. How was she involved?"

"She was one of several women who were violently attacked by the same perpetrator."

"Oh, and you are looking for him?"

As he spoke, he typed on the keyboard of a computer standing to his left. "We already know him. We are looking for evidence against him."

"I see. Well, I get it, of course. I need his name because he may be involved in this homicide as well as the assaults."

Aggie gave the cop Dougal Toomey's name and address.

The cop said, "The detectives who looked at this case may need to speak to you and whoever is investigating the assaults case. Do you know anyone?"

Aggie gave Jack's name and number, thinking that he would not mind.

"Well, anything to add that would help here?"

"No, that's it really."

"OK. I'll pass it on. By the way, you might have told me the truth from the start."

"I know. I'm sorry. Just habit. Bye."

"Good afternoon, ma'am."

Outside, Aggie sat in her car for several minutes digesting this new path in her inquiry. Georgia Kaplan gone, murdered some time ago, not even the satisfaction of a killer brought to justice. Toomey obviously figured as a potential suspect. A possible motive was to keep Georgia Kaplan quiet. But why? She was out of sight and mind with a new name. One possibility thought Aggie, was money. She had bought a small property but probably had no job. The time would surely come when she ran out of money. Maybe she asked for more. Aggie was certain that she had been paid off—and substantially. Anyway, time to head home, but first some food. She hadn't eaten all day since the apple. She found a thriving roadside diner in Ocean Beach and ordered coffee, an egg, cheese and bacon sandwich and ice cream. Stuff the diet again for today. she said to herself.

Half an hour later, well-fortified because the sandwich was huge, she left a message for Jack which said that she had good news and bad news but that was better than no news. Then, she began the return journey to New York with lots to think about. She felt that Jack could find out the homicide circumstances, which she could not, and listen to her theories. After an hour of driving, Aggie felt sleepiness coming on so she switched on her music and the Lumineers were soon blasting away in the confined space of her cab, especially Classy Girls which she loved, and the second half of the journey soon passed. Back in her apartment, she opted for TV and a glass of Fiji water, wanting her system to be cleansed after the loaded diner fare. TV turned out to be a great movie called 'Bandits' which was funny and satisfying and put her in an upbeat mood. She turned in at about midnight and fell into a dreamless sleep.

Sunday showed up soon enough and, as she mulled things over with a cup of coffee, she realized that it was time to talk to Jonathan Black. She eventually tracked down a telephone number for him and, although it was mid-morning on a Sunday, she decided to call him. He picked up on the second ring.

"Hello," was the only word to break the silence.

On the spur of the moment Aggie said, "Jonathan?"

"Yes."

"It's…"

"I know who it is, how could I not?"

"Um, I would like to talk to you."

Jonathan Black sighed and said, "I believe that is exactly what you are doing."

Aggie paused and said, "I mean that I would like to meet up with you and discuss something."

"Something?"

"Yes, a few things have come up."

"Can you elaborate?"

"I'd rather not."

"Do you mean a few things that are to our mutual benefit?"

Aggie thought that it would be to her benefit anyway.

She said, "Exactly."

"You know, I cannot imagine what would be to my benefit right now. That is, among those choices that affect us both."

"OK. Look, I need to talk to you, see you, and meet up with you."

"Ah, to the point. Matters are improving by the minute. A meeting would be most enjoyable. At least, I trust that it will."

"Good. Brunch today somewhere? I'll pay."

"Even better…Agnes, but I do not need the incentive."

He named a place on Broadway in the nineties at 12:30 pm.

Aggie said, "Great, see you then."

Aggie cleared away the coffee things and then settled on the couch to write up the events of the past two days on her iPad. A lot had happened in both cases. She still had not made a decision on how to proceed with Maisie and did not want to call her yet. She could just lay out her findings for Maisie to interpret or, she could first discover what was going on with absolute certainty. Either way, she did not intend to be intimidated by David. She would let it sit for a while. She did call Jack but his phone went to message. She did not leave one.

She spent an hour or more reading through all of her notes so far and trying to define a plan of action. Finding Georgia Kaplan was positive. Finding that she was dead was not. There was no real evidence that the attacks and her murder were connected. That is by Dougal Toomey. She sensed that there was a connection, almost knew it, but proving it was another matter entirely.

The cops may get somewhere with it now and would, in fact, be better placed to get at the truth but, on the other hand, this was now something of a cold case and who knew what priority it had in the general scheme of things, police wise?

Time to meet Jonathan Black.

Aggie dressed quickly in a white tank top, black jeans and dark brown jacket. She shook her hair into shape, grabbed her bag and set off down the stairs to the street. Fifteen minutes later, she arrived at the restaurant to find Jonathan Black waiting outside.

He said, "Agnes. How nice to see you."

Aggie said, "Good to see you too." She actually felt it.

They were soon seated in a booth off to one side of the restaurant floor near the kitchens. They ordered coffee and began to scan the menu. After a couple of minutes, they placed orders for omelets, both vegetarian, hers cheese and peppers, his cheese, mushrooms and asparagus.

Jonathan said, "Well now, Agnes, to what do I owe this unexpected pleasure?"

Aggie took a deep breath. "Well, you know what I've been chasing up?"

"I do."

"You said that I would not find our missing woman, Georgia Kaplan."

"I didn't realize that I had been that definitive."

"You were. I have found her."

"Well done. What did she have to say, may I ask?"

"Nothing. She's dead."

"What?"

"I'm sorry that was a bit abrupt."

"What happened?"

Aggie went through the events of the last day or so, including the name change Jonathan listened intently without interruption, their food arriving as she neared the end.

"I had no idea," said Jonathan.

Aggie threw him a penetrating glance. "Didn't you?"

"I did not. A sad affair, indeed. You thought that I was involved?"

They both began sampling their omelets as she answered.

"It had crossed my mind and you certainly indicated something along those lines."

"I am not a violent man Agnes."

"But?"

"I did not provide a but."

"You paused as if you were about to."

"One pauses in conversation now and again. To marshal one's thoughts."

"Ah. Do you know violent people then?"

"Of course. We all know violent people Agnes. Even you, including those who wish to do you harm."

They ate in silence for a spell.

Aggie said, "This is going nowhere is it?"

"There's nowhere to go. I was not involved in any way with this woman's demise."

"OK. OK. I think I believe you."

The omelets were exceptional and they finished up in a comfortable silence. Finally, Jonathan said, "The cops have no leads?"

"Apparently not. They didn't know of any relatives because she had assumed a different name. No acquaintances known either. So, I suppose no motive known."

They sipped their coffees.

Jonathan said, "Do you think the cops put enough effort into the investigation?"

"No way of knowing really. I suppose that they could have done more in terms of investigating her past life but I imagine life there was very hectic at that time, with the storm damage, looting, getting things back together, all that."

The waiter came by to clean up and to ask if they had further requests. They both declined and Aggie asked for the check.

Jonathan stared into space for a few moments and then turned his gaze upon her.

She said, "What?"

"I want to be honest with you."

Aggie nodded.

"As you already know, I negotiated situations a few times on behalf of the Toomey family."

"By Toomey, you mean Katherine Toomey."

"Yes."

"And by negotiate, you mean paid off someone."

"Yes. That was the extent of my involvement. I would discuss, persuade even, and then afford some recompense for the incident. I don't think I was the only person doing that."

"And you paid off Georgia Kaplan?"

"I did. A very significant amount, much more than the others. I also suggested that she leave the city."

"Why? Was she in danger?"

"No. It wasn't that. My employer wanted her completely away. Just didn't want her anywhere near."

"You didn't know her new name?"

"No. I suggested that she changed it though and that she begin a completely new life somewhere else."

"Well, she didn't choose the right place or, worse, did not go far enough."

"Unfortunately not."

"Thanks for that. I would like us to be honest with each other."

"My sentiment too."

"You said that you think somebody else works for Katherine Toomey. Doing the same kind of thing as you."

"Yes. Just a feeling. I think there were more assaults than I dealt with."

Aggie smiled and said, "Hah. You said assaults."

"Yes, I did. What's wrong?"

"Well, you prefer euphemisms, like events or incidents. As if you don't like the word assaults because it is too descriptive."

Jonathan's eyes twinkled. "You are beginning to read me. I don't know if that is good or bad."

The check arrived and as Aggie signed and gave her credit card, she said, "I don't know either. Let's just say that we are getting to know each other."

Jonathan smiled and they rose from their booth.

He said, "Thank you for brunch."

Aggie said, "You're welcome," as they filed out of the restaurant.

On the street they faced each other and Aggie said, "That was nice. I'd better get going."

Jonathan, "Yes, I enjoyed it very much. What are you doing next?"

"I'm not sure. Find out all I can about Georgia Kaplan, I suppose. Get as much inside information as possible about the murder. I can do that."

"Good. Well, keep in touch. Maybe we should do this again."

And with that, he set off up Broadway without looking back. Aggie watched him for a few moments and then began walking home.

When she was almost at her apartment block, her cell knocked out the Stones again. She made a mental note to change it before the day was over, again. She read private caller on the screen and answered.

"Hi," a woman's voice said.

Aggie said, "Hi," thinking that she recognized the voice.

"Is this Agnes?"

"Yes, who's this?"

"Adele. You know we met a week or so ago."

"Oh yes. Hi Adele. What's up?"

"Well, I don't have long but I've been thinking."

"About what?"

"Well, you know that I don't want to get involved in your work on the case you spoke about?"

"Yes. I understand that."

"I did recall a bit of information that might be useful."

"Yes?"

"You can't call me back or anything."

"No. I won't do that."

"I heard of another woman who was assaulted. Not as bad as you but she got punched and it sounded like the same guy. Had a knife, wore a mask this time and waved his thing around. You know?"

"Yes. Who was the woman?"

"Her name is Lisa Begu. She's at my gym. I feel bad about giving her name out so, if you see her, don't mention me."

"OK. I won't. What gym is this?"

Adele Morris gave Aggie the name and address. Aggie said, "Thanks Adele. This means a lot."

"Good. OK. Hope it works out."

And then she was gone.

Aggie found that she had stopped on the sidewalk to listen to Adele and now she set off for home, deep in thought. She was soon on her couch bringing her notes and thoughts up to date.

She wanted to believe that Jonathan was not involved in any way with Georgia Kaplan's death. Could he lie to her so directly? Many people could do just that but her instinct was that he was being truthful. That is not to say that there was a lot more to be truthful about. There had to be. But today was a good start and, in fact, a very pleasant one. Of course, he could have offered information to develop the illusion of honesty but she didn't think so. Anyway, Georgia Kaplan had received big money which explained the modest property that she appeared to own. Modest but in a decent and desirable location. Aggie resolved to check whether she bought it outright or used a mortgage. Even modest properties were expensive in that area. Aggie's theory, that Georgia Kaplan had run through her payoff quickly, seemed to be gaining traction. Aggie thought that Kaplan should have rented and saved capital, which would have allowed her to remain financially flexible. The overall structure of her investigation, that Toomey perpetrated a series of criminal acts which were papered over by his mother through payoffs and/or intimidation seemed solid now. There was also the possibility of a fixer associated with Katherine Toomey who had a more menacing view of life. One, perhaps, who was capable of violence. Finding out if he existed and his identity would be difficult and needed some thought.

Aggie's thoughts turned to her telephone and with what she might replace the Stones ring tone. She ran through the offerings given by the telephone company, most of which were innocuous or just plain annoying. In the end she decided that she needed simple and peaceful so she chose a tone called Ripple which fitted the bill. It seemed to have been some time since she had read a book. She recalled that she was into The Life of Pi but felt more like a Peter Robinson, one of her favorite authors. She would read it in parallel and promised herself time to read, a pastime she thoroughly enjoyed. She would call Jack and then take time off to read and have a glass of wine. What a thought. She called Jack who picked up after several rings.

"Hi Ag. How's things? Meant to call but I've been busy."

"Hi Jack. When aren't you busy? This is Sunday."

"I know, but I'm making progress. I got your message. What's up with that?"

"Well, do you have time?"

"Yes, go ahead."

Aggie summarized her trip to the Jersey shore. Jack was silent throughout.

"Wow," he said. "That is something. No wonder I didn't find out anything about Georgia Kaplan. Dead end then."

No hint of humor.

"Maybe."

"You gave the guys there my name?"

"Not the guys. A station cop who took lots of notes and chastised me a bit."

"What about?"

"Not identifying myself as I came in the door."

"Right. Well, that's fair."

Aggie didn't respond.

"Jack, will you have a moment to check on the murder? You know, the autopsy, what they found out about what happened and whether they got anywhere."

"It'll be more than a moment. They'll want to know if I know anything relevant too. Also, they don't just give out their findings, even to a cop. This'll be a quid pro quo do but it might work. I can't do much right now but I'll give it a shot when I can. Name was Sandra Taylor, right?"

"Yes. Thanks Jack. Good luck with your case."

"OK. Bye for now."

He was gone before Aggie could respond.

Aggie changed into her robe and snacked on some nuts and raisins, before pouring a glass of Chardonnay and looking among her bookshelves for the Robinson, but in the end, she couldn't find it and settled for a John Harvey of which she had also read a few pages. It involved a rather endearing detective of Polish descent who was investigating a murder aboard a canal barge.

Aggie had been to England on three occasions in the past and, on the second visit, had met her friend, Archie, a tall, rangy guy, who lived on a barge. He had converted what was a coal barge, in its dotage, into a reasonable kind of rail home with two bedrooms, a kitchen, a bathroom with no shower but a large bath and a living area. She remembered that electricity could be piped in from a facility on the canal bank but Archie had his own generator on board which, although a little on the noisy side, was far enough from the bedrooms not to be disturbing.

Water came from the barge's internal tanks, which had to be replenished every so often. Archie said, with great pride, that he had reconditioned and maintained the engine and that the barge could travel on the canal network with no problem if he so desired. Aggie had liked him a lot but found him to be a trifle eccentric and very set in his ways. He had, though, been an interesting and engaging companion, as well as an excellent cook. A vague, esoteric thought flitted through her mind. Quite a number of people she had met in England had baths, even exotic baths, but many of the older folks had no showers or, if they did, those showers only paid lip service to the practice of showering. It struck her as a little odd to soak in one's own dirty water without rinsing off but, she thought, it takes all sorts and a luxurious hot bath was certainly better than no bath.

Aggie made no telephone calls and received none, having what amounted to a quiet, relaxing evening of reading and wine with no interruptions. Her peace of mind and deep, rewarding sleep ended when she was awakened at about 3 am by loud, blaring sirens passing by in the street. She estimated two or three fire engines and some ancillary vehicles, which were accompanied by an abundance of flashing lights which seemed headed somewhere close by. She turned over and went to sleep again, giving it no more thought. Just after 5:30 am, her telephone began to assail her with its new Ripple tone which was not, she thought, too invasive. In fact, it was quite pleasant.

Aggie did not recognize the number and said, "Who is this?"

A female voice said, "Am I speaking to Agnes Trout?"

"Yes, you are. Who are you?"

"I am a police officer ma'am. Detective Sharon Penn."

"Oh. What's up?"

There was a pause of a couple of beats and then the voice said, "Are you the owner of a BMW vehicle?" Then she gave the registration details.

"Yes, I am. Why do want to know?"

Again, there was a pause and, ignoring her question, the voice continued with, "Do you garage it in Park Davis Garage?"

"I do. What is going on?" Aggie was wide awake now.

"Ma'am, can you come to the garage please. It would be very helpful."

"What? Now?"

"Yes, or as soon as you can."

"I don't know. Is my car OK?"

The voice said, "I'd rather discuss this at the garage if you don't mind."

Aggie felt annoyed and said, "I do mind. I don't know if you are who say you are for one thing. I'm not sure I want to come out to the garage right now."

"Ma'am, I can give you a number to call if you wish to confirm my identity. You can also call my precinct."

Aggie thought for a moment or two and said, "No, that's OK I suppose. I can be there in ten minutes."

"If you are concerned, ma'am, bring someone with you."

"OK. Thanks. See you in a bit."

Aggie threw on a large, loose sweater, jeans and sneakers, grabbed her keys and headed for the street. There was early morning light and it felt cooler than she had expected. There were people walking and a trickle of cars passed her as she walked to the parking garage. As she turned the last corner leading down to the garage, she saw a lot of activity. The fire engines were there with firemen moving around who appeared to be tidying up and putting equipment away. There were three police cars and an SUV with New York Fire Department printed on its side. Two small groups of people stood around talking earnestly, one or two on handsets or telephones. As she approached, she began to realize that something serious had happened and, somehow, she must be involved. Onlookers were being kept at a generous distance from the garage by barricades and yellow tape.

Aggie reached a barricade, manned by a cop carrying a handset, who was talking into it and staring at a line of viewers, two deep.

She called out, "Excuse me," to him.

He ignored her and she called out again and waved her arm. He came over more than reluctantly and said, "Yes, ma'am?"

Aggie said, "I am here at the request of Detective Sharon Penn."

"Who's that?"

"She is here somewhere and called me to come over as soon as possible."

"OK. What's your name?"

"Agnes Trout."

"Do you have ID?"

Aggie said in an irritated tone, "No. I came straight here with nothing."

The cop said, "Wait there."

He turned away and after several minutes on his handset said, "Someone is coming to get you."

Less than three minutes later a youngish guy in a leather jacket, jeans and a collar and tie came over to the cop who pointed her out.

He said, "Agnes Trout?"

"Yes."

"Come through and come with me." He did not introduce himself.

Aggie slipped under the barricade and followed the rather dapper guy across the street and into the parking garage. The air smelled of wet smoke. They walked down a ramp to where Aggie knew her car was kept on the lower floor. They turned into the lower level and, as she walked along the center aisle with her escort, she saw three people standing to one side and watching her approach. There were two men and a woman. One of the men she recognized as Roberto, the garage manager. The smell of burnt rubber and plastic was now pervasive. She looked for the source and saw it among the cars near the group. A burnt-out car. She reached them and took in the scene. A frame and bodywork of blackened metal, wheel rims and some melted glass surrounded by pools of water was all that was left of her Beamer.

Chapter 18

Aggie stared at the remains of her car in disbelief, hardly able to take in the spectacle. The inside looked to be a charred mess from where she was standing. She barely noticed as the woman stepped away from the group towards her, her escort sliding to one side. The woman, who was tall, erect and slightly imposing with a sharp, serious looking face said, "Detective Sharon Penn." She did not offer to shake hands and continued, "I take it that you are Agnes Trout."

Aggie dragged her eyes away from the wreckage and nodded thinking that it was pretty obvious since Penn's guy had just brought her down.

She said, "What's all this?"

Penn looked at her with no expression and said, "Well, my guess is that it looks like a burnt-out car. Is it yours?"

"Yes. What happened?"

Penn looked impatient and said, "Someone set it on fire."

"Set?"

"Yes. Set. It was deliberate. Can I confirm when you brought it in?"

Aggie was aware that Roberto must have supplied that information and she said, "About mid evening on Saturday."

"Good. You left it with Mr. Martinez as usual?"

"Yes. The guys here park it."

"Right. You saw no one follow you in?"

"No. But, then I wasn't looking. I was tired."

"Where had you come from?"

"The Jersey shore."

"Vacation?"

"No. Just visiting."

Penn seemed to be deciding whether to continue that line of questioning. Instead she said, "Do you know who might do this?"

Aggie said, "What, set fire to my car?"

"That's right."

Aggie paused and said, "Not really, no."

Penn's expression sharpened. "What do you mean, not really? You don't know someone who would do this?"

"No. But, I am a private investigator and so there are those who are not fond of me."

Penn sighed and looked Aggie over slowly.

"A private investigator. How nice. Well, that gives us a wide field of possible perps to follow up."

Aggie said, "Does it?"

"Well. How many people have you pissed off do you think?"

Aggie glared at her. "Plenty I would think. But that doesn't mean that they are going to set fire to my car. Have you pissed anybody off?"

Penn ignored the comment. "Right. This is arson. Someone came into the garage, found your car and torched it while Mr. Martinez," she gestured towards him, "was otherwise engaged on, no doubt, important duties."

Roberto looked concerned, his eyes on Penn. Penn continued. "It looks like this person poured gasoline on the driver's seat and ignited it. It doesn't take much to start a fire."

Aggie said, "Well, it could have been that someone wanted to start a fire and chose my car at random."

Penn gave Aggie a patronizing glance. "Yes, it could have been but unlikely."

"Why unlikely?"

"If you are an arsonist you want to see your workmanship. You wouldn't go the lower level of a garage, start a fire, leave and not see any of it. I think your car was chosen deliberately."

Partially convinced Aggie said, "What about cameras?"

Penn again enveloped Roberto with one of her withering looks. "Nothing. One camera down here that's not working and one on the ramp that was not in operation on Saturday evening. The perp left the garage, again unseen, because Mr. Martinez was obviously still very busy, at something."

"Nobody saw him, or her?"

"No. At some point Mr. Martinez dispensed with his pressing duties and observed that a fire was in progress. So, here we are."

Aggie glanced around. On the passenger side of her car was a space while on the other side a Chevrolet had sustained blistered paint and looked to be soaked with water internally. The wall in front of her car and the ceiling above were blackened with smoke.

She said, "Only one other car damaged then?"

"That's correct. Small fire but a fire nevertheless."

Aggie knew that all parked cars in the garage had both front windows wound down for safety reasons, no keys locked in the cars.

She said, "Are you sure that the fire was started? There could have been an electrical problem or something."

Penn sounded like someone who was confronted with a slowish rate of comprehension. "As I have already stated, the fire was started in the driver's area. What electrical problem do you think that you have there?"

"OK. Just asking. And if there is a space next to my car on the driver's side, wouldn't it be easier to start a fire with space to work in? A good choice, if this was random."

"Ah. Very clever but no; we think your car was chosen deliberately. Just your car with, basically, minimum collateral damage."

Aggie felt angry and was feeling upset because of the loss of her Beamer.

Penn continued. "Since you were not in, or near your car, this must be some kind of statement or message. Any clues?"

"No," was all Aggie could manage.

"Right then, I want you to give as much information as you can to Detective Powers here." He was the third person in the group. "Your current case or cases and, say, any you have had in the last year. I'm sure that Mr. Martinez will make his office available. We will be in touch."

Aggie had a passing thought. "Have you informed the owner of the other car?"

Penn rolled her eyes. "No. Mr. Martinez is going to fit that in to his schedule somewhere."

Roberto was now looking exceedingly uncomfortable.

Aggie said, "What's next then?"

"Well, I hope that you are fully insured. I would suggest that you deal with it."

"I meant in your investigation."

An edge appeared in Penn's voice.

"As I said, we will be in touch. We will be making inquiries."

Aggie could not resist. "No clues here then?"

Penn raised her voice a notch. "No cameras. No photographs. No decent lighting. No footprints. No convenient gas cans with fingerprints on them. What do you think?"

"OK," said Aggie, also with an edge to her voice.

Penn stared at her for several moments and then turned and walked away, followed by the guy in the leather jacket.

Roberto looked at Aggie and, with concern in his voice, said, "I'm sorry about all this Ms. Trout."

Aggie responded, "Don't worry, Roberto. It will all get sorted out. It wasn't your fault."

Roberto found the glimmer of a smile and said, "You'd both better come to my cubicle then."

Aggie looked at Detective Powers who nodded and said in a deep, rich voice, "Yes, that would be very helpful. It shouldn't take long."

They arrived at Roberto's cubicle which lived up to its name. It was basically a glass box with an open, sliding window in the front for transactions with the public and a glass side door for entry. Inside, there was a metal desk with two side drawers and a revolving stool. Roberto showed them in and left. Detective Powers indicated the stool for Aggie while he pushed aside papers and newspapers and perched on the corner of the desk. An hour later they were done. Detective Powers or Ron, as he told Aggie to call him, proved to be an entertaining and thorough questioner. He was fiftyish, carried a magnificent mustache and had a full head of salt and pepper hair above a thinnish face. Aggie wrote a brief statement and signed it.

As the verbal intercourse came to a close, he said, "Well, Ms. Trout," Aggie had not offered her first name, "we'll be in touch."

Aggie doubted that. Her cynical brain cells were too dominant in this case. Perhaps, she mused, someone would take a look at it for a spell, come up with nothing substantial and move on to bigger things.

She hadn't felt any positive vibes from anyone, although Detective Powers, Ron, had tried to project earnestness and efficiency. She looked away, glancing through the glass walls at nothing in particular. Finally, she decided to ask a couple of questions of her own.

She said, "Is she always like that? Detective Penn?"

"Like what?"

"Unpleasant, aggressive, unfriendly."

Powers sighed and said, "She is a very good detective. She doesn't suffer fools gladly." He paused and continued, "And she doesn't like PI's." Then he added, "Most of us don't."

Aggie returned his gaze and said, "Are you in that club?"

"For the most part, yes. You are a little different though."

"What, a woman?"

"No, I didn't mean that."

"What then?"

Powers puffed out his cheeks. "In my experience, private investigators, of either sex, tend to be devious and sleazy. Not all, but let's say, the majority."

Aggie looked directly at him.

"Two ways to answer that. I can be devious and sleazy if I have to. And, how many in your profession are devious and sleazy, do you think?"

"OK, OK. Let's stop right there. Point taken."

He slid off the desk and stood up, brushing down his jacket and pants to make things presentable. "Well, nice to have met you."

He put his hand out and Aggie shook it from her perch on the stool.

She just said, "Yes."

With that Powers said, "I'll be off, then." And he turned, opened the door and strode away.

Aggie sat in the almost palpable silence, apart from the distance chug of the occasional exhaust coughing up its fumes. She tried to gather her thoughts, figure out what had just happened and to decide what to do next. Nothing seemed to be falling into any kind of ordered reasoning. She became aware that Roberto was standing in the doorway, concern etched into his face along with a heavy frown as he regarded her silently. "I'm sorry," he apologized again. "What will you do?"

Aggie looked up. "I don't know Roberto. What a mess. I suppose that I'll have to call my insurance company right away. See what they have to say."

Roberto said, "I have to call management right away too. Or I could be in trouble. They will want the car moved and everything cleaned up. The smell too."

Aggie stood with a long sigh. "Don't move the car yet, Roberto. The insurance people may want to see it."

"Oh. What about painting the wall and ceiling?"

"I'll let you know as soon as I can. Today, probably. I can't see why that would matter, but you never know."

She left his cubicle and trudged up the ramp.

Outside, the fire trucks had already gone and the onlookers were reduced to just a handful. One uniform remained to make sure that all street encumbrances were removed. It was time for everyone to move on. Back in her apartment Aggie checked her landline for messages but there were none, and slumped onto her couch, cell phone in hand. First things first. Reluctantly, she dialed her insurance company. After several of the usual press this number or that number, she reached a live person and explained that her car had burnt out.

The live person, a guy with a flat, bored voice, said, "Caught fire did it?"

"Well, not exactly. Someone torched it."

The voice perked up a tad. "You mean deliberately?"

Aggie sighed. "Yes, I do mean that."

"Really. Well, whatever, you will need to go to our website, download the forms and put your claim in motion."

"OK, I get that. So, when I've done that, how long does the claim take to go through?"

The voice went back to neutral. "We send an assessor within a few days so that the claim can be processed."

Aggie was feeling the first pangs of frustration. "But, there is nothing to assess. There is no car left."

"I understand. You know that but we don't know that. We still need to confirm the claim."

"Will a police report do? That would seem like adequate confirmation to me?"

"No. The assessor has to assess. That's what he does."

Aggie hit the irritated mode. "I don't believe this. I have a business to run. What am I paying for? I need a car."

"I'm sorry ma'am. There is a procedure in place. I will try to speed things up for you. If you can complete the claim today, I will flag it for expediency."

Aggie grunted unenthusiastically. Small victories.

The voice said, "Ma'am, have you considered contents. The loss of items left in your car?"

Aggie had not. She suddenly realized no GPS, no music, no several things. Somewhat mollified, she said, "No I hadn't. How do I claim for them?"

"Well, you will need receipts for most of them. There is a form for that too."

"Of course, there is."

"Ma'am. One more thing. Once the assessor has been, you can have a replacement car for two weeks."

"Oh. That's helpful. Two weeks?"

"Yes, that's the limit."

"OK. Thanks. Who removes what's left of the car? Do I do that?"

"No ma'am. The assessor will arrange that. He will contact you about the claim, the replacement and the other stuff."

Aggie hung up, reasonably satisfied with the outcome so far. She completed the claim online, car contents being a bit of a problem as far as finding receipts went but she finally managed to sit back to begin again to confront what had happened. She called the garage and told Roberto that an assessor would be in within a couple of days, hopefully, and that he, if it was a he, would have the car remains removed. She said that she could see no reason why repainting could not begin. It was already late morning and so much seemed to have happened that Aggie felt disoriented. A shower and coffee seemed to be in order while she turned the events over in her mind. Her car had been destroyed and it had been done deliberately, not as an inconvenience to slow her down for some reason but, she thought, as an unmistakable warning to her. Warning about what?

Her pursuit of Toomey, her inquiries about Georgia Kaplan, her observations of David Hamilton? Who would warn her and why? Assuming that nobody from her previous cases had suddenly acquired the need to threaten her, this nasty little incident was down to someone connected to the Toomey's, mother or son, or David Hamilton himself. Until her brush with David's significant and aggressive behavior, she had thought of him as a fairly normal human being, a little flirtatious perhaps, but decent and every day. Could he have done this? She tried to visualize him in an angry and malicious mood, dousing her car with gasoline and setting fire to it in a flurry of triumph and vicious delight. Anything was possible. She showered, dressed and brewed some coffee. She felt more inclined to believe that Katherine Toomey had put one of her factotums to work but with what end in mind? Just to get her to back off from trying to bring her son to justice? Yes, probably that was enough motivation, who knew? Anyway, the mundane, the car insurance chore, had been accomplished, although, she had to get another car soon.

She hoped that the insurance compensation would be both timely and enough to replace the Beamer. She couldn't afford to buy a newish car outright. A case for wait and see, nothing else could be done. Aggie dragged her thoughts back to her cases. She wasn't looking forward to calling Maisie and, besides, she felt that she needed more solid confirmation of what she had witnessed in terms of David's apparent double life. Plus, she wanted to speak to Lisa Begu as soon as possible. Probably, she should also call Jack and bring him up to date and see if he had any news about Georgia Kaplan. She also felt the urge to call Jonathan Black which caused her to have a momentary thought as to whether he could have set fire to her car. She felt embarrassed to even be going there and dismissed the idea immediately. In the end, she decided to call Jack. For once he answered on the second ring. "Hi Ag, you're back. What's up?"

Aggie said, "Not a lot. I don't have a car any more though."

"Why? Don't tell me you crashed it."

Aggie smiled to herself. "No, of course not. Somebody torched it."

"What? When?"

"Last night. In the garage."

"What for? That's dangerous, arson."

"Well, the cops didn't seem too bothered."

"Ah, you should have called me. I could have come over. Who's in charge?"

"Woman called Penn. Not too nice."

"Oh yes, I know her. Well, I know of her. Decent reputation. She wasn't helpful?"

Aggie paused and said, "Let's say a little indifferent. Patronizing too."

"Probably her way. She should come through, see how it goes. No idea who did it?"

"No. Could have been anybody but she thought that I was the target."

Jack said, "Oh-oh, that's not good. A warning then."

Aggie said, "Yeah, probably. One of the Toomey bunch I would think."

"Maybe. Look, do you want to stay at my place for a bit, until this blows over. It's an escalation."

Aggie felt appreciative. "No, but thanks. I'll be OK."

Jack said, "I don't like it, you could be in danger. What about your friend's husband? Could he be in on this?"

"Hard to say. Anything is possible. He's already had a shot at threatening me."

Jack said, "What? When did this happen?"

"A couple of days or so ago. In the car park of his office building."

"What did he do?"

Aggie kept it simple. "Basically, he told me to stop following him."

"And?"

"And, so I followed him."

"Of course, you did. Anything?"

"Yes. He could be leading a double life. I've got to check it out some more."

Jack sighed knowingly and said, "Look, I've got to go. Be careful and come and stay with me if you want to. This car thing could be serious."

"OK, thanks. Any other news?"

"Yes, a bit. I'll get back to you later today. Bye." He rang off.

Aggie sat back. Jack was concerned which was nice. She would have liked some news on the Georgia Kaplan front but maybe later. She made some more coffee as her mind picked through her next moves. She wanted to research the property visited by David Hamilton, find out who owned it and how everything fitted together. She felt anxious about the whole setup because, if it checked out along the lines that intuition was telling her, she would have to break it to Maisie. She was not ready to do that either emotionally or factually. She also wanted to look at the financial background of Georgia Kaplan/Sandra Taylor. According to Jonathan Black, she had money but where did it go? Is it in a bank account or has it gone? Was her death connected to Aggie's case? That was an unknown. She reflected ruefully that all of her current time was being used pro bono for the first time in her career. She would need another case or two soon.

As she sipped her coffee, her cell phone pumped out its new offering. She checked the screen which presented private caller. That usually meant some kind of sales call but she picked up anyway, ready to switch off if that was the case.

She said, "Agnes Trout."

In response, a fairly high voice, reminiscent of Truman Capote and with a faint mid-western accent, said, "How's your car doing?"

A slight ripple of shock ran up Aggie's spine. "Not well. Who's this?"

The voice said, "Next time it will be you. Nice and crispy."

Aggie drew a quick breath. "I don't do well with threats."

The voice was matter of fact.

"This is not a threat. This is a promise."

Aggie said, "You said next time. Next time for what?"

The voice said, "Lady, drop your current cases. Take a break. It'll be good for your health."

Aggie was calm now. "All of my cases? Who are you?"

"Keep poking around and you will become a barbecue, or worse. I won't call again."

The phone went dead.

Chapter 19

Aggie tossed the phone down and sat back on the couch.

Well, there was not much doubt about that. An unequivocal warning.

She noted that the caller had not targeted a particular case of hers, reasonably assuming that she was working more than one. Whomever was behind the warning did not want to have any pointers in their direction. Some reticence then, to being identified. A good thing? Maybe. It meant that as soon as she knew the case, she would know who was threatening her. As it happens, she had only two cases and so her choices were still the same. The call hadn't changed that. But, things had clearly escalated. Being made into a barbecue was a death threat. Why the escalation? Did either case warrant such intense feelings? Evidently, but who was responsible? Suddenly, Aggie thought phone, caller ID but immediately recalled that there had not been one. The phone used to call her was undoubtedly a throwaway anyway. It was no surprise that the caller had her telephone number. She had shared that information many times, both her land line and her cell. Aggie's next thought was that she needed professional advice on how to process her situation. Her instinct was to ignore it because she did not like intimidation nor was she moved by it. She decided not to call Jack yet because, somehow, Jonathan Black felt like the way to go, although she needed to allow her thoughts to crystallize before doing that. Meanwhile, to take her mind off the last few hours and to allow it to percolate, she proposed to pursue the next steps in her research. She settled in on her couch with her iPad and chose to start with Sandra Taylor, the former Georgia Kaplan. She wanted to know if Sandra Taylor owned the destroyed house and, if so, how much it had cost her. Aggie had no real sense of the 'settlement' sum of money that Sandra Taylor had received. She needed to ask Jonathan about that, but she doubted that it would have amounted to the cost of a seaside cottage. It took her less than twenty minutes to determine that Sandra Taylor was the registered owner of the cottage and that she had taken out a mortgage on the property, which, in turn, probably meant that a deposit had been placed. She couldn't yet get any numbers. Mortgage payments had ceased but the mortgage was still outstanding. She could find no record of any insurance although it was her understanding that the mortgage had to be insured. It also meant that there should be named beneficiaries to recover the insured value and clear the mortgage but that was not in the public record.

Aggie discovered that Sandra Taylor had a checking account but she could not determine how much cash there was in that account. The bottom line was that Sandra Taylor had probably put most, or all, of her 'settlement' into the cottage with little income to support the future of it. A possible outcome of that could have been a request for more money and hence a motive for her murder. All guesswork, maybe fanciful but that was how cases got solved. Aggie put all of those thoughts in the back of her mind for now, although she wondered if Sandra Taylor had ever entertained any regrets about taking money for her silence. Anyway, in the end it hadn't worked out too well for her. That twinge of cynicism made her feel guilty and so she turned her thoughts away. When Jack was able to add something new to Sandra Taylor's shortened life, she would return to that part of her case. Meanwhile, she reviewed her notes on the Toomey family structure. Right at the top sat Ardal Toomey, resident of North Carolina, the de facto head of the Toomey progeny and apparent current source of the family wealth. He was subsidizing Dougal Toomey's lifestyle according to his mother and, no doubt, was of some financial use to her also. Katherine Toomey had been divorced from her husband Floyd, the orthopedist, and had acquired her apartment and an unknown income from him. He had moved on without looking back and was basically out of the Toomey picture, probably with no regrets about the mess that was once his family. Aggie had no record of any contact between Floyd and his son in the aftermath of the divorce and thought how sad it was that there was apparently no love or decent emotion anywhere in this family. Aggie confirmed that Ardal Toomey had been married to and divorced from a Margaret Nesmith, had not remarried and she could find no further information on his ex-wife. She wondered if it would be helpful to talk to Ardal Toomey but, what would be the point? She was, in effect, casting around in the dark, looking for any indication of who had threatened her or, at least, who had set the wheels in motion. Ardal Toomey certainly had the resources and the clout, as did Katherine Toomey but they weren't about to inform her of any malicious intent on their part. At a pinch, Dougal Toomey probably also had contacts of the required inclination to do her harm.

Her eyes then settled on a name. Ana Toomey, the sister of Dougal, married to a teacher and living with her husband and two children in New England. Calling her might have a productive outcome, although what that might be she didn't know but the idea, at least, appealed to her.

Maybe she could add some substance to the family relationships which would alleviate her growing frustration with her lack of progress. It was only hours since she had been threatened and she told herself to show some patience, although patience had never come easily to her. She felt the need to act, to move on, to be doing something useful. As it turned out, Ana had kept the Toomey name after marriage, forgoing the Plunkett label. Aggie soon found an address and telephone number that corresponded to this Ana Toomey. There were still, apparently, many people who clung to landlines in the telephone world. She took a deep breath and dialed the number.

After four rings there was a response. "Hello?"
"Hi, I am trying to reach Ana Toomey."
"You have, and who are you?"
"I am Agnes Trout. I am a private investigator."
"Oh. And who or what are you privately investigating?"

Coming straight to the point seemed to be the way to go so Aggie said, "I am making inquiries about your brother, Dougal Toomey. He is part of a case that I am investigating." Almost true but not quite.

Ana Toomey responded, "And you expect me to talk to you about my brother?"

"Well, as you probably know, he could do with some professional help."

"Professional help? In whose opinion?"

Aggie said, "Mine, law enforcement," again, not quite the truth, "and several women who have been subjected to his antics. Assaulted, in fact."

Ana Toomey paused for a few moments and said haltingly, "Well, that may be but we have nothing to do with him. I don't even want to talk about him. Goodbye."

Aggie raised her voice. "Wait, wait. Your mother is involved. She's supporting him and covering his tracks, his assaults on women. Do you think that's right?"

"What do you mean? I don't speak to my mother and I don't really care what she does."

Aggie pushed a little harder. "Your mother pays off women that your brother has attacked so that they will go away and forget it. You are a woman and you are his sister."

"So what. You have no right to lay this on me. I don't want to know."

There was a period of silence.

"Look, I have to go my own way. I am effectively ostracized by my family and I am perfectly happy with that. As far as I am concerned, they are all screwed up, so just leave us alone."

Aggie could feel the conversation ending so she slipped in one last shot. "What about your father and grandfather?"

"My father and grandfather? What about them?" Ana paused. "My father was smart. He got out and I don't see him either."

Aggie threw in some sympathy. "That's sad."

"No, it's not. My grandfather thinks he is God. I don't miss any of them. I don't want them and I don't need them. I am happy the way things are." She paused for breath. "So, I imagine, as a private investigator, you get the picture."

Before Aggie could respond the phone went dead.

Aggie sat quietly for a few moments absorbing the call. Had it been worth it? On the whole, she thought it had. Katherine Toomey had lied about being in touch with her daughter. Her daughter and her family had effectively been cut off from the rest of the Toomeys and with no regrets it seemed. Ana, Aggie surmised, knew about her brother's proclivities and probably about her mother's covering them up. Her sense of Ardal Toomey was that he was a manipulative patriarchal kind of figure whose money, even if he was unaware of his grandson's actions, found its way into some kind of slush fund used by Katherine Toomey. All in all, not much new except the family was, indeed, screwed up. Aggie was no closer to finding out who had threatened her. Time was moving along and she thought a little more research could be fitted in while she was waiting to hear from Jack and before she called Jonathan Black. She also wanted to locate Lisa Begu and talk to her. She turned her thoughts to David Hamilton. She had noted the name of the street to which she had followed him, along with the number of the house at the end of the street where she had parked. She made an educated guess as to the house number having counted the homes along her side of the street. She felt that she had the address. It took only a few minutes to figure out who owned the house where David Hamilton had parked his car and entered the home in such a familiar way. The name of the owner of the house was Elizabeth Starkey.

Aggie gazed at the name in both astonishment and disbelief. Elizabeth Starkey was the name of one of the two college friends that she and Maisie met up with occasionally. She tried not to jump to conclusions but she thought that now she knew why David Hamilton had warned her off, maybe even torched her car. All the implications of this were staring her in the face and, not for the first time, she felt saddened by her work.

Chapter 20

Aggie's discovery about Maisie's husband weighed heavily on her mind. There could be little doubt about his situation. Well, there was always doubt but everything pointed to a double life. It all fitted together, the absences, the familiarity with the child at his homecoming, the warning to Aggie, all underscored Maisie's suspicions. David Hamilton had another family, another life. It was Aggie's responsibility to tell Maisie so that she could make decisions about her life at this point. That was not something that she wanted to do over the telephone. She decided that she would arrange to meet with Maisie soon. Meanwhile, she wanted to be productive while waiting for Jack to call. She looked up the address of the gym that Adele Morris had given her and found that it was only twenty blocks away. She decided to visit it on the off chance that she could find Lisa Begu.

She slipped on jeans, a thin polo neck and her faux leather jacket, grabbed her bag and headed for the door. It was a very pleasant walk to the gym. The air was fresh, the sun was casting a streaky light through the sidewalk trees and noise was at a manageable level for once. The gym was a double store front at street level. Aggie passed through the double glass doors into an open area dominated on one side by a glass counter full of pastries, sandwiches and fruit with a strong smell of coffee permeating the air. In front of her was a utility, wooden counter behind which stood a tall woman with dyed, short blonde hair, a thin face, bright blue eyes and wearing a grey hoodie and sweats. She looked very fit and vigorous. Behind her, a busy area was in full exercise mode. Aggie thought that nobody looked especially happy when they were attacking machines; it was all rather grim and intense. As she walked over to the counter, she saw that the woman had a nameplate pinned to her hoodie which declared her to be Cat Jensen. The only time that Aggie had seen the name Cat had been in reference to rock singers, two in fact, one male and one female.

She said, "I'm trying to locate someone whom I think is a member here called Lisa Begu."

The woman said, "And who are you?"

"My name is Agnes Trout and I am a private investigator."

The woman stared intently at her and said, "What do you want to see her about?"

Aggie said, "Ah. It's a personal matter and I can't discuss it."

"If it's a personal matter then I'm involved. I'm her partner."

Aggie said, "I see. Well, even so, I would like to speak to her privately, unless, of course, she is happy to have you present."

Cat Jensen gave Aggie a long look and said, "She's not here now."

"OK. I dropped in on the off chance anyway. Could you give her a message for me?"

"I could. What is it?"

"Tell her that I would like to meet her. I can come in when she is here next."

"OK. But she might not want to see you. You are not saying what it is about."

"I suppose that's fair. I think that she can help me with a case that I am working on. It's very important. I can't say more than that."

Aggie gave her name and cell phone number. "Please have her call me or let me know when she will be in."

"OK."

"Thanks. I appreciate it."

And with that, Aggie turned and strode out of the gym. She was going to talk to Lisa Begu one way or another. She headed back to her apartment.

Back home, Aggie saw that she had a couple of messages and checked them out. The first was from Jack. He said that he had a little news and would call again later. The second message was from her mother who called about once a month to chat and check on her. Her message was brief and just said that she was checking in and hoped all was well. Her parents had long retired to Florida where they walked the beach every day and talked to their bronzed, aging friends about early bird dinners, their finances and health issues.

Maybe that was unfair but that was the way that it seemed to Aggie. They lived in an over 55 community in a detached cottage with no stairs and with all the gardening taken care of and a decent patio out back where they could read and sip wine for several months of the year. The advent of the ubiquitous iPad kept them in touch with the outside world and their small family. Aggie was an only child and had no complaints about her liberal and mostly happy upbringing. Once in a while, she succumbed to an awkward Skype chat with them and saw them perhaps twice a year at Thanksgiving or for a weekend in the summer or a birthday.

They were only in their late sixties, her father having been a malpractice lawyer and her mother a math teacher. The local medical profession was not endeared to them or, at least, not to her father but they had excellent health coverage and facilities. Aggie often thought that surely, surely, they were bored but it never seemed that way. They enjoyed their life together, her mother doing daily exercises in the swimming pool with her friends while her father intermittently labored over writing a legal text book. Aggie promised herself that she would call back later in the day. Meanwhile, she felt that it was time to call Jonathan Black to see if he had any perspective on what had happened. She picked up her cell and dialed. He picked up on the second ring.

"Ah. Ms. Trout. Agnes. How are you?"

"I've been better. You?"

"Relaxing. All the better for your call though, a nice surprise." After a moment's pause, he said, "To what do I owe this pleasure?"

Aggie took a deep breath and said, "Well, I think I need some advice. From you that is."

Johnathan Black's response was, "I'm always available for that. What can I do to help?"

Aggie paused and decided to go one step at a time. "Well, my car has been destroyed. Wiped out. Gone."

"What? Are you OK?" There was immediate concern in his voice.

"Yes, for the time being. The car was basically firebombed in the garage. I was not there. It was quite specific and complete."

"You are safe, though?"

"I'm fine but I have been threatened. It's been a busy time."

"Threatened how and by whom?"

"By phone. I don't know who it was. Could have been anybody. I was told to drop my current cases or else."

"Or else what?"

"I'd be treated like my car."

"Oh. That's terrible. Not too big on threats are you."

There was a smile in his voice.

"No, I'm not. I'm just figuring out how to deal with it."

"OK. I understand. Look it's getting on towards late afternoon. Would you come over to my place and I'll rustle up a meal. We can talk and you can relax a bit."

Aggie was taken aback. This sounded like a good idea. Talking the whole thing through was a welcome thought.

"You're going to cook? You don't have to."

"It would be my pleasure. Are you OK with fish? Didn't know if you were vegetarian. It wouldn't surprise me."

"Fish would be great."

Aggie felt relieved and grateful.

"OK then, about an hour and a half should do it."

He gave Aggie his address. Aggie sat back on the couch, put the cell down and closed her eyes. The prospect of having a dinner cooked for her was something that she really looked forward to, a treat, in fact. She was curious as to how Jonathan Black lived his life and what his home would be like. He seemed at peace with life and she could not imagine him ever being rattled or even ruffled by circumstances. Anyway, it would be an interesting evening, perhaps entertaining as well. She opened her eyes and decided to shower and make an effort to look decent. The shower was also the place where she could think clearly and get things in perspective.

Half an hour later, Aggie was out of the shower, in her robe and actually drying her hair with a blower for a change. Her investigations were at a point where she could not do much to advance them. She was waiting on calls from Jack and Cat Jensen. She wasn't ready to talk to Maisie but knew that would mean getting together and breaking the news. She also put off calling her mother because she felt unable to have that chat. She slipped out of her robe, put on blue jeans and a faded T shirt declaring the remnant details of a Bob Dylan concert from eight years back. Socks and sneakers completed the assemblage with a maroon hoodie ready on the couch with her bag. She picked up the John Harvey mystery and settled in for half an hour of enjoyable reading. After twenty-five minutes it crossed her mind out of the blue to install an Uber app on her cell phone. She had been told by friends to do it, enjoy the comfort and, on occasion, get a cheaper ride than the yellow cabs. It took less than three minutes and she immediately put it to the test. The screen gave her four minutes to get downstairs for the pickup. She threw on the hoodie, grabbed her bag and keys and headed for the street.

Aggie's trip took just a few minutes, her young driver regaling her with his reasons for driving, which were to get him through his last eighteen months of college. It was a cheerful, comfortable drive and as she exited the Camry, she took in the Amsterdam building of her destination. It was a relatively new high rise sporting a long wedge shape at its summit which must have encompassed the penthouse and, perhaps, a pool. She had seen many similar glass and steel towers appearing all over Manhattan and wondered idly how it felt at the top in a storm with gusts of wind of over 100mph. She remembered something from her high school physics that indicated that these buildings could move safely for two or three feet in any direction at the top. Good luck with that. She pushed her way through one of two revolving doors into an expansive marble floored lobby flooded with bright light from several chandeliers. Just inside the door she was greeted by a uniformed doorman who directed her towards a long marble topped reception counter to one side of the lobby and behind which sat a man and a woman, both in uniform. She addressed the man. "Hi, I am visiting Jonathan Black. He's expecting me."

In a rich sonorous voice, the man said, "Good evening ma'am. Your name please."

"Agnes Trout."

He picked up the house phone and announced her presence, nodding at the response.

"Go straight up ma'am. Apartment 42B. The elevators are just around that corner." He indicated a recessed area behind a group of couches, chairs and coffee tables.

She found the elevators and was soon on her way up to the forty second floor. Apart from a small initial thrust, she was unaware of any movement in the elevator. The floor numbers flew by quickly and she soon felt some minor deceleration as she came to her floor. She stepped out of the elevator into a small carpeted hallway which boasted two ferns in jardinières and four doors, one of which was ajar, apartment 42B. She tapped on the door and pushed it open, stepping inside and closing the door.

Ahead of her was a long hallway and, as she walked down it past what must be bedrooms on the left and a bathroom on the right,

She called out, "Jonathan. I'm here."

Almost immediately his head popped out of a doorway just ahead on her right which was evidently the kitchen.

He said, "Hi Agnes, go right in. Drop your stuff anywhere you like."

She drew parallel to the doorway and looked into a well-equipped kitchen with Jonathan Black standing over the cooker on which she could see fish and sliced lemons in a large frying pan. He wore blue jeans and a thin black crew neck. His feet were bare.

"I'll be with you in a sec." He checked inside a shoulder high oven next to him, opening and closing the door after a brief look inside.

Aggie said, "Thanks," and walked on into a huge living room with a dining area next to a wall of windows. She glanced back through the hatch into the kitchen and said, "Sorry Jonathan. I should have brought some wine. I didn't think of it."

His head appeared at the hatch and he said, "All taken care of. I've got a couple of bottles of Blue Nun. Could you open one?" He proffered a bottle through the hatch and she reached over and took it.

Moisture was already appearing on its cool surface. He said, "There's an opener on the table with our glasses."

Aggie walked over to the table, which was laid for two, and picked up the opener. Nothing fancy, just a regular opener. She was immediately taken by the magnificent view towards the River Hudson, over rooftops and past a couple of other tower blocks. Light was fading but the river twinkled and reflected lights and buildings from the New Jersey banks. Two or three sailboats were visible on the river. The scene was truly beautiful and peaceful. She took off her hoodie and laid it on an easy chair alongside her bag. She opened the wine and poured out a generous helping into each of two glasses. Jonathan arrived at her side as if by magic, perfectly in time for the wine.

He glanced at her and said, "I can't help noticing that you are now calling me Jonathan with some regularity. I'm getting quite used to it."

Aggie smiled and said, "Well, that's good. We are getting to know each other quite quickly, aren't we? And you can call me Aggie if you prefer, that's up to you. Either is OK."

"I would like to. Thank you. Excellent. Shall we drink. Here's to good times ahead."

Aggie said, "Good times. I hope so."

They waved their glasses for a moment and then drank deeply.

Jonathan said, "Have a look around if you like while I serve up dinner. It's ready. I won't be long."

Aggie said, "The view from here is really beautiful."

Jonathan nodded.

"Yes. At certain times of day, it is spectacular. I never tire of it."

He headed for the kitchen. Aggie glanced around the room. The floor was almost totally covered with a well-worn antique patterned carpet colored in various browns and gold. One wall was almost entirely books, in mahogany bookcases from floor to ceiling, the one anomaly being an iPod with speakers.

The opposite wall from the Hudson River view had more modest windows looking East while the remaining wall carried a flat screen TV. There were framed, old water colors and oils squeezed into every available wall space, along with three African masks. Easy chairs, including the one on which she had dropped her hoodie and bag, and a non-matching couch with a coffee table filled the central area. Aggie walked over to the books, carrying her glass and taking an occasional sip. Art history, military history and biographies stood alongside some classics and many mystery novels. The latter ranged from S.S. Van Dine and Sax Rohmer to Lee Child and Peter Lovesey. Ha, something in common, then. Jonathan slipped out of the kitchen with two hot plates and some candles. He set them up on the table and lit the candles beneath the plates. He bustled back to the kitchen and emerged with two platters, one of fish and one of roasted carrots and Brussels sprouts, and placed them on the hot plates, along with servers.

Aggie poured more wine and Jonathan said, thoughtfully, "I think we're set to partake."

Aggie sat facing the window and the view in the failing light while Jonathan sat to her right on the table's adjacent side. The fish was halibut and was covered with sliced lemons, capers and sliced olives.

Jonathan said, "Go ahead—dive in."

Aggie said, "This looks delicious." And helped herself to some fish with some olives and capers. She added some sprouts and carrots and waited while Jonathan did the same.

He said, "Would you like some music? I have eclectic tastes."

Aggie responded, "No thanks, I love the quiet and the peaceful view. It's very relaxing."

Aggie broke the silence after a minute or two of eating and said, "You are a great chef Jonathan. This is a really wonderful meal."

He smiled, his eyes twinkling and responded, "Thanks, I was hoping that you would like it."

They picked up their glasses, chinked and sipped the wine. Jonathan, noticing the bottle was now empty, jumped up and retrieved another bottle from the kitchen.

They finished eating and both carried their plates and the empty platters to the kitchen where Jonathan put them and other utensils into the dish washer, switching it on.

"OK," he said with a flourish, "I've put together a fresh fruit medley," which he then pulled out of the refrigerator. He handed the bowl to Aggie, gathered two small bowls and spoons and they headed back to the table. Aggie helped herself to raspberries, strawberries, pineapple and kiwi fruit and waited for Jonathan to put some in his bowl. He did so and turned to her with a concerned look on his face.

He said, "Well, now, how do you feel about enlightening me on the recent past?"

Aggie sighed, ate a spoonful of fruit and said, "OK, I'm ready; there's quite a story to get through."

Jonathan said, "Let's take our fruit and wine over to the couch and get comfortable."

They repaired to the couch complete with fruit and wine.

Aggie took a sip of wine and said "Well, early on Sunday morning I got a call from the police to go over to my garage. They would not say why, just to get over there. I went over to find firemen and a load of equipment and some police. I was taken down to my parking spot where what was left of my car was sitting there. It had been fire bombed."

Jonathan said, "By that you mean…?"

"Someone had poured gas into the front driver's area and set light to it."

"Ah. Did the police say that your car was the target?"

"Well, it was pretty obvious. Of all the cars there at different levels, mine was the one picked out for treatment. It seemed straight forward at the time."

"Did the police think so?"

"Yes. I suggested otherwise but was rather rudely put down, especially when they knew that I was a PI."

"Did they have any ideas about who might have done it? Was it professional?"

Aggie looked up at Jonathan. "They didn't seem to care that much. I suppose that it wasn't that professional but it was precise and deliberate." Aggie suddenly felt saddened by the loss of her car. "It was an unpleasant experience and I was very fond of that car."

Jonathan looked genuinely sympathetic. "I know or, at least, I understand that. How did they leave it?"

"Oh. They took my information and said that they would be in touch. I didn't get any feeling that they were concerned too much. It seemed more of a nuisance really."

Jonathan frowned and said, "Did you get any names?"

"I did. Powers and Penn."

"Right, I know of them. They have decent reputations."

Aggie pulled a face and said, "Must have got them on a bad day then."

Jonathan paused a moment and said, "What's next on the car agenda?"

Aggie said, "I've been in touch with the insurers and they will hire me a car for two weeks while they assess the value of my car."

"When do you get the hire car?"

"I am waiting to hear from them. It means that I will have two weeks to find another car."

Jonathan said, "You know, you may not get a settlement before the two weeks are up. In fact, I am sure that you won't. That kind of thing moves very slowly."

They ate some more fruit in silence and then Aggie said, "I hadn't thought of that. I'm not thinking ahead too clearly."

"Not surprising after what you have been through. Look, here's the thing. I could lend you the money to buy another car. You could pay it back when the insurers settle. You would not have to worry about not having a car."

Aggie smiled briefly. "Thanks, but I couldn't do that. Besides we don't know what the insurers will value my car at."

Jonathan eased back on the couch, glass in hand.

"Why not, we can guess or ask them. In the end it will work out."

Aggie responded, "Well, let me think about it. It's all a little overwhelming. I can probably push them a bit."

"OK. But, either way, allow me to accompany you, when you look for another car. I might be useful."

"That sounds good. Thank you. I will take you up on that."

"Good."

They had finished the fruit and were halfway through the second bottle of wine.

Jonathan said, "Now, what happened with this phone call? Can you elucidate carefully so that I can follow?"

Aggie glanced at him questioningly but did not comment.

"OK. The phone rang and I picked up. A voice said something like how's your car doing?"

Jonathan said, "Sorry about interrupting but I would like to get a sense of this as you go along."

Aggie said, "Well, there isn't much to go along."

"Nevertheless…."

"OK."

"Was the line clear or, say, distorted?"

"A bit in and out I would say."

"So, cell? Throwaway. No indication of source on your cell, of course."

"No. I believe it said out of area."

"Good. Go on."

"I said that my car was not good and asked who he was. Yes, it was a he."

"What kind of voice was it? Accent? Slow or fast diction? Anything."

Aggie said, "It was a highish voice. I thought Truman Capote, something like that. It was firm, I thought menacing too. Could have been a mid-western accent, not that I could be that accurate but I thought so. The vowels made me think that way."

"Good. What was said next?"

He said, "That I would be treated like my car, done all nice and crispy."

"Ah. Not nice at all. And you said…"

"I don't take to threats. Then he said that it wasn't a threat, it was a promise."

"What came next?"

"Well, he had used the words 'next time' so I asked what next time but he ignored it and told me to drop my cases."

"He used the plural?"

"Yes. Well, I suppose if I had only one case, I would know who was threatening me. He was lucky that I have more than one. Only two, admittedly."

"True. So, he wants to preserve his anonymity. Anything else?"

"Not really, just that I would be barbecued or worse."

"Did you feel that he meant it?"

Aggie smiled. "Oh, he meant it, yes."

Jonathan's brow was wrinkled with concern. "This has been rough for you. I know that you don't scare easily or, at least, you won't be intimidated. But this has a serious ring to it."

Aggie sipped some more wine and then her eyes held his. "Do you have any ideas?"

Jonathan did not reply but sipped his wine thoughtfully. He said, "Look, I would like you to stay here for the time being."

Aggie sat up. "What? I can't do that. I have a home. I will be vigilant. I can look after myself."

Jonathan said, "I have a spare bedroom. You could come and go as you please. Check that you are not followed. No strings attached, of course."

Aggie said, "I don't think so."

Jonathan pressed on. "It might be for a very short time, a few days. I'm not so bad to live with. I'd like to make some inquiries with some folks that I know. Meanwhile, it would mean a lot to me to know that you are safe."

Aggie looked very doubtful. "I don't know."

"Well, look at it this way. You're not going to stop investigating, are you?"

"No."

"Well, the threat will be real then. It is only a threat but it has substance. I'd like to figure out who is behind it. It might not take too much to do that."

"You do have some ideas then."

"Perhaps. I can't say more than that. Tell me that it's a deal."

Aggie felt that she had little resistance. She felt mellow, happy for once and rather enjoyed the attention and care that Jonathan was bestowing upon her. It crossed her mind that she must be getting old to let her guard down like this. She said, "Now you've given me something else to think about."

"I have. I just want you to be safe, that's all."

"OK I will think about it. This has been a lovely time. It was so nice of you to do all of this and dinner was amazing. It's been good for me."

"But…"

"Well, I should be getting back, even if only for a night."

Jonathan sighed, "You are so difficult to convince of something if you have doubts."

Aggie laughed and said, "Tell me about it."

Jonathan said, "One request then?"

Aggie looked at his open face. "What's that?"

"Allow me accompany you back to your apartment, please."

Aggie paused, smiled and said, "Can't see much wrong with that."

Within a few minutes they were on the street together. Because the late evening was so pleasant, they decided to walk to Aggie's apartment. Jonathan chose to remain on the curbside of Aggie whichever side of the street they walked on. Mostly they walked in a comfortable silence.

As they were approaching her block, she said, "One of these days Jonathan, you will have to tell me what you do all day."

He laughed quietly and said, "Yes, one of these days perhaps I will."

At her walk up, she opened the small lobby front door and inner door and they tramped up to her apartment. The building was quiet and, for once, all the landing lights were functioning well. Jonathan was the first to notice that her apartment door was ajar. He moved forward quickly and pushed it open gently, reaching inside to find the lights. Aggie's living area was immediately flooded with light. The bathroom and kitchen doors to the left were open and clearly empty and her bedroom door to the right was also open. Aggie followed Jonathan through the living room into the bedroom where he put the light on. All seemed OK. Nothing seemed to have been touched.

Jonathan said, "Strange. Anything different from when you left?"

Aggie looked around and then saw a small package on her coffee table. Anxiously, she said, "There, that."

Jonathan walked over to the table, reached down and carefully picked it up.

Aggie said, "What is it?"

Jonathan said, "It looks like a delivery from a Chinese restaurant."

"Weird."

The package had the name of a local Chinese restaurant on the outside of the bag. He opened it and looked inside.

Aggie said, "What is it?"

He said, his expression tight and angry, "It looks like an order of spare ribs."

Chapter 21

Aggie looked at the bag and gasped as realization set in, her mellow disposition disappearing in an instant.

She tossed her bag onto the couch and said, "Another warning, how the hell did he get in?"

Jonathan glanced at the door. "Not too difficult with that lock. A minute or so at the most."

Aggie felt shaken but rallied determinedly.

"I'm not going to be put off. Fuck it. This creep can't even show himself."

Jonathan nodded but added, "He may be a little more than a creep. A professional perhaps."

Aggie looked questioningly into his face. "You know him?"

"No, I'm not saying that. It's just the methodology, intimidation by increments."

Aggie gathered her feelings. "Increments? You mean that there's more to come?"

"Probably. Likely I would venture."

Aggie puffed out her cheeks.

"What's next then?"

Jonathan paused. "I don't know. Another reminder. The point being that these events are reminders. You are not being physically harmed, yet. The clear intent for now is to frighten you."

Aggie looked from Jonathan to the bag and back again. "Yet. Not physically harmed, yet."

"Yes. Yet. One's sense is that that moment has not arrived."

"Comforting."

Jonathan sighed and said, "I'm really sorry Aggie. You could have done without this."

He put down the spare ribs and put his arm around her shoulders. She did not resist. He said, "You will need new locks. Plural."

Aggie looked at the door. "OK, I'll take care of it."

Jonathan gave her shoulders a gentle squeeze and removed his arm.

"Let me do it. You need to stay at my place. I can get it done quickly."

Aggie's eyes widened, "I'm still not sure about this staying at your apartment thing."

"Well, as I said, I'm not difficult to live with."

"It's not that. It feels as though I'm giving in."

"Aggie, you would not be giving in. Just being sensible. You have already said that you will not be put off."

Aggie was silent. She turned and walked around the room, looked at the door lock and then came back to the table and couch. She sat down.

She said, "Do you think that I am in any danger tonight?"

"I doubt it. The point has been made, very clearly, including this guy somehow getting access to your building and into your apartment. I imagine a pause in the proceedings is under way to see how effective the warnings have been."

Aggie said, "To see if I stop working on the relevant case, whichever one that is?"

"Yes."

Aggie reflected for a few moments, "OK. How about this. I stay here tonight, give it all some thought and tell you tomorrow if I agree."

Jonathan smiled for the first time since they had arrived at Aggie's apartment. "Fair enough. Look, I'll get a friend around here in the morning to do the locks. I'll aim for about nine, if that's OK."

Aggie nodded, having no resistance left.

"Right. And then I will await your call. Any clues as to which way you are leaning?"

Aggie found a smile too. "Perhaps just a tiny bit towards a change in habitat. That's all I can say right now."

"Wonderful. I'll be off then. Anything I can do before I go?"

"No thanks."

"OK then."

Jonathan paused for just a moment, glanced at Aggie and then turned for the door.

Aggie said, "Thanks for a wonderful evening. It was very thoughtful of you."

"My pleasure."

As he headed for the stairs he said, "Call me at any time if you need to. I mean it."

Aggie closed the door gently and thought what a fat lot of use the door had been. May as well not have had one at all. She threw the spare ribs into the garbage, sat down and tried to focus her thoughts. There were no telephone messages and it was much too late to call either Jack or her mother. She went to the kitchen and filled a glass with ice water from the refrigerator and headed back towards her bedroom. On the way, she paused mid-room, grabbed a chair with her free hand and propped it against the apartment door, it's back just beneath the door knob. Satisfied, she walked slowly to the bedroom, which was somewhat stuffy but she had no inclination to open a window. Within minutes, she was in bed, slowing down her racing brain and looking for a solid night of rest. Eventually, after tossing back and forth for half an hour, she fell asleep.

Aggie awoke at 6:30 am with just a touch of a headache and a dry mouth. Time for coffee and an early start. She dragged herself out of bed and to the bathroom. After a shower and a mouthwash, she went to the kitchen in her robe and made coffee, taking it to the couch. She put Channel 1 on the TV but found the sound too much, preferring silence, although the outside sounds of the occasional horn blowing, sirens and helicopter engines permeated her space. She sipped her coffee ruminatively and decided to call her mother after the locks had been fixed. Getting that out of the way seemed a good idea. She would also call Jack, thinking he must be overwhelmed, not having called her again yet. She wanted to bring him up to date and to find out what he had dug up about Sandra Taylor. She realized that she was using that name mentally rather than her given name. Interesting. She rose, took the chair away from the door and went into the bedroom to change. All sweats and sneakers today. She sat on her bed and reread her iPad notes with no new ideas or flights of fancy. Her mind was a bit sluggish today which was not surprising.

When her doorbell buzzed fifteen minutes early, she called down, received a cheery response and was soon joined by a large man with a small bag and a big smile. "I'm Cedric," he said with a strong Jamaican accent. "I'm here for the locks."

The big smile flooded his face again.

Aggie said, "Well, this is it. Do you need anything? I'm Aggie by the way."

"Hi Aggie," he said. "No, I'm fine, it won't take long. I'd like to check the bedroom window though, just for size, if that's OK."

"The bedroom window?"

"Yes, Jonathan said that you need a bar set, even if it is only temporary."

Aggie was a little taken aback. "Well, I suppose so. How temporary is it?"

Cedric smiled. "I can remove it in about ten minutes."

"Are you a locksmith?"

As he put his bag down and began looking at Aggie's single lock he said, "Sort of, I'm a jack-of-all-smith really."

"Ah," said Aggie, "multitalented."

"You could say that."

He removed the lock, laid out some tools on the floor and began unwrapping two new locks.

Aggie said, "I'll leave you to it then."

Cedric nodded.

She went back to the bedroom and sat on the bed. She thought that it would be a good idea to call her mother—something to do while the locks were being fitted.

Her mother answered straight away. "Hi, is that you Agnes?"

Aggie thought that the ID would have given that away.

She said, "Hi Mom. Sorry, I missed you."

"Hi Agnes." Her mom did not use sweetie or honey, sometimes, love. "It's so nice to hear your voice. How are you?"

"Oh, I'm getting by, plugging away."

"Still working cases I suppose?"

"Yes, I have a couple going, keeping me busy. How's Dad?"

"He's well. Fit as ever. We both are. So, you are still investigating people?"

Serious drilling noises emerged from the other room.

"What's that Agnes? Is that in your apartment?"

"Yes Mom. I'm having my lock changed. Good to do once in a while."

"Well, I've never heard of that idea."

"I'm having an upgrade. Can't be too careful."

She didn't want her parents to worry about her. She would tell them when all this had blown over.

"You know Agnes, you should join the police force or some kind of security, if you like that kind of thing. Investigating can be dangerous. Anyway, your friend is a cop, isn't he?"

"Yes Mom, my friend is a cop but I like working for myself." She must have had this conversation or something like it a dozen times. "Besides, a cop or security is a dangerous job too."

Her mom said, "OK, OK. Just thinking of you. As long as you are happy, I suppose. I am." Her mom continued. "You're still on your own, are you?"

"What? Oh yes, nobody steady but I do have a life. So, not entirely on my own."

"Good. We all need someone you know. Look at me and your father."

"Yes Mom, I know. Some people are lucky. It works out for them."

A few moments of silence followed. "We've just seen a Judi Dench movie about a hotel. You'd love it."

Aggie said, "I've heard of it. The Marigold or something I think. I'll try to see it."

"OK love, well take care won't you. Call us soon."

"OK Mom. Love you."

"Love you too. Bye."

So, there it was, a chat with her mother. Telephones were sometimes difficult. One had to keep thinking of things to say. It didn't seem to come naturally. She loved her parents and they clearly loved her, so why was it so awkward to talk? It was always easier face to face. When she thought about it, Aggie knew there were many things to talk about but it just didn't happen. Maybe she should have been forthcoming about her recent adventures but they would only worry. She thought that next time she would tell them most of what was going on and not second guess them.

Cedric called from the front door. "Aggie, door's done."

She went out of the bedroom to find Cedric. He was standing by the door beaming. Agnes looked at the two new locks one above the other.

Cedric pointed to the top one and said, "This is a motorized electronic entry door deadbolt with a keypad." It looked magnificent and a bit daunting. "You can prime the lock by remote or use the keypad and then use your key. Of course, you could just use the key, that is, nobody would know that the keypad isn't in operation. Doesn't make a lot of sense to do that but it's up to you. Now, would you please put in five numbers that you can remember and I'll prime it."

Aggie put in the five numbers and Cedric ceremoniously pressed a couple buttons on the remote and gave it to her. She tried the keypad and used her key, working the lock perfectly.

Cedric said, "When you go out you just close the door and plug in some numbers, not your code, of course."

Aggie nodded.

He said, "Good," and turned his attention to the second lock. "This one is a regular deadbolt and this is the key. No bells and whistles for this one."

He handed her another key.

"Now, can I measure up in the bedroom?"

Aggie took him through and after a couple of minutes with a tiny tape measure, Cedric said, "Got it. I'll be back shortly."

After a few minutes, she heard him climbing nimbly up the stairs before he arrived, carrying a set of bars and a small package which, she thought, probably were the brackets. Cedric was barely breathing after that expenditure of energy. He passed through into the bedroom, calling out that it would not take long. As she cleaned up her kitchen, she heard the whine of a small drill motor and some light banging as Cedric labored away with, she imagined, customary efficiency. After what seemed a very short period, he was in the living area calling out, "All done."

Aggie said, "That was quick," and they walked through to the bedroom. It was impossible to disguise the fact that the window now had bars on it but they were, surprisingly, not intrusive.

Cedric said, "The bars are thin but are high quality steel and will be more than adequate. Black is the usual color but you could paint them. Here is the key plus a spare to that lock too."

Cedric handed her two small silver keys.

Aggie said, "Wow, thanks for doing all this Cedric. Life has turned into locks, bars and keys all of a sudden."

"The world we live in." Cedric flashed his smile again. "It's not so bad."

"True. Cedric, what do I owe you for all of this?"

"All taken care of. Jonathan has covered it all."

"Oh dear. He's going to be in trouble. I'll pay him. Thanks so much. Do you want a coffee or anything?"

"No ma'am. Aggie. I'm good."

Aggie said, "Do you know Jonathan well?"

"I do," Cedric said with a smile. "Very well. We go back years. Many years. Well, good luck with the locks. Bye."

Aggie said, "Bye," as he moved swiftly and smoothly down the stairs. She closed the door and, not without some amusement, operated the two new locks in her door from the inside.

Chapter 22

Aggie stood by her door for a few moments and then drifted into the bedroom to take a second look at the window. It didn't look so bad and the bars were thin but were unmistakably preventing entry, or exit for that matter, unless she was in possession of a key at the desired moment. Kind of ironic, trying to escape a fire and finding the way out blocked to stop someone uninvited from going the other way.

She wandered back into the living room, sat on the couch and decided that she would take the initiative and call Jack as she had not heard from him. She was aware that a lot had happened in a relatively short time and that he would want to know what was going on. As she dialed his number, her gaze rested on the two new locks, glinting brightly on her old door. She hoped that she would not notice them after a while. Jack's phone rang and, to her surprise, he answered after one ring.

"Hi Ag."

"Hi Jack. Have you got a few minutes?"

"Yes. Yes, of course. Just give me a moment." There was a sound of vague shuffling and a door closing.

"OK. I was in the hallway. I'm in the conference room now."

Aggie recalled the room. "Good."

Jack said, "Aggie, I'm really sorry that I haven't got back to you. It's been a bit crazy."

"That's OK Jack. I know what it's like."

"Yes, but you have been having a rough time and I feel so badly about not keeping in touch with you. I did try a couple of times."

It crossed Aggie's mind that some telephone conversations seemed rushed these days, at least between people that mattered to each other. There was usually so much to say and one was almost forced to prioritize to make sure that the most important things got said.

She said, "Don't worry Jack, I understand. You know that I do."

Jack heaved a sigh, "OK. Well, how are things? Is the car situation going anywhere?"

"I hope it is. My dead car is being assessed and it looks as though I will get a rental for a couple of weeks."

"No cost to you?"

"It would seem so, so that's good."

"Ah, so you are going to find another car?"

Aggie sighed, "That's the plan."

"Do you need help with that? I know a bit about cars."

"No thanks. I'll be OK."

Aggie was about to introduce Jonathan Black into the conversation but stopped herself, deciding to ease him in a little later. For some reason, she felt awkward about it which raised her irritation level with herself. Jack said, "Well, let me know if you need me. I might be able to help."

"I will."

There was a pause and then Jack said, "Anything from the cops who checked out your car?"

Aggie said, "No, nothing but it's only a day or so and I'm sure that I am low priority."

"Perhaps. They are good people though. You never know."

Aggie smiled mentally. "Fingers crossed then." She took a deep breath, "Jack, there is something else."

"What? What else?" He suddenly sounded worried.

"I received a phone threat."

"Threat. What kind of threat?" There was urgency in his voice.

"Well, straightforward really. If I don't drop my current cases, I'll finish up like my car. That was the gist of it."

"Fuck. All of your cases?"

"Yes. Well I only have two, but yes, all of my cases."

"Was it a man? Did he sound serious?"

"Yes. And I would say very serious. Nasty, in fact."

Jack had become anxious. "Oh Ag, you have to be careful. I don't like this. You should stay with me or drop your cases or both until we can sort this out."

Aggie felt that this conversation was going where she did not want it to go. She began to feel uncomfortable. Suddenly, everyone was getting protective and there was just too much to explain over the phone. New locks, dinners, places to sleep over, threats, spare ribs showing up.

Saying that her situation was overwhelming did not seem to fully describe her feelings but it was certainly much more than complicated. She wanted space and to be able to think, to gather herself.

"Thanks Jack. But I feel that I am OK for the time being. Nothing is going to happen just yet."

"Why not?"

"Well, the threat has been made. Who is going to know whether I have complied? It will take time."

Jack sighed, "Look, whoever it is may not wait for confirmation. If you present some kind of risk, it might be safer or more expedient to put an end to it."

"Thanks."

"No, no Ag. I'm being practical. I'm trying to help. I don't want you to be in any danger or anything to happen to you."

"Sorry, Jack. That was unfair. But I do think that I am safe, at least for a few days."

"Ag, shall I come around tonight so that we can talk? It also looks good to see that you have visitors."

"I'll be fine. We can talk more tomorrow."

Jack heaved a big sigh, "OK. Stubborn as always."

"I am. I didn't ask about your case. Is it moving along?"

"Oh, yes. Been busy with arraignments but I get a few hours here and there now. It's good. Look, I have to go. Still haven't given you the info, sorry. I'll try to call later today and catch you up. Take care."

"Bye."

And that was it. Aggie had no further information on Sandra Taylor and she hadn't put Jack in the picture; whatever that now happened to be.

Chapter 23

Aggie began once again to feel stymied. It was already close to midday and she needed progress, needed to dispel her mood of frustration and irritation. Her mind settled on the car situation and she grabbed her cell and called the insurance guy. He answered on the second ring with just the single iteration of his name. Aggie introduced herself and listened as he stabbed at the keys of his computer.

Eventually he said, "Ah, yes. Your assessment is not complete at this point. We are still working on it."

Aggie jumped in, "What's to work on? My car has a specific market value which anyone can look up. Don't you just pay me?"

There was a pause and the guy said, "It is not as simple as that. There's a lot of paperwork involved."

"You don't use paper any more, do you?"

"You know what I mean. Assessment takes time."

Aggie sighed loudly, slapping her knee with her right hand. "Well, meanwhile I don't have a car. You said I would get one for two weeks. Is there one?"

"Just a moment."

More keys being tapped.

"OK. Yes, there is. You can pick it up today."

Aggie immediately thought that if she hadn't called, he would not have told her.

He gave her the name of a dealer with an address on Tenth Avenue.

"What kind of car is it?"

"I don't know ma'am. If you go there, they will give you a car for two weeks. Take your ID and license."

Aggie felt slightly mollified, thankful for small mercies. "How long will the assessment take now?"

She heard a pen tapping on teeth and then the assessor said, "A couple of days. You will receive a summary and a check in the mail. It is non-negotiable."

"Really. OK. Thanks. Bye."

So, progress. She decided to head over to Tenth Avenue straight away.

In a little over an hour, she was driving to her parking garage in a seven-year-old maroon and grey Subaru Outback with 115000 miles on the clock. It was very clean and shiny with custom mats and a GPS and was, presumably, very safe. All of the paperwork and arrangements had gone surprisingly smoothly. Maybe they always did, this was her first experience. An affable, efficient stalwart of the dealership had quickly sent her on her way, after he had made a crass attempt to date her. She arrived at her parking garage and stopped to pass the time with Roberto, who seemed very excited to see her and told her that her parking space was still open. She parked the car herself, for once, got out and surveyed all of the fresh paint and new parking bay lines, the air still giving up a faint whiff of fresh paintwork. She left the keys on the seat and the window open. As she walked towards the exit, she spotted new cameras mounted at several locations in the garage.

Cynical thoughts of closed stable doors and all that crossed her mind. Within minutes, she was back in her apartment, having negotiated the locking system with no problem. She now had a car for two weeks which was much better than not having a car. Even though she had used her Beamer infrequently, it had felt strange not having a car. Things were looking up. Maybe a call to Jonathan Black would help her mood even further. She had not decided on whether to stay at his apartment yet but it did not feel like the right way to go. She didn't know why, that's just the way things are sometimes. She dialed up his number and he answered after two rings. Not a busy day then.

"Hi Aggie. This is a nice surprise."

She smiled to herself, "Hi Jonathan. Look, thanks so much for the locks and bars, it was very kind of you."

"Hope you didn't mind the bedroom idea, belt and braces, you know."

"No, it's all good. They look very expensive and I want to repay you for them."

With a smile in his voice he said, "The least I could do. Can we leave the financial aspects of this for the time being, at least, until you have your own four wheels under you again?"

Aggie paused for a moment, "OK. I am not real comfortable with that but thank you."

"Good."

"I will come back to it, you know."

"I do know." Jonathan chuckled lightly. "I wouldn't expect anything less."

"Cedric is a very nice man."

"Yes. He is indeed. And a very valued friend."

After a comfortable pause Jonathan said, "Any more hints from untoward sources?"

"Hints?"

"Yes. Unwanted advice shall we say."

"No, none. I'm planning on going ahead on both current fronts but I haven't gone public yet. Too early probably. I mean for repercussions."

Jonathan said light heartedly, "Promising, though, don't you think?"

"Well, yes. I suppose that it is. I'm still being cautious though. I have to be."

"I know. But it is a strain to keep that up. It can be destructive. Perhaps you should worry less."

Aggie heaved a big sigh, "I have no choice really. Comes with the job and all that."

Jonathan said, "Look, time has passed and nothing further has happened. Not much time, admittedly, but you might consider that the danger has diminished or concluded."

Aggie laughed outright and said, "Why would I do that?" She paused in mid-thought, her awareness heightened.

"Jonathan. Do you know something?"

"I know many things. Aggie, I'm just trying to allay your misgivings."

Aggie almost yelled, "You do know something!"

"Aggie, I'm being realistic. Nothing more has materialized."

Aggie decided to try a new tack, "OK. Look at it this way, then. Did you make any inquiries among your copious contacts?"

Jonathan Black sighed heavily, "I did, and some were fruitful. An indication here and there. The world of persuasion is a small one and its participants are not unknown to each other."

Aggie said, "And?"

"And nothing, Aggie. I feel that we should continue this conversation some other time if you have no objection."

Aggie said, "Oh, I don't know about that. I like to know about everything that I am dealing with. I don't like little pockets of 'I can't go there'."

Jonathan Black, his voice tinged with concern, said, "I understand that but can we have a pocket or two for the time being."

Aggie said, "OK. You do realize that you love the words time being, don't you? It's your way of distancing yourself or avoiding situations."

"Indeed. You have me to rights."

Aggie said, "Can't you say something? It's me you know."

There was a long silence followed by a "Dear me" whispered quietly.

Finally, Jonathan said, "Let's say this. Inquiries are ongoing. The origin, that is to say, the instigator of all this is unknown. My good friend Cedric has taken appropriate action to stem what is a fluid situation. Further threats are less likely but not entirely eliminated because, as I indicated, the threat source is unidentified. Can we leave it at that?"

Aggie sighed resignedly, "We can but to be clear, if that is possible, I might be safe now but, on the other hand, I might not."

"Look, OK, here's the bottom line. Your caller will no longer be making calls. However, he was paid via a drop box with no knowledge of his benefactor. His final, or last, assignment was a monitoring one, to observe your compliance or noncompliance."

"I see. So, that's not to say that there isn't another caller out there."

"Exactly. But that is unlikely."

"And, of course, Mr. or Mrs. Mastermind is still out there."

"That is true, also. There is our unknown."

Aggie suppressed any further questions on her part. "Thank you for your candor Jonathan. I really do appreciate it."

"My pleasure. Now, I suppose that you are not, unfortunately, disposed to stay at my apartment."

"True." Aggie did not reveal her intention of not going in that direction anyway. She added, "But, I could do dinner for us at my apartment sometime soon. A thank you, if you like."

"I do like. An excellent idea. I'll look forward to it."

"Good. We'll talk about it soon, then. Thank you, Jonathan. For everything. Bye."

"Bye Aggie."

Aggie put the phone down feeling a little overwhelmed at the turn of events. She had more than surprised herself with the dinner offer.

Was it professional or personal? She didn't know and, moreover, she didn't want to know. Also, the possibility that perhaps, no more threats were heading her way was a relief. She needed to get her mind around all of this, and quickly.

Chapter 24

Dougal Toomey sprawled in an easy chair in his apartment, his head resting against the stained upper cushions, his hand gripping a half empty beer bottle which was resting on the arm of the chair. His dark, thinning hair flopped across his nose and left eye. There was a small red scar next to the eye and a dirty band aid around two of his fingers. He was close to reflective, allowing fleeting thoughts of self-assessment to percolate through his mind. He thought that he was a reasonably attractive person with something to offer once someone came to know and understand him. He conceded that he had a tendency toward a reclusive nature, that he didn't get out and about enough but, even so, he was not bad company for women. He could talk about video games, Star Wars, pro wrestling and reincarnation in an engaging and forthright way. The problem was that he had had only one date in the last two years and maybe only one in the three years before that. He recalled that the last one, Ursula, didn't like the smell in his apartment. He had never been aware of any particular smell, but she said that it was like sweaty socks and sausage. She had even said that he didn't smell great either and there was no call for that.

She was a bit crazy and had been aghast, yes aghast, when she observed that he didn't wash his hands when he went to the bathroom.

Didn't she know that too much washing removes natural bacteria from the skin and renders one more vulnerable to all kinds of infection? Anyway, Ursula came and went with no real intercourse—physical or otherwise. So, all in all, nothing much was happening in his relationships with women. He'd watched a few of them but had not got close or personal. He was not sure that he even wanted any kind of social interaction. He tossed his hair back so that it fell across his left ear and took a long pull at the bottle remnants, burping loudly after he did so. His solution to all of this was very simple. At some point he had realized that he didn't like the sex act. It took too much proximity, too much work and too much commitment, even though he had felt it to be nice once in a while, vaguely satisfying but overrated. No, he had discovered that stalking for long periods, learning all about a particular woman was much more satisfying; especially when he added exposing himself in that scenario, along with frightening her with a Lone Ranger mask and a knife. He thought that this behavior was entirely logical, that is when he gave it any thought. He tried not to think about it because there was nothing to be gained by that. In fact, he was concerned that he might conceive of the idea that there was something wrong with his behavior and that wouldn't do at all. He preferred to stalk vibrant, confident and experienced women because he wanted to spoil all of that; bring them down a peg or two. He drained the beer, got up a little unsteadily and headed for the kitchen, tossing the empty into a bin and taking a new one from the fridge. He screwed off the top, took a swig and returned to his chair. He was rather enjoying his reverie, feeling as though he was undergoing some kind of intellectual exercise. He smirked to himself as he guessed that he had enacted scenes in one form or another about a dozen times or more, refining his techniques as his desires and behavior changed. He became aware at some point that his focus had begun to center around the physical feelings that he engendered in himself by frightening his victims, along with a predisposition toward violence. The Kaplan woman proved that.

His mother, whom he knew despised him, couldn't put in the effort to understand him. It wasn't so difficult. How could a mother despise her progeny? Anyway, she was stuck with him and forced to protect him in order to save face, not to have to admit to his existence publicly. How exquisite he thought. What goes around comes around. There he was with the potential to sully the family name. He liked that. She would, he thought, be happy if he was dead but he wasn't. Too bad. She had to put up with that. He took another pull at some beer and grimaced; he would need the bathroom soon. His mother seemed to like his stupid sister and her stupid husband and their stupid children but here he was in the same city, carrying the same name and a threat to her high rise, superficial existence. Good. Poor mother trying to disown her sexual predator of a son. That's what he had been called by her tough guy fixer after the Kaplan affair. Ship him off to Europe or South Africa he had said. He's getting out of hand. Kaplan's gone but who's next? Something had to be done.

As it turned out, his next project had been a private investigator. He looked down at his stained band aid which had partially peeled back from the cut across his fingers. No infection there, of course. He rubbed the small itching scar next to his eye. Just his luck, he thought, to pick some kind of kick boxer to assault. He sipped some more beer as he recalled Aggie. He had seen her weeks before in a bar with a tall, lean guy who had cop stamped all over him. He had followed her from the bar just to see where she lived and had later checked her name and Googled up a private investigator. She had looked like the perfect challenge. No apparent routine to her life, intermittent trips to Whole Foods, a gym, a couple of bars and a coffee shop on her own or with that guy or with odd people who must have been clients or acquaintances. He had liked the lack of routine which kept him on his toes, made him more observant, tested his faculties and scouting abilities. He had found that he really enjoyed watching her, trying to anticipate her moves, analyzing her lifestyle and challenging his observational powers. He burped and took a long pull at his beer. Then it had happened. He grimaced at the memory and ran his tongue around his plaque covered teeth. She had met up in a bar with a group of four or five people of about his own age. He had been able to see them dimly through the grimy window, partially shaded by a heavy curtain and he had clearly seen her getting overly sweet and flirtatious with one of the two guys in the group. That had been extremely disturbing for him. She was part of his life now and should not be sending out signals to other men. He had begun to feel a mounting agitation, surging disbelief and burgeoning anger. Eventually, the party—it was a party—had broken up and he had watched the two of them, hand in hand, make their way to a parked car in a corner of the lot and climb in. He had watched in deepening frustration as nothing seemed to be happening and the car had remained in place with its windows lightly misted up in the semi darkness. Then, suddenly, there had been a couple of muffled bumps as the car moved on its suspension, and then it had begun to jiggle rhythmically. Realization had dawned remarkably quickly, his head spinning as he cried out through clenched teeth and pounded his fists against his chest, squeezing his eyes shut as he did so. A hot tear had randomly trickled down his cheek as he had turned, head down and shuffled down the street away from the lot, trying desperately to force the unwanted images from his mind. He had returned home to his apartment feeling devastated. How could she? She had to pay. This was betrayal of the worst kind, right in front of him, so thoughtless and so insensitive, an unbearable insult. He had felt an overwhelming need to cause her pain, to pay her back for making him seem foolish and ineffectual.

He had on two previous occasions located her fire escape at the back of her walk up and had managed just once to climb up late in the evening to watch her undress and read in bed. There had been something charming and peaceful about it all, something he had treasured and owned. Now, all that had gone and he had felt a massive compulsion to do her harm. He finished up the rest of the beer in one gulp. Well, he thought, it had not gone well. He had been knocked out for the first time in his life, been dragged around by a huge cop, been intimidated and questioned and finally set free by his socialite excuse for a mother. Once again, she had bought her way out of trouble. He ran his eyes blearily over his fingers which were still sore and found that revenge or even the concept of revenge had faded. It was just too much to contemplate, too much effort, too little return. He knew that the PI was making all kinds of inquiries about his activities. Well, good luck with that. She would get nowhere. His tracks were covered. Time to move on, to lower expectations a bit, to go back to exposing and frightening which he enjoyed, keeping at a distance, never getting attached to someone ever again. What a master of self-control and understanding oneself he was. There were not many in this world with his acumen, his perception and his understanding of human nature. How blessed he was. He soon fell asleep.

Chapter 25

Aggie turned all of this new information over in her mind. There had, then, been a hired intimidator put in place expressly for her benefit. She wondered vaguely who he was and what had become of him but she decided that she did not have the time to consider any of that or its implications in terms of Jonathan and Cedric. If someone had been paid to force her to back off from her investigations, that meant money.

She imagined that that kind of hiring did not come cheaply. That, she thought, pointed towards the Toomey clan. The money was there, whomever was electing to use it. David Hamilton, on the other hand, was very unlikely to have that kind of money. She suddenly realized that she had no idea what it would cost to hire a heavy but, surely, it must be substantial. In any case, he could have fire bombed her car himself. It was not difficult to do but he would have had to pay for a caller. Jonathan, she thought, had hinted at a professional being involved in that. He had certainly sounded like one. Probably not hired by David then. Somewhere, in the further reaches of her mind, she held the thought that she did not want David to be this crass and violent. He was understandably upset at having his secrets exposed so that he would have to face Maisie at some point with all of the emotion that would suffuse that discussion but she still hoped that he would not resort to real violence. The more she thought about it the more she could not see David in that role. No, she liked the Toomeys for all of this. Dougal or Douglas venting his spleen on her because she had exposed his weaknesses, his ineffectuality and his pathetic proclivities. He had, in the heat of his embarrassment, threatened her after all. His mother, the ultimate self-absorbed, self-aggrandized, unemotional and nasty matriarchal figure, living in her nest atop her building. Or, maybe the grandfather, Ardal, who sprayed money throughout the family. Well, interestingly, not to his granddaughter who probably needed it the most, and who could have learned of Aggie through either Dougal or his mother. He sounded like the kind of manipulative person who would try to put a stop to Aggie's activities, just because he thought that he could do so. Oh, well, there was nothing much to be gained by all of this speculation, except perhaps, that she was beginning to find it hard to envision David being physically involved.

Aggie wanted to know more about Sandra Taylor. Could there be a motive for her murder by this loveless family?

Blackmail perhaps? It was not such a huge step between employing a facilitator and commissioning a murder, was it? Perhaps the key to all of this was, indeed, the demise of Sandra Taylor. Her death was, in effect, a cold case, muted, forgotten and reduced to a couple of files in someone's filing cabinet or some archive. Maybe, just maybe, Aggie had stirred up unwanted interest in the case again by unearthing facts and asking questions; that being the reason for the attempts at intimidation. An interesting thought and one that appealed to her as an investigator. It was certainly worth more follow up. At the very least, she felt that she was doing something for Sandra Taylor, finding some justice on her behalf. In addition to all of that, there was the fact that she was causing consternation and irritation to the Toomey family by following up on the string of assaults and lewd behavior attributed to Dougal Toomey. Great. Publicity was complete anathema for these people.

She decided that today's modest dinner would be a toasted cheese sandwich plus one of two tomatoes that lay in her fruit bowl. She scattered some Celtic salt and black pepper on the cut tomato and sat on the couch with this repast and a half glass of Chardonnay. She was just consuming the last morsel of tomato when her cell 'Rippled'. Yes, she was quite satisfied with that sound. It was Jack. She picked up.

"Hi Ag."

"Hi Jack. What's up?"

"Well, first things first. I know that you want info on Sandra Taylor, so I'll start there."

"Great. OK." Aggie waited expectantly.

Jack said, "I spoke to a couple of guys who were involved with the initial investigation. Mostly one guy actually and he was quite guarded, which is understandable really because they didn't come up with much."

Aggie said, "They were defensive?"

"Yes, well this guy was, anyway. They didn't exactly pull out all the stops; priority it seems."

Aggie interjected, "Sad, you know, really sad."

"Yeah, it is but that's the way it is too."

"Was there anything helpful?"

Jack paused.

"I think so. At least, I've got some of the details and a basic timeline."

He continued, "They got to the body after Sandy, a couple of days later, during the cleanup. It was clear from the autopsy that she was murdered before Sandy happened."

"Hah. I had wondered if it happened during or after Sandy but that makes no sense does it?"

"No, but there is some irony at work here isn't there."

Aggie said, "Is there?"

There was a slight pause before Jack said, "You know, if he had waited, or she, Sandy would probably have done the job."

"Jack!"

Jack said, "I know. Sorry."

Aggie said, "Any idea how long before Sandy, that she was murdered?"

"Less than a day. Could have been deliberate timing with Sandy coming. Upheaval, confusion and her staying put. Apparently, she didn't think there was too much danger or she just didn't want to move." Jack paused while turning something over in his mind. He said, "On second thoughts, I think this was independent of Sandy. It was premeditated and opportunistic at the same time. The chance just came up."

"It was planned. Sandy or no Sandy."

"Yes."

Aggie said, "Anything else? This is really helpful."

"A bit. It was not that professional. That is, not a hit, if that is where you were going. Two knife wounds, one of which was fatal."

Aggie puffed out some air. "Really? I had been thinking along the lines of a Toomey hitman."

Jack laughed aloud, "Wow. What? That's a huge leap. Rather high blown if you ask me."

Aggie said, "Well, I was moving towards blackmail by Sandra Taylor. For more money."

Jack said, "A decent idea but they could have shut her down just as well with a couple of warnings, dead rabbit on the door sort of thing."

Aggie said, "Jack, today really is your cynical day."

"Ah, sorry. I feel cynical. Anyway, this is all helpful, isn't it?"

"Yes. Yes, it is. Thanks so much. I'm going to follow up a bit more for Sandra Taylor's sake."

"Good. OK, to other things. How is the car situation?"

Aggie said, "I've got a rental for two weeks. A Subaru. It all worked out, they actually came through."

"Surprise, surprise. What about a permanent replacement?"

"Don't know yet. I'm going to work on that."

Jack said, "Do you like the rental? What about buying that?"

"I hadn't thought of that. I might. I'll look around a bit first. The rental is not sporty, of course, but that's not a big deal."

"OK. Had you thought any more about staying with me for a while. Till things have settled down?"

Aggie drew in a deep breath, "I've taken a step or two on the safety front. I've installed two more door locks and barred my bedroom window."

Jack said, "What?"

"Yes, I had some help. Jonathan Black arranged it for me."

"Jonathan Black did? How did that come about?"

"Well, we had dinner a couple of days ago to talk things over. He was concerned about the escalation of events, the car firebombing and all of that."

"Dinner? That sounds awfully cozy. Didn't you think that he could be involved?" There was a long pause. Then Jack said, "Look, I'm just thinking of you. I want you to be safe."

Aggie said, "I know but my apartment was broken into. Jonathan had asked to see me home and we found the door open and a bag of spare ribs on my coffee table. Another warning. That's what led to the lock changes."

"Well, he could still be involved. You should be careful. He worked for the Toomeys you know."

"I know but that seems to be over. He has been trying to find out who my caller is."

"Has he. Well, I suppose he can do that. Please take care though, he could still be involved. Tread carefully."

"OK Jack. Thanks for all of this. Are you managing?"

"Yes. Things are good. The fraud case is almost done, the hard work, anyway. I'm going to have a bit more free time for a day or two, mostly paperwork. We could get together if you like."

Aggie said, "Sounds good. I'll go to New Jersey tomorrow and then we can see how things are."

They rang off.

Aggie hadn't known that she was going to New Jersey the next day. The idea had crystallized on its own during her conversation with Jack. As she sipped her wine and watched a little TV, a Seinfeld rerun, the idea took off and seemed like a good one. She would put follow ups on Lisa Begu and Maisie on hold, try out the new rental and see if she could pull up any new ideas on Sandra Taylor.

Chapter 26

Aggie opted for an early night, relatively speaking, that is before midnight; and was up, showered, refreshed and into her second cup of coffee while Morning Joe was still in mid-flight. She felt vigorous and ready to take on what the day offered. She called Roberto so that her new rental would be ready and, within the hour, she was threading her way through heavy traffic on her way to the Jersey shore. The Subaru was comfortable, not at all clunky, clean and reasonably powerful, as much as she needed anyway. All of the controls were simple and easy to use because this model was only on the cusp of those that she knew came with their computer primed, for example, to stop the car in its tracks. Or, to react to a finger straying near to a sensitive button and causing mode changes or fans to burst into life. Correcting any of this could mean stopping and taking out the instruction manual. She liked the simplicity and was soon in the environs of the shore with a mid-morning NPR call-in discussion in full swing on the car air waves. She found the small, bumpy, sandy street in Seaside Heights, where Sandra Taylor had ended her days, with no difficulty. It must once have looked cheerful and attractive here in mid-summer with the small brightly painted terraced and small detached houses nestling in the sunlight. It really had been a pleasant place to live, just off the beaten track and close to the beach and local amenities.

    Now, the houses, or what was left of them, looked quite forlorn, although, the furthest away was showing signs of activity, a heap of sheet rock, wood and plaster stacked at the edge of the property. Sandra Taylor's house was just the rubble strewn space that Aggie had seen on her last visit and it would probably go on looking that way for some time to come. Why on earth had she and others decided to stay after so many warnings? An element of 'cry wolf', perhaps; although these days meteorologists were fairly accurate. Would she have been killed if she had decided not to stay? Probably, because it seemed like a planned murder with, presumably, a strong motive but what was that motive? After a final glance at the devastation, Aggie decided that there was nothing more to be gained there amid an overwhelming sense of sadness and loss that made her even more determined to find justice for Sandra Taylor, someone she had never met but felt a deep sympathy for. As she negotiated a three-point turn, she glimpsed sections of the ocean through the buildings that survived Sandy and failed to protect this little street. She had a vague memory of reading about the local Ferris Wheel rolling out to sea like some section of a paddle driven steamship. How bizarre and otherworldly.

As she drove away, she had to decide what to do next. It was time to pay a visit to the self-proclaimed dental implant specialist, Dr. Samuel Parker.

He was only a few minutes away and was most likely probing someone's mouth right at this moment. She parked her rental in the tiny car park to one side of the dental practice and headed for the shell encrusted building. To her surprise, as she opened the door, an old-fashioned bell attached to the door jangled her entry. There were two elderly people in the open plan waiting room and, as she made her way to the counter, she saw a blonde woman seated behind the obligatory computer. She had a tight face with her hair pulled back, large brown eyes and a small rosebud mouth. Her hair was all at the back of her head, not as a pony tail, a French roll or a bun, just tied up back there with pins. Aggie's view was why have long hair if you weren't going to show it?

She said, "Hi, I'd like to speak with Dr. Parker, please."

The blonde woman said, "Oh, do you have an appointment?"

"No. I'm not a patient. I just want to have a word with him."

Consternation made an appearance on the tight face. "Have a word?"

"Yes. I'm making ongoing inquiries about a matter. I've spoken to Dr. Parker before."

"You mean here? I don't remember you. What is your name please?"

Aggie felt the first stirrings of irritation. "Agnes Trout. I spoke to him a few days ago on the telephone." She added, "We have not met in person."

"Right. Would you take a seat for a moment and I will see if and when he is free?"

If and when? She sat down in the waiting area.

After a couple of minutes, the blonde woman returned and Aggie went to the counter. The blonde woman said, "He's with a patient now and has two more to see this morning. He said, can you come back in about three quarters of an hour?"

Aggie could see that she had no choice and so she said, "OK. I'll be back then. Thanks."

She went out, complete with the bell jangle, and sat in her car. Good time to get some eats. She drove back to the diner in Ocean Beach and settled in to a table with an egg and cheese sandwich, replete with tomato ketchup, salt and pepper and a cup of coffee. There were some empty tables but quite a line for lunchtime sandwiches. She realized that she was very hungry and enjoyed the sandwich so much that she thought of another but knew that she would regret it. She finished up her coffee and headed back to the dental practice. When she arrived, she pushed open the door with the accompanying jangle of the bell and discovered an empty waiting room and no blonde woman behind the reception counter. Within seconds a door, presumably leading to the examination and surgery rooms in the back, opened and a stocky, powerful looking man, wearing a white coat, came into the reception area. He had carefully groomed white hair ringing a bald pate and falling into a pony tail at his back. His grey, small eyes peered out at Aggie through a pair of heavy framed spectacles.

His thin, bluish lips said, "Ah, Ms. Trout I presume."

Aggie recognized the voice from their telephone conversation. She said, "It is. You are Dr. Parker I presume."

"Yes. Shall we sit down."

They sat on opposite sides of a small table in padded chairs with wooden arms.

Aggie said, "Thanks for seeing me. You seem to be having a busy time."

"Today, yes. It's up and down. Early in the week is often busy. Broken bridges, lost fillings and more, over the weekend." He paused and, looking directly at her and said, "What can I do for you?"

Aggie, returning the look said, "Well, I was hoping that you could help me further with my inquiries about Sandra Taylor, the former Georgia Kaplan, as you know."

"Yes, well, I don't know how. I told you all I knew on the telephone."

Aggie noticed long, thick, dark hair protruding from under his watch and creeping out from under both sleeves of his white coat. She had a passing thought that Parker had a hairy back, not among her favorite attributes for a man.

She said, "I know and I appreciate that. I did find her house in Seaside Heights."

Parker raised his eyebrows. "Oh, really. I wonder why she hasn't been in touch lately, then."

Aggie took a deep breath. "Well, her house was destroyed by Sandy." She looked carefully at Parker as she said this but there was no reaction except that he made a sucking sound as he pulled air in through his closed lips.

He said, "Do you know where she finished up?" He paused. "I mean I wondered whether she was still in the area."

Aggie said, "She finished up in a mortuary." This was brutal, she knew, but she was curious about this guy. It wasn't really hanging together but she didn't know why.

Parker said, "Oh dear. I am sorry. Dead. Hard to believe." He turned his grey eyes to look through the front window of the surgery. Then he said, "Didn't she try to get away before the hurricane came? We all did. It wasn't safe. It was well known that it wasn't safe."

Aggie glanced out of the window too and then returned her gaze to Parker. She said, "She wasn't killed by the storm Dr. Parker. She was murdered."

His face registered surprise but his eyes were expressionless. "She was murdered? What do you mean, murdered?"

"She was stabbed to death."

Parker said, "That's awful. Poor Sandra. Who did it?"

Aggie shook her head. "I don't know. No one has been charged as far as I know." In the silence that followed Aggie became aware of a clock ticking quietly somewhere.

Parker said, "Who would do something like that? She was a good person."

"That's why I am here Dr. Parker. I was hoping that you might have some information on her friends or her financial situation. It sounds as though you were comfortable with her work for you."

He shifted in his seat. "Well, I don't know about all that. Yes, she was good at her job here. Other matters are more personal."

Aggie said, "Anything might be helpful, if it is not too personal."

Parker uncrossed and re-crossed his legs and Aggie caught sight of more, rather repulsive thick hair on his lower limbs. He drew in a breath, "Ms. Trout. If you don't mind me saying so, you are being a bit pushy." He grimaced a sort of half smile, "I mean, I feel limited about what I can tell you. I really don't know where all this is going."

Aggie said, "It's me. I'm trying to understand her better."

Parker clasped his hands together around one knee. "But why? You are not with the police, are you? Why do you need to understand her?"

"You are right. I am not with the police. I came across her misfortune by accident while I was working on something else and wanted to find out more about her."

Parker released his fingers. "Right. I recall that you said that she was attacked by someone."

Aggie said, "I did. I was too, so I felt that we had something in common."

Almost true. Close enough for this conversation anyway.

Parker's eyebrows moved upwards marginally with no other expression of surprise. "You were attacked?"

Aggie said, "Yes, but I don't want to talk about it. It was enough to make me interested in Sandra."

"I wondered. Well, she was a nice person, the patients liked her, she did some reception and some lab work. She was reliable and I was sorry to see her go."

"Did she leave suddenly?"

"No. She gave me notice. There was this guy, came out of the blue and off they went."

"Did you meet him?"

"No. As you told me, he was, or is, a musician."

Aggie said, "Did you ever get any sense of her finances?"

"Look, I really don't know. She had the house so, some money, I suppose." Parker looked at his watch in a pointed way and twisted a ring back and forth around a finger.

"But she did tell you that she needed a job."

"Yes. Although, I believe that the reason for that was social rather than financial. She may have been lonely. Something like that."

There was a lengthy silence and then Aggie said, "You think that she wanted company? Perhaps to meet people?"

Parker scratched his ankle moving his forefinger down inside his sock revealing hair once again. Aggie dragged her eyes away as Parker continued. "No real reason to say that, you know. Just a feeling. Look, I have to get ready for my next patient."

Aggie did her best to smile engagingly. "I understand. Thank you for your help and taking the time to see me."

Parker looked relieved and they both stood up but did not shake hands, for which Aggie was grateful.

Parker ventured, "If there is anything further that I can do, give me a call."

Aggie said, "Thanks, I will." And, after one final glance at the cool, grey eyes, headed through the door and the bell to the parking lot.

She walked to her car, wondering if she was being watched, taking in the only other car in the lot, a black Highlander with MD plates, parked in a corner. A fine drizzle was drifting over the general area dampening her face with a cool, gentle touch. She climbed into the rental, fired up the engine and put on the wipers. Something about this whole visit and the exchange with Parker was amiss but she could not identify what that was. As she reversed and drove out of the lot with no sign of a new patient yet, she had an idea. She turned the rental's nose back in the direction of Seaside Heights. Within minutes, she was back in Sandra Taylor's road and parked in front of the terraced house that she had called on previously. The drizzle had eased off and Aggie climbed out of the car and, once again, made her way up the short pathway and tapped on the door. It opened and the same elderly lady appeared wearing the same floral dress that she had worn the last time Aggie had visited. She smiled warmly as she dabbed a tissue to her eyes and nose.

She said, "Hello, so you are back. Sorry, I've been sneezing a bit."

Aggie said, "Yes. May I ask you a couple of questions about your neighbors?"

The old lady slipped her tissue into a dress pocket. "You can but, if it's about someone in those three houses, as your friend, I didn't know them."

The smell of chili drifted out from the inside of the house. Aggie said, "I understand that. I have a more general question or two if you are OK with that."

"Fire away young lady, and be quick. It's getting cool out here."

"OK. Did you ever see any regular visitors to the end house?"

"Is that where the lady lived? The one you knew."

Aggie said, "Yes, it is."

"Well, some time ago there used to be a visitor. It's very quiet here for much of the year so one would notice things like that. I'm not nosey you know."

Aggie said, "Of course not. How long ago?"

"In the fall, winter time, three or so years ago maybe. I don't know. It's hard to gauge time these days. It was a man."

"Did this man visit often?"

The old lady blinked her eyes several times. "It seemed often. I mean I didn't see every visit. Let's say every week."

"Was he on foot or in a car?"

"Both, really. He parked the car up there." She pointed up the street to the entrance. "And he walked down to the house."

"Can you describe him to me?"

The old lady looked at Aggie quizzically.

"Lot of questions then."

"Sorry. Just trying to sort a few family things out. I won't be long."

"Well, he was just a man. He wore red baseball cap and a coat, always. He wasn't too tall, sort of average."

"OK. What was the car like?"

"I don't know cars. Big and black I suppose."

"Thanks," said Aggie. "You've been very helpful. I do appreciate it."

As she turned away to head for her car the old lady said, "Oh, there is one thing."

Aggie stopped and said, "Yes?"

"He had a white pony tail."

Chapter 27

As Aggie made her way back to the city, she had a lot to think about. She now had another candidate who may have done harm to Sandra Taylor. A number of visits to her in some secrecy, or at least, apparent secrecy, suggested clandestine trysts, a lover for Sandra Taylor. Something could have gone wrong. Perhaps she needed permanence or commitment of some sort but that was not a motive for murder, surely. Aggie knew that she did not like Dr. Parker and she tried not to let it color her thoughts or cloud this issue. He wasn't exactly defensive but he wasn't forthright either. He was cautious, measured in his conversation and carefully controlled his emotions so that they appeared appropriate at the right moments. What was it about him that rankled so much? Everything, she thought with some humor. How could he not have known about the death of Sandra Taylor in a community where all local news of any import must have been viral in nature. Well, if Sandra Taylor had not been named or if Parker had been away and not picked up the news, there was still something off about him. How had the affair ended? Sandra Taylor had suddenly taken off with a new, probably younger, lover but had eventually come back, looking for work. Maybe her return posed some threat to Parker. Aggie decided to poke around in his background a little more. Meanwhile, the Toomey clan were not off the hook. They could well be involved in Sandra Taylor's death. Of course, it could also have been a complete stranger or, at least, a stranger to Aggie's case. Her instincts did not point in that direction though. She felt that her investigation was taking her towards a Toomey, with Dr. Parker hovering in the background somewhere. Suddenly, she was crossing the George Washington bridge and was shocked to realize that she recalled hardly any of her journey. The automatic pilot syndrome for her journey was very unnerving and showed how intense her thinking had been. She dropped off the rental in her garage, feeling that it had been quite comfortable and trouble free. As she walked to her apartment, she thought that, perhaps, she would consider a deal for the car or, at least, inquire about one. Jack's idea had been a good one. In her apartment, locks all negotiated, she sat on her couch, writing out her notes on her iPad. It had been a productive and worthwhile trip that had generated more follow up action but that was what she did best and why she was an investigator. There were no messages on her landline and so no chat with Lisa Begu. That left calling Maisie and arranging a meeting. Before she could get to that, her cell rang. She immediately thought Maisie but the screen indicated Jonathan Black.

She picked up and said, "Hi Jonathan. How's it going?"

Jonathan said, "Hi Aggie. I'm just seeing if all went well today."

"Checking up on me?"

"Yes, perhaps I am. Anyway, any luck?"

Aggie smiled to herself. "I think so. There's a guy there, a dentist actually, who was apparently having an affair with Sandra Taylor.

"Really. Did he remind you of Olivier in Marathon Man?"

Aggie said, "Well, let's just say that I didn't take to him. She took off with the musician and then went back. You know some of this."

"Ah. Yes, never go back!"

"Well, sometimes it works Jonathan but whether things went sour or not I don't know."

"More work to be done then. Do you like him for her death?"

Aggie paused. "I just don't know. He is a bit creepy, something's a bit off. Anyway, how about your end? Any new revelations for me?"

"Mm."

"You know, those pockets."

"Well, the gentleman involved has been dissuaded from further activity."

Aggie sighed. "No more calls then. Not from him, anyway."

She added "Does he have a name, if you can tell me."

"He does. He is one Peach Dekker."

"Peach or Pete?"

"Peach. I don't know how that came about. He is definitely not a peach. Ex-army. He's moved on to pastures anew to ply his trade."

Aggie took this in, wondering what it meant. Nothing bad it seemed.

"That's nice. He should have paid for my car. Did you find out who hired him?"

"No, it was all done by mail box in a post office on 83rd. It's not difficult to communicate that way. Almost standard practice. The less anybody knows, the better. Interestingly, he does not claim responsibility for the rapid oxidation of your car."

"Funny. But I'm not sure I like that. Do you believe him?"

"I think so. A trifle odd that he did the calls and not the car job. Plus, he was dumb enough to use his own voice."

"Well, if he's telling the truth, there's still somebody dangerous out there."

"Perhaps. I'm working on it."

"What about the cops?"

"The cops?"

"Yes, what do they know about all of this?"

"These negotiations have been entirely independent of the police. I doubt that much will come of their investigation."

Aggie was genuinely curious. "How do you figure all this out when they can't?"

Jonathan gave a muted chuckle, "Resources, inside information and a brilliant strategic mind. The usual."

"I should not have asked, silly of me."

"Sorry. . By the way, is that dinner arrangement looming, may I ask?"

"It is, just be patient. Thanks for calling Jonathan."

"You are welcome. Bye for now."

"Bye." Aggie rang off and put her cell next to her on the couch. It was time for a bite to eat and so she decided to put off the call to Maisie. It was not a difficult decision.

There was nothing in the fridge that even bordered on enticing. Maybe cheese and crackers which, at times, filled the bill but not this evening. Chinese just reminded her of the spare ribs episode so that was out very quickly. She decided to hit the soup and sandwich delivery outlet and an hour later was munching on a chicken salad with avocado sandwich and thinking that there was no way that she could attack the noodle soup afterwards. That would go into the fridge. No wine left for an accompaniment and so she settled for smart water. Part way though her sandwich, she began, once again, to mull over the recent past, looking for clarity or even an epiphany moment. She felt that part of her problem was that she had conflated two issues; Sandra Taylor's murder and her own torched car warning. They were not necessarily connected but they could be. What, she thought, if David had become so incensed with her inquiries that he set fire to her car, knowing as he must, that it was special to her.

He would still have needed to hire Peach to call her and frighten her off the case. What would that cost? She had no idea but thought that David didn't have much cash available with two families to run, unless he had a source. Aggie thought no, she liked a Toomey for all of this and, by extension, the death of Sandra Taylor. They had the connections and the money. She was convincing herself that someone in that family wanted her out of it, one way or another. Too bad because it had become a personal crusade for her. Stir the pot, she mused with customary determination, see Lisa Begu, see Maisie, see what happens and find out who put old Peachy in the mix. Time for a bit of TV and bed.

Chapter 28

The next morning, Aggie awoke later than she had expected and it was almost 10:00 am before she had showered, dressed and made some coffee. She had no cereal left which meant that she would, unfortunately, have to submit to a round of shopping. Cross legged on the couch, she sipped her coffee and ruminated on her chat with Jonathan. She remembered her question about the police. Why not call them and see what they had achieved, if anything? At least she would be keeping some kind of contact with them, or more specifically, with the Powers guy.

She dug her wallet out of her purse and, after very little poking around, flipped out his card and dialed his office number. She did have Powers' cell number but elected to go the office route. To Aggie's surprise, he picked up after, perhaps, eight or nine rings. "Powers."

Aggie said, "Hi, this is Agnes Trout."

There was a short pause. "And who is Agnes Trout?"

"My car was firebombed a few days ago. We spoke at the garage."

"Ah. Sorry. I did not remember the name. You'd think I would."

Aggie's face tightened a little. "Why? Woman or the fish?"

Again, there was a pause. "This is not going well. Let's start over."

Aggie said, "OK."

"Powers. How can I help you?"

Aggie smiled in spite of herself. "Pretty good. I'm calling to see if there have been any developments. You know, progress."

Powers became marginally warmer. "Yes. Well, not a lot."

Aggie said, "Back burner?"

Powers did not seem put out. "Not exactly. We have spoken to several people."

"You mean interviewed them?"

"No. I mean spoken to them, phone calls."

"I see. Any luck with all these people?"

Powers said, "Ms. Trout, do I detect a trace of skepticism in your voice?"

Aggie half smiled as she drained her coffee. "Well, to be honest, I didn't expect a lot."

Powers drew in a breath loudly, "I'll tell you this. We do, of course, prioritize our cases, my cases, and I have done what I can on your fire. It doesn't amount to much at this point."

Aggie liked honesty when she heard it. "I understand. Is there anything, then?"

"I do not believe that the Toomey family is involved, if that's where you are going."

"Why is that? I think that there is every chance that they are involved."

Powers said, "The guy you tangled with has been in hospital for a while from just before your car was torched."

Aggie took this in quickly, barely registering the 'tangled with' which would have set her off under most circumstances. "What? Taken ill?"

"You might say that. Fell down a flight of stairs to the basement of a building."

"Just fell?"

"Said he was pushed while taking a leak. Broken bones, leg as I recall. Look, I have to get going."

Aggie said, "OK. By the way, I didn't tangle with him. He attacked me."

"Whatever. Either way."

Aggie said, "Before you go, what about the rest of the Toomeys?"

"All respectable people who said that they had no part in it."

Aggie said quickly, "Their word is enough?"

Powers began to sound irritated, "Correct. It is enough when obtained by people with experience in doing this kind of thing."

"What kind of thing?"

"Listening to conversations carefully, nuances, pauses, breathing. That sort of thing. I got to go."

"Just a moment. Will you talk to anyone else?"

"I will, we will."

"No names?"

"No names. Goodbye Ms. Trout."

"Thanks for your time and talking to me."

"My pleasure."

They hung up.

Aggie felt that she had certainly kept in contact with Powers but the outcome of the conversation had turned out to be frustrating because Toomey might not be involved in destroying her car. That is, if the hospital thing checked out. He could have hired someone anyway but the cops, or Powers, seemed to give any Toomey a clean slate. Intuition or Toomey clout? Who knew? She had to do her own follow up, then. She had learnt something though. It was possible that Toomey had been given a helping hand to dive into a basement or he was just drunk enough to fall down on his own. If he fell, he deserved that sort of poetic justice. If he was pushed, he still deserved it. She began to feel a rising compulsion to visit Dougal Toomey, if he was still in hospital. She might be able to pick up an odd vibe or two from him by giving him a surprise visit. Quite a thought and not as outlandish as it first sounded. Aggie put that idea aside for the moment to figure out her day but she liked it and would come back to it soon. She began to write up the Powers discussion. It felt right to have kept in touch and it did seem that he, personally, was trying to make some headway on who was behind the warning. She had not let on that she already knew who the messenger was but not the source, hoping that would be revealed at some point. A bit unfair on Powers, perhaps, but she could not tell him where her information came from. And, anyway, a second confirmation, if it transpired, would be useful. In addition, she now knew that Toomey was in hospital and, apart from a possible visit, that news was satisfying. Her reverie was interrupted by her cell performing its new musical offering. She picked it up, scanned the screen and saw Maisie's name backed up with an unfamiliar number which she vaguely recalled as Maisie's home phone.

She picked up. "Hi Maisie."

"Hi Aggie. I hope that this is not a bad time. How are you?"

Aggie thought that Maisie sounded rushed, a little breathless and she was speaking very quietly. "I'm fine, thanks. You're not using your cell? You OK?"

"Yes. I'm good. I've lost my cell. It's just disappeared. I don't know where it is."

Aggie said, "You should call it. If it's at home you will hear it and if someone has it you might get it back, if you're lucky."

"Of course, I knew all that, I just forgot. I'll do that later."

Aggie said, "Have you got company or something?"

"Yes. But not in here."

"Ah. Look, we should have lunch so that we can talk."

There was a long silence, laden with expectancy, but Aggie had no intention of talking about David over the phone. "Maisie, I am in a position to give you some answers which are not entirely definitive but I do think that I am on firm ground."

There was continued silence and then Maisie said, "Well, if it was all good you would tell me so a lunch seems to be in order."

Aggie thought that she should have seen that coming.

"Maisie, you are my friend and whatever this turns out to be, I don't think now on the phone works. I'd like to talk about it with you when we are together."

Maisie sighed deeply. "OK. But this evening is not too easy, you know."

She lowered her voice further. "Actually, David is off tomorrow. A day or so. In fact, I think it's just an overnight. He is working Friday and coming back sometime Saturday." Several thoughts immediately coursed through Aggie's mind, the most prominent being that she might have a chance of confirming David's other lifestyle. She said, "How about the day after tomorrow, then? Saturday. A late lunch."

Aggie needed time to get back after running her checks in Delaware.

"Will that even be possible?"

Maisie said, "Yes, I think so. I should be able to work it."

"That will let me tidy up a couple of things before we meet. You can just call me with a place and time and I'll meet up with you."

"That sounds good. Thank you Aggie."

"Great, I'll see you then."

They hung up.

Aggie wondered why Maisie had called today when she could have called when David was away the next day. She must have felt pressure of some kind to find out the truth. Living day to day in her current circumstances must be very difficult and she had sounded strung out, which was understandable with him somewhere nearby. It was a sad fact, she thought, that a lot of marriages fail or were in crisis. One in three she had read somewhere. She felt her mood moving towards the melancholy. Surely, it was possible to do better than that. Who knew? She had not given it a shot and didn't know if she would ever. With an effort she dragged her mind back to the rest of the day ahead. She had to do some shopping straight away and she really had the urge to do a workout at the gym, having been too busy for too long now. Also, she had to think the David situation through, the plan forming in her mind being to drive to his apparent second home overnight and just watch what happened at the start of the day there.

For the moment, coffee and lemon cake at Starbucks, followed by some shopping at Whole Foods seemed in order. As always, the lemon cake was magnificent and Aggie eventually returned home with plenty of groceries and produce. Her dinner in the evening consisted of strawberries, goat cheese and a chunk of sourdough boule with some Sancerre white wine. She spent the rest of the evening reading and occasionally sipping wine, leaving her cases alone in their entirety. It was a luxurious experience.

Chapter 29

Dougal Toomey had spent his day, whatever day that was, playing video games, looking at porn and drinking beer, none of which was in the least satisfying for him. His lank, unwashed hair hung around his head like that of some bedraggled dog, climbing out of a ditch. Stubble coated most of his lower face. He had often toyed with the idea of a beard but, whenever he had tried it, the beard only grew in patches which was another small failure to add to the many that he felt he owned. A mustache didn't look too bad, He was seeking an unobtainable debonair effect and, at least, it was complete when trimmed. But, in the end, it disappointed him. It made him look like some caricature, like an actor with a bad fake mustache. He recalled that he once tried a Hitler mustache which he thought looked pretty good and he liked it but, outside, people seemed to avoid him which was unfathomable. As the day grew into early evening, he decided to go to a bar and get some food. His remaining Stouffers frozen meal, a meatloaf, was several months past the due date, not that he normally concerned himself with that. He didn't fancy it anyway. He felt like going out. There was a version of an Irish pub about seven or eight blocks away that he had been to before and which did decent food. It did not take the usual effort to get himself up and out. He was already wearing a check patterned shirt and soon found a pair of balled up socks, his jeans and his sneakers and pulled on a stained leather bomber jacket. He threw his hair back and ran his hands over it and checked his wallet, which had three credit cards and quite a lot of cash in it. He had never been short of ready money thanks to his grandfather and, while he liked never being short of cash, he had vague twinges of easily suppressible feelings about his dependence on the old boy. His grandfather felt like an old-fashioned patriarchal figure who enjoyed his family's dependence upon him but he didn't rub it in too much and so his beneficence was bearable.

He was soon on the street and reached the pub after an uneventful walk, hands in pockets, head down. He was pleased to see that it was not crowded, about a dozen people on stools at the long counter and three of the seven dining tables, placed along two walls, occupied. He found a stool just around the bend at the end of the counter which was far enough away from the nearest drinker to dissuade socialization. He ordered beer after beer for an hour or so and then decided that it was time to eat. He was shown to one of the two remaining tables by an accommodating waitress who assisted him gently to his seat. He hadn't noticed the place becoming more populated as he had drunk his way through the past hour or more. He grabbed the menu which swam before his eyes for a minute or two until he focused. He drank the glass of water on the table as he scanned the offerings, which included bangers and mash, shepherd's pie and steak and kidney pie, as well as burger varieties. He thought fuck this British shit and ordered a double cheeseburger with curly fries and pickles. His glass of water was also replenished. While eating gustily what turned out to be an excellent burger, he glanced at the people around him. The tables were occupied by two or four people and the counter was now full of earnest drinkers, none of whom seemed to have any interest in him whatever, which was just as he liked it. Feeling full and imbued with a feeling that bordered on happiness which only came along once in a while, he left a big tip and meandered and negotiated his way to the door and into the night air.

He began walking in his usual slouch when an intense urge to empty his bladder engulfed him. He should have gone at the bar but had not thought of it. There was no way he was going to make it home. He was passing sets of steps leading down to basements of the brownstones on the street and found one with railings but no gate.

It looked very inviting. He looked around. There were plenty of lights in windows but the street was not too well lit. He stepped quickly onto the top step, which was wider than those below and began to pee. The relief was palpable. He was only partially aware of a presence behind him and by the time it had registered, he received a solid push between his shoulder blades. Sometimes, when people are drunk and they fall, they are so floppy or loose jointed that their injuries are minimal. Dougal Toomey did not turn out to be one of those people. He went flying through the air, spraying urine all over himself and the steps. As he turned over and crashed down the steps, his head hit a rail and he landed on a small, flat area of concrete at the bottom with one leg awkwardly bent beneath him, producing a sickening crack somewhere below his knee, while his shoulders and the back of his head struck a wall. As he slid over to one side, overwhelmed by nausea, he vomited and just before his cheek touched the cool concrete, he caught sight of a large, dark figure standing at the top of the steps.

Chapter 30

Aggie spent the morning of the next day cleaning her apartment or, rather, her small bathroom and kitchen, as she had had enough by the time that she had finished both of them. The work allowed her to continue her break from the night before, giving her mind free reign to gain some perspective on her cases. The foremost thought, which kept surfacing with increasing persistence, pushing itself into her mental field of view, was one of visiting Dougal Toomey in hospital if he was still there. The prospect of shocking him and confronting him head on in any way that would add to his misery was very appealing. She didn't know whether he was still in hospital or even in which hospital he might be but she decided to find out. There were a couple of possibilities. After several telephone calls she established that he was, indeed, still in the hospital and that hospital was Mount Sinai. No other information was forthcoming and so she decided to give it a go that afternoon. She ate a bunch of celery sticks with a slice of Cambozola, the best part of which was the front wedge and began to prepare herself for the trip. She was soon at the reception desk offering Toomey's name up for visitation.

When asked she said, "I am his step sister."

The receptionist said, "He has had no visitors."

Aggie responded, "He will be pleased to see me then."

She was given floor and room. She checked in at the floor and soon found the room. It contained two beds, the nearest to the door having curtains drawn around it. The first thing she saw when the second bed came into view was a set of pulleys and a plaster encased leg partially suspended from them. Dougal Toomey was propped up on pillows with his eyes closed. His hair hung to the opposite side of his head from a richly colored eye and cheekbone. There was some kind of dressing attached to the back of his head that was barely visible. His arms and hands rested at his side on the bedclothes and appeared unharmed. Aggie walked around the foot of the bed and stood there for a few moments, her abhorrence mounting markedly. She thought what an unpleasant and pathetic excuse for a man. Toomey sensed her presence and opened his eyes which immediately flooded with alarm.

Aggie said, "How's the pervert doing today? Badly, I hope."

Toomey swallowed several times. "What are you doing here? How did you get in?"

Aggie gazed directly at him.

"Came to see if you were suffering enough."

"What? I'll call the nurse and have you thrown out."

"Well, before you do, tell me how many women you have assaulted."

Toomey paled, "You're crazy."

Aggie ignored him, "Go on, tell me how many."

Toomey's hand rose involuntarily to his damaged cheek. "Go away. I'm not going to talk to you."

Aggie said, "Does Mom know about all this. I'm sure that she could find you a private facility. I could call her."

Toomey said, "None of your business. Just go away."

Aggie pressed on, "You know that I am going to get you put away don't you. You will have plenty of time in prison to remember those women."

Toomey showed the first signs of anger. "I'm not going to prison."

Aggie said, "Oh but you are. I've been in touch with several women who do not like you at all."

"No way."

"Why? Because you paid them off? You'd be surprised."

Toomey pushed himself a little more upright. "None of it is true. I haven't done anything."

"Really? What about me? Forgotten that have you? Let me ask you this. Did you murder a woman?"

Toomey looked genuinely shocked, taken aback and frightened.

"What do you mean? You are crazy."

"You don't know the half of it. I'm just getting started."

"Leave me alone. I've got a terrible headache."

Aggie nodded appreciatively. "I am so glad to hear that. You should not get drunk and fall down steps."

Toomey responded quickly.

"How do you know about that?"

Aggie allowed herself a brief smile, "Spoke to the cops, they know about it. Must be checking up on you."

Toomey drew in a loud breath.

"I was pushed."

"Who would push you down some steps?"

"Was it you? Did you get someone to do it?"

"Wish I had." Aggie reached over to the cast and tapped it. "Only one leg broken? I would have done better than that."

"Don't do that."

"Little nervous, are we?"

Aggie tapped the cast again and stared at him until he looked away.

"I'll be off, then. See you when you get out. More bad things ahead!"

Toomey did not respond. He continued to look away. Aggie turned and left without looking back.

Back in her apartment, she felt pleased with her decision to go to the hospital. Toomey had looked miserable and had received quite a bit of damage through his fall. Could have been a mugger but she didn't think so. She would have to ask Powers if Toomey had been robbed. It seemed more like an act of malice, either intended or opportunist. The one interesting part of the visit had been Toomey's look of genuine surprise when Aggie had virtually accused him of murder. He was clearly shocked, enough so that she believed that he had not personally been involved in Sandra Taylor's murder, although he could have been party to it.

She felt on a roll again and decided that she would drive to David's second address in the early morning to see if his car was there and what transpired at that time, if anything. It was a lot of commitment but it could pay off if she was lucky. She watched some TV, ate some buttered toast with some orange juice and settled in on the couch for a nap, setting her alarm for 2:00 am.

There was something relaxing about driving in the early morning hours on a dry night, the lights from New Jersey reflecting and flickering off the river and all the buildings off the West Side Highway swathed in darkness with occasional shafts of light emanating from brightened windows and signage. Thousands of people were living their lives behind many of those windows, piled one above the other into the night sky. There were only a handful of cars on the road, an occasional set of headlights coming up behind her and easing by with barely a sound above her own motor and the approaching beams of a couple or so cars on the other side of the divide pushing downriver. Aggie crossed an almost deserted George Washington bridge, knowing it would have made more sense to use a tunnel but enjoying this route. She was soon well on her way, experiencing the quiet and musing on the possibility of future self-drive cars when drivers could sit back, read or take in the views. How is it possible, she thought, to map out the whole country in real time fine detail for all of that to work? Of course, sometime, somebody would do just that. After a time, she tuned in a classical station on the radio and found the darkness and low volume Schubert conducive to relaxing and clearing her mind. It was therapeutic to let her mind flicker over the mundane, like shopping, cleaning her apartment and getting herself into shape, as well as fleeting images of her parents, Jonathan and his lifestyle and Jack's work driven life.

As she drove on, she gradually became aware of a set of headlights that were a long way behind her, perhaps half a mile or more but they had not, noticeably, gained on her or dropped back. She thought of someone else enjoying a night drive without being in a hurry. She knew that, sometimes, drivers used the lights of the car in front of them as a guide to relax a bit while eating up some mileage. These lights though, were too far back to make any use of her rear lights. Faint starlight and a quarter moon, partially hidden by clouds, revealed that any buildings adjacent to the road had long disappeared from her journey and had been replaced by grass verges, banks and troughs, some dense with trees and bushes, and some with more sporadic coverage. The median was now solid guard rail with occasional grassy areas and bushes too. She had been driving in the middle lane and, once in a while, a car would appear in her rear-view mirror and drift by her to be swallowed up in the darkness, the rear lights becoming pinpricks of red light dying away to nothing. She decided to move over to the slow lane because it felt comfortable with the hard shoulder sliding by close to her right. She checked on the distant vehicle and realized that it was a little closer to her. She could see two dipped main beams and two smaller beams lower down but she could not identify the type of vehicle, guessing that was an SUV, truck or van. She allowed herself to speculate about being followed but that seemed impossible. Who would know that she was out at this time of night and where she might be going? Nobody was the inevitable answer. Still, she switched off the radio so that she could give her attention to the following vehicle trying to figure out if her imagination was getting the better of her, or not. The lights behind were clearly closer now and in the middle lane and she thought that she could make out the shadowy outline of a van. What were the odds that two cars were traveling in the thick of the night in the same direction with almost no other traffic on the road and just a couple of hundred yards apart for several miles? In fact, Aggie had lost track of the miles but the van had been behind her for a substantial period of time. Once again, she thought who would want to follow her? The idea seemed silly, preposterous and paranoid even. Her speed had been consistently just a few mph's above the limit, fairly expedient and not fast enough to attract any traffic cops. The van was now gradually making up the distance between them, still in the middle lane and yielding a dark color, maybe brown or navy blue. It was hard to tell. It slowly began to overtake her with only a ten or fifteen mph differential in speed and Aggie suddenly thought what if the driver or passenger had a gun? What a crazy idea. But she just could not help herself, paranoia or not.

    She carefully applied the brakes so that she dropped back, leaving the van almost half past her Subaru. The van began to slow too and then eased over so that it was almost touching her car and then turned into it striking just in front of the windshield and forcing her car across the hard shoulder. She was immediately aware of loud noises, screaming tires and crunching metal as the van pulled clear and broke contact while her car careened across the grass verge and plunged down a bank, the bushes and small trees creating horrific cracking and slashing sounds. Braking had no effect as the car was skidding and bouncing into a tree line having hardly reduced speed. As she desperately struggled for control, trees loomed up and, by sheer luck, the car plowed between two large oaks, barely missing them and through a pool of stagnant water, slewing around and striking a bank and a small tree with the driver's side wing before stopping. Aggie's shoulder and head struck the window but her seat belt kept her in place. The engine had died on its own and her first thought was surprisingly clear in her mind. Get out of the car and get away from it. There could be intrinsic danger from the crash such as a fire but she wanted to get away in case anyone came back to look at their handiwork. She unbuckled her safety belt and tried to open the driver's side door. Pain seared through her shoulder and on the other side of her neck as she found that the door would not budge. Calmly, she turned and gingerly climbed over to the passenger side and tried the door. It opened. She grabbed her bag and coat and crawled out of the car and pulled herself upright, feeling spasms of pain all over her body, as well as some dizziness and nausea.

The car headlights were stabbing beams of light into the trees but, apart from them, she was surrounded by darkness.

She took off resolutely towards the rear of the car and beyond, pushing through bushes and mud for about twenty yards or so until she found a large tree and leaned her back against it in some exhaustion. Almost immediately, she heard the whine of a high gear up on the road and realized that the van was reversing back down the road. It stopped near the point where her car had crossed the grass verge and she could see a pool of light up at road level. She heard a door creaking open and the sound of footsteps on gravel and then silence. Either the driver was walking across the grass or was staring in the direction of her car headlights and listening for movement. She held her breath, wincing with the pain, and continued to listen. Soft gusts of wind whispered through the trees but there was no other sound. The time ticked by interminably until suddenly she heard footsteps on gravel again and the van door squeaked open and slammed shut. The engine fired up and the van pulled away leaving Aggie shaking in her small, dark portion of nature's environs.

Chapter 31

Aggie sucked in her breath and let out a huge sigh of relief. She was beginning to tremble slightly from the shock and the pain in her shoulder. Also, she had a serious headache and ran the tips of her fingers over the side of her head and face. There was no broken skin but it was definitely bruised and tender. She dug out her phone trying to decide who to call and, in the end, it seemed that the police were the best solution. She had nothing to hide and they could get her to a hospital and alert a towing company for her car. She went through the emergency system and had cops for company, along with very bright flashlights, in less than fifteen minutes. After ascertaining that she was not seriously hurt, they listened to her carefully, checked the road and her car's final resting place, gave her a breathalyzer test and took her to the local emergency room. One cop remained while she received treatment which included X-rays, painkillers and a sling to support her arm. When she was sitting quietly in an ante room, he took a statement along with her personal information which she signed.

She had learned from the female emergency room doctor that the acromioclavicular joint had been severely impacted but remained intact with significant bruising and swelling around the joint which was now very painful. She had been given an ice pack to hold against the side of her head and told to drink lots of water. Since, in her opinion, Aggie would not have to be admitted, the doctor asked if she had someone to call to drive her home. Aggie decided to call Jonathan who, clearly, had been asleep. After a very quick explanation and details of her dilemma and condition, he promised to be at the hospital in just over an hour. While she waited, sipping some dreadful black coffee from the hospital coffee machine, she thought about the last couple of hours. It had not taken much observation on Aggie's part to see that the cops had initial reservations about her story, clearly entertaining the thought that she was impaired by alcohol or drugs or had fallen asleep at the wheel, or both. After all, what were the odds that someone would force another driver off the road in the middle of the night in their jurisdiction? But, after examination of the road and the skid marks plus her negative alcohol test, they had attached some credence to her view that a second vehicle was involved. She supposed that the damage to the impact side of her car had masked any signs of a forced exit from the road. They had contacted a local towing company to take care of her car, giving her all of their contact telephone numbers. Where all of that would lead financially with the rental company, she had no idea. She had not checked the contract that she had signed, being so pleased to get a car again. All of that was in the future and she could do nothing about it for the time being.

She was just beginning to consider who had been responsible for trying to injure her or worse, when Jonathan came through the door, dressed in a blue open neck shirt, blue jacket and jeans, looking very concerned as he walked swiftly over to her. She stood up and, without a word being said, he held her for a few moments, carefully avoiding squeezing her damaged arm and shoulder.

He muttered, "Oh, I'm so sorry. Let's get you home."

Aggie did not respond. She allowed herself to be led from the hospital to Jonathan's maroon colored Highlander parked nearby and not in the parking lot. He carefully and gently arranged her in the passenger seat and then went around the car to the driver's seat. He fired up the engine, gave her a long, concerned look and pulled away from the hospital. She closed her eyes.

Aggie awoke with a start not knowing where she was or what was going on. Looking around she saw that they were just parking in an underground car park. Jonathan switched off the engine and turned to her.

"Look, I took the liberty of bringing you to my apartment."

Aggie glanced at him. "So, I see."

"If you would rather not stay here tonight, I will gladly take you to your place."

Aggie looked at him with some resignation in her expression.

Jonathan said, "You will be safe and you will get a good night's sleep. Well, actually a good half night's sleep. It's getting near dawn."

Aggie sighed, "OK. But I have no clothes, no toothpaste, all those things."

Jonathan smiled, "I can find all that you need. You'll manage. I have a robe, odd clothes, dental paraphernalia plus anything else that you need."

Aggie said, "Of course."

Jonathan helped her out of the wagon and the elevator took them up to his apartment in a comfortable silence. He opened the door and, once inside, said, "This bathroom is yours," indicating the bathroom near the entrance door. "You will find new toothbrushes and toothpaste in one of the drawers and there are clean towels—and a shower if you want it."

Aggie said, "Is there another bathroom then?"

"I have a small en suite in my room."

"Lucky you."

Jonathan smiled, "You could say that."

Aggie said, "Sorry, that didn't come out right. I was trying to be funny."

Jonathan said, "That's OK. Here is the bedroom."

He indicated the nearest of the closed doors that Aggie had seen on her last visit. He opened the door onto a medium sized room with a window, a Queen-sized bed, three chests of drawers and several prints on the walls. At least, she assumed that they were prints. The room was painted a pale green. Jonathan walked over to one of the chests and produced a white Terry cloth robe, a couple of tee shirts and a pair of light sweats.

"The best I can do." he said.

Aggie said, "Thanks." She sat down on the bed feeling utterly exhausted.

Jonathan went out for a few moments and returned with some bottled water, for which she was truly grateful and thanked him.

"I'll leave you then."

Aggie said, "Don't you want to hear a bit more about what happened?"

"Not now, no. You need some rest. Plenty of time for that later. Are you all set?"

"Yes, thanks for all of this."

"Once again, my pleasure."

He left the room, closing the door quietly behind him.

Aggie threw off her clothes, climbed into the bed and went straight to sleep. The bed was gloriously comfortable but it would not have mattered.

Chapter 32

Toomey lay in his hospital bed with his eyes closed, thinking about the veiled threats delivered by that vindictive woman. Well, the threats were not veiled really, they were explicit. He was still in some pain when he tried to move his leg but it was the itching under the cast that he could barely endure. His head and cheekbone were also still very sore so that he found it difficult to sleep. He couldn't turn over and the back of his head hurt against the pillows so that he was obliged to hold his head up or rest his chin on his chest to doze off and get some sleep. Plus, the guy in the next bed snored all day and all night, or that was how it seemed. His life was unquestionably miserable he thought. Why were some people so unlucky when they did not deserve it? Good people always seemed to get the worst out of life. There seemed to be some law of physics or some other science that designated that, a kind of fate that was uncaring and indiscriminate. He called his mother to unload some of his woes, including the recent visit of that PI, but her attitude conveyed to him that she had stopped caring about his predicaments, the unjustifiable nature of his problems. She had even suggested, with some persuasion, that it was time for him to leave the country or go to somewhere like Montana or Alaska; all of which was spectacularly unhelpful to him. Yes, she really was an excuse for a mother but she could still help him, however unsympathetically. He ruminated some more. Maybe, just maybe, it was time to start over, go somewhere where nobody knew him, meet people who appreciated his talents, who might see him for the good person that he actually was. The idea began to gather momentum. It looked like a perfect solution, no more aggravation, no more impending problems or threats, a new life. Why hadn't he thought of this before? Perhaps, because he had been so busy coming up with new game ideas, trying to live a productive life. His mother would be only too pleased to arrange it and his grandfather would pay for it and continue to support him. There was that, at least. He gave a deep sigh. There was no justice in this world, but there might be soon.

Chapter 33

Aggie was aware of a light knocking entering her dreams and, with quite an effort, she dragged herself awake, remembering where she was with a start. The knocking was at her bedroom door and she called out that she was awake. Jonathan responded that he had coffee made and asked how she liked her scrambled eggs.

Aggie said, "Dry, thanks."

She climbed out of bed and put on the robe. There was no mirror in the room so she opened the door and headed to the bathroom to wash up. She decided to shower later, cleaned her teeth and ran a set of fingers through her hair, shaking it into some sort of order and wishing that she hadn't because of the bruising. Finally, realizing that there was nothing more that she could do, she padded into the living room passing the kitchen where Jonathan was at the cooker.

Jonathan called out, "I'll be with you in a moment, take a seat."

Aggie headed to the table where two places were laid. There were two glasses of orange juice, two mugs and a pot of coffee on a pad near the center of the table. She sat down and took a quick sip of the orange juice. In a couple of minutes, Jonathan came breezing into the room carrying a platter of scrambled egg which he placed on the table. He was wearing jeans and a white tee shirt. He then went back to the kitchen and reappeared with a plate of toast and a dish of butter.

He said, "Well, that's it. Nice and simple. Tuck in."

Aggie had not eaten for a long time and breakfast smelled delicious. She helped herself to some scrambled eggs and buttered a slice of toast.

"Thanks so much Jonathan. I really need this."

"So do I. You must have slept well, it's after eleven."

"I did. I was totally knocked out. The bed was very comfortable. I'm glad that you did this. Thanks so much."

Jonathan smiled and said, "Good."

After a few minutes of eating, Jonathan broke an easy silence. "Aggie, do you feel like talking yet? About what happened?"

Aggie said, "Yes. It will be good to go through it all. To see if anything stands out."

Jonathan said, "OK, let's start at the beginning. How did you come to be on the road at that time in the morning?"

Aggie gathered her thoughts. "For various reasons, I decided to visit the house in Delaware where my friend's husband seems to be living with a second family."

"One good reason for doing that?"

Aggie sighed, "I wanted a sort of final confirmation of the second family. I thought I might see him leave the house in the morning, saying goodbye to the kid and the second wife, so to speak."

"Were you sure he was there?"

"Not sure, no. I just knew that he was going to be away for a couple of days. For work."

"Mm. Who else knew that you were going?"

"No one. I decided to do it on the spur of the moment. When I was chatting with Maisie."

They both paused and sipped at their coffees. Aggie suddenly remembered that Maisie was going to text her about lunch and it was already lunchtime.

She said, "Jonathan, sorry, I have to check my phone."

She got up quickly and went to the bedroom to retrieve her phone. Sure enough there was a text from Maisie but it was to say that she couldn't make it. So, she now had her cell phone back. The text message said, 'would tomorrow work at 12:30?' She proposed the same diner at which Aggie had met Adele Morris. Aggie texted back that she would be there and returned to the breakfast table.

Jonathan said, "All OK?"

Aggie said, "Yes, fine. I had to text my friend."

He said, "Talking of your friend, did you tell her you were going to take the trip?"

"No."

Jonathan looked puzzled, "So, this guy could not have found out that you were going?"

"No. Well, there was one odd thing."

"Ah, what was that?"

"She called me. But not from her cell, from her home phone."

"Is that unusual?"

"I suppose not but she said that her cell had vanished. I mean, people lose phones but I got the impression that it disappeared at home."

Jonathan leaned forward, "So, her husband could have taken it? Perhaps to check it out."

"That's right. But I think that there is an extension to the landline phone. In the office in the other room at her apartment. To do with her business."

Jonathan said, "So you are thinking that he could have listened in?"

Aggie put her cup down. "Yes, but I did not say that I was going there. Ah, but he could have deduced that I might, from our conversation."

"Good, so we have one possibility for your driver."

"It's not really his style but yes, I suppose so."

Jonathan leaned back, "What about the Toomey story? Anything new there?"

Aggie took a deep breath and looked directly at Jonathan. "I went to see him in hospital."

A flash of disbelief crossed Jonathan's face.

"What? Aggie, when was this?"

"Yesterday. I wanted to confront him, make him suffer a bit."

Jonathan glanced at her anew. "That took a lot of moxie. Talk about stirring things up. Do you think it was wise in the circumstances?"

Aggie smiled. They had finished everything on the table now.

"Perhaps not but it was worth it. I gave him something to think about."

"I expect you did. Maybe it prompted him into action too."

"What? You mean set that guy onto me, I thought he had moved on."

"He has. The word, so to speak, is out there. Not to get involved, I mean." He paused. "That is not to say that there are not unscrupulous actors available."

Aggie smiled, "I see. Not adhering to the code?"

"Exactly. Well, now we have two possibilities for the attack on you. Even so, it would mean extensive surveillance in order to catch you leaving your apartment. I see no other way that it could have been done."

Aggie's amusement turned to some concern.

"Wow. That is creepy. Someone has been watching my apartment for quite a time, then."

"I would say so. That, in turn, means that the situation is serious. Someone has a compelling reason to dissuade you from your activities. I think that this was an attempt to kill you." Jonathan continued, "What they do not know is where you are now. We would not have been followed from the hospital. The guy was long gone I'm sure. You should not go back to your apartment."

Aggie tossed her head, "Jonathan, I'm not going to be intimidated. I will carry on my life as usual."

He smiled knowingly, "You are so stubborn."

"Of course, you know that."

"OK, I'll make some inquiries, see what I can find out. If you don't mind, Cedric will keep an occasional eye on your apartment. He can spot trouble long before it happens."

"No, I don't mind. I rather like the idea of Cedric being nearby."

"Good. I did not ask you much about the actual crash, did I? What happened?"

Aggie thought back. "Well, I was followed for quite a few miles from a long way back. Then, the van, I think it was a van, came up quickly and pushed me off the road."

Jonathan said, "So for a long time it remained behind at the same distance?"

"Yes."

"What was the area like where you were driven off the road?"

"There were lots of trees and bushes and a bank that I went down."

"Then, would you say that the van accelerated rapidly to get to you almost before you realized it?"

"Yes, why do you ask?"

"Because it suggests that the driver knew the road and had chosen that spot to drive you off. In other words, lots of trees down a bank, the terrain was right for a nasty crash. Or, maybe the driver could see enough of the terrain to give it a shot."

"That could be true. Somehow, I missed all the trees, just, and eventually hit another bank in the middle of them. I remember the car spinning around because of water and mud."

"What happened next?"

"Mm. I was actually worried about a fire. You hear about that sort of thing. And I thought that the driver might come and finish the job, so I got out quickly."

"So, he did not come back?"

"He did. The van reversed and someone got out and stood there for a long time. Well, it seemed like a long time."

"But he did not come into the woods?"

"No. You think I could have identified him?"

"Perhaps. He could have just killed you though, so it would not have mattered."

"Nice."

"He didn't come to the car because at best you would have expired and, at worst, been out of commission for a bit and duly warned, again."

They both sat in thought for a minute or two.

Eventually, Jonathan said, "It looks like the same person is behind all of this. He, or she, has hired help once and, perhaps, again or taken on the task himself, or herself."

"What could I have done that warrants killing me? I can see getting mad, wanting some kind of revenge but not this. I've had threats before but that is what they have usually been, just threats."

An expression approaching anger, a hardening of the features, crossed Jonathan's face. "I don't know but, believe me, I'm going to try to find out."

Chapter 34

Aggie had helped Jonathan clear up the breakfast dishes as best she could with one arm in a sling. It had been a companionable chore and they had not spoken further about her exploits. After some thought, she had decided to take her shower at home. In some shoulder pain, she donned her used clothing as best as she could. In spite of the difficulty, she also made the bed and laid out the robe and unused clothes. In the bathroom, she had freshened up, noting that the mirror was not too complimentary as she had fluffed up her hair with her free hand. There had seemed to be no visible swelling but the side of her head had felt painful to the touch. Jonathan had offered to see her home but she had gracefully declined and had thanked him profusely for all of his help and support in the last day or so.

Back in her apartment, she carefully slipped out of her clothes and sank into a hot bath until the water was only lukewarm and then followed that with a hot shower. Relaxing on her couch in her robe and an ice bag, held to her shoulder, she probed the mental noise in her thoughts, looking for some clear perspective. With some amusement, she remembered a quote that she had heard when she was just starting out in the business. It said that private investigators think, ruminate or mull a lot because that is what they do. Whatever the truth of that statement, the bottom line here, however unpalatable, was that someone was trying to kill her and she had no real idea who that someone might be. As Jonathan had pointed out, it could be David or a Toomey connection and she was betting on the latter.

Toomey and, more significantly, his family had very good reason to want her gone. She was much too close to providing adverse publicity which, she thought, affected Katherine Toomey more than anyone else in the family. She had gone to a lot of trouble to keep her son out of the spotlight, not for his benefit but her own. Aggie doubted whether she cared at all about him, now or ever. So, there it was. An actual attempt on her life. Well, it would not stop her. For the moment it was time to regroup and then move on with her cases. It was also time to tell Jack what had happened. For some reason, she felt a vague sense of guilt about not doing so yet, a feeling that she had not kept him fully in the loop, although that was not an obligation.

First things first though. She had to call the rental company to tell them where their hurt car was. It was a nice, comfortable car too and she had been moving towards the idea of trying to buy it. After a lengthy conversation with a rental company employee, she learnt that she would be paying a deductible of over $500 which would be charged to her credit card. She had to supply details of the police report, largely it seemed, because she had somehow contrived not to obtain the other driver's information after the incident. The guy at the rental place did not seem to understand the difficulties involved in attempting to do that. Anyway, it could have been worse in terms of what it cost her. Once again, she did not have a car and would have to manage without one for the time being. She had not thought to ask the rental place if there was another car available. She wondered what their response would have been. Aggie's thoughts turned to Jack. It was now well towards late afternoon and she expected that there was a good chance of catching him in the office, even at the weekend. He answered on the third ring.

"Hi Ag. This is a nice surprise. How's things?"

"Hi Jack. Well, the last day or two have been rather hectic, to say the least."

"Why, what happened? Are you OK?"

"Yes. I'm fine now but I got banged up a bit."

Jack sucked in a deep breath.

"Banged up how?"

Aggie said, "Long story but I was forced off the road last night."

"Forced off? Fuck. But you are alright though?" It was too much information in one jolt. Jack said, "Look, can I come around in a couple of hours so that we can talk?"

Aggie had not expected that but she found it immensely appealing at this point. She would have some time to catch up with Jack without being rushed and instead of just exchanging words through electronic devices.

She said, "That sounds good Jack. Shall I order out?"

"No. I'll bring a pizza—pepperoni and sausage?"

Aggie said, "Great, I'll get some ice cream and some wine then."

"OK. See you at seven. Bye."

They hung up. Aggie had forgotten about her shoulder but the swelling had diminished significantly. She gingerly slipped into a sweat suit and in less than an hour, was back in her apartment with Italian Mediterranean Mint ice cream, two bottles of Shiraz and a bottle of Chardonnay as a backup.

She laid out the coffee table for the pizza and wine, checked her appearance briefly in the bathroom and settled in to wait for Jack with a few pages of her book. It was less than two hours since Jack's call when her buzzer signaled his arrival and he was at the door. She opened up, took in his cheerful smile and they gave each other an awkward hug with the pizza box held high and her arm pushed out sideways.

Jack said, "Looks like Fort Knox out there, just need some guard dogs and you will be home free."

Aggie laughed, "A bit of overkill you think?"

"Not really. Good to be safe. What's up with the arm, is it OK?"

"Shoulder is a bit sore but getting better. Tell you in a bit."

They sat down on the couch, opened up the pizza box and extracted their first slices, munching in silence.

After sipping some wine Jack said, "Good to see you Ag. You look good."

It felt good to hear that. She liked Jack's earnest demeanor and warmth. "So, do you. Seems like a while, doesn't it?"

"Yes, it does." he said with a smile. He paused. "Do you feel up to talking about all this? The last day or two?"

Over the next few slices of pizza and the remainder of the first bottle of Shiraz, Aggie related her adventures up to the time that she was taken to the hospital. Jack had of course, known about the crash but he had still been shocked to hear how it went down.

He had said, "Whomever it was, then, was trying to kill you."

"Looks like it."

"This is bad stuff Aggie."

"I suppose it is but it will not put me off."

Aggie had also elicited a strong reaction from Jack when she had told him about the Toomey hospital visit. He had invoked the idea of deliberate provocation but Aggie had dismissed that premise firmly.

Eventually, as he opened the second bottle of Shiraz, Jack came up with the obvious question.

"How did you get home from the hospital then?"

Aggie gave a small sigh, "I called Jonathan Black."

Jack looked at her in disbelief, "Jonathan Black?"

"Yes. At the time I thought it was the best way to go. I thought it might put you in a spot, workwise, if I called you."

"Second guessing me?"

"Yes, I suppose so. Sorry Jack."

"You know that I would have come for you."

"I do. Anyway, he was there quickly and brought me back."

Aggie moved the conversation on, "I think the rental car has had it. Cost me quite a bit."

"I expect it did."

Jack paused a moment or two.

"Anything going on between you two?"

Before Aggie could reply he raised both his hands, "Sorry. None of my business, I know. I asked because I have some information."

"Well, nothing is going on, as you put it. What's the information?"

"Right. Mm. Jonathan Black may not be his real name. He turns out to have several names."

"Does he. Such as?"

All the pizza had been consumed and they were sipping the wine sparingly. "Jonathan Groom, Alexander Kowolski, Henry Penn. And those are the ones that I know about."

Aggie mused, "I see. So, you have been checking him out."

"I have. Just making sure that you are not in danger. At least, not from him."

"I appreciate that, I do. But do aka's make someone dangerous?"

Jack looked at her over the top of his glass, "You know the answer to that. It depends on the reason for them. I mean, he is, after all, a fixer by profession."

"A nonviolent one."

"As far as we know." Jack leaned forward. "Let's be crazy for a moment. Could he have been the driver that got to you? Could he still be working for the Toomeys?"

Aggie felt annoyed. "Jack. That's absurd. He is not that kind of person."

"OK. OK. But you should consider all of the options. To do his kind of work, he has to be engaging, manipulative, believable and, perhaps, ruthless."

Aggie did not like this at all. It questioned the foundation of her intuition about people. "That is a distant option. In fact, it is a nonstarter."

Jack pressed on, "You know him that well, do you?"

"Not that well, no. I just think that I am a decent judge of character."

As she was saying that, Aggie had multiple thoughts skittering through her mind. She had not judged David that well. She knew on some level, that Jonathan had put a stop to Peach Dekker's activities, and maybe others. How he had achieved that she had not considered too much. Someone had shoved Toomey down some steps. Random or planned? Could that have been Jonathan, or Cedric? Misgivings began to have legs but she pushed them away.

She must have looked uncertain because Jack said, "Ag, you are a good judge of character. I am making suggestions, that's all. Covering the bases so to speak. You make the choices."

Aggie said, "Let's have some ice cream."

They cleaned up the dishes and the empty bottles but left the glasses in case the Chardonnay looked inviting.

They dished up the Mediterranean Mint which had a particularly cleansing of the palate effect after the pizza.

Jack said, "What's next do you think?"

"I would have liked to have gone through a bit more on my friend's husband. You know, that was what I was doing when the crash happened. I'd also like to know why he left Turner and Bowden. There is a guy there I might have got to talk. But I think that I have enough. I'm seeing my friend tomorrow. Plus, I've been given the name of another woman who was assaulted by Toomey. I need to talk to her. It would be nice to get someone to testify or confirm that this guy is a nasty predator. That's about it. Getting near the end of both cases now."

"Sounds good. You've found somebody else, then."

"Yes. Adele Morris put me onto her."

"Right. Anything you want from me that would help?"

"Yes. Open that bottle and bring it to the bedroom, if that works."

Jack laughed out loud, "Are you kidding?"

And it did work, really well. Aggie barely noticed her shoulder pain or her bruises.

Chapter 35

The next morning, which was a Sunday, Aggie and Jack lingered for more love making which was less strenuous than the night before but very satisfying. Aggie put on her robe and made coffee and buttered toast for them both while Jack was taking a shower. Sitting on the couch they demolished both in short order and Jack rose to make his way to the office. Weekdays and weekends seemed to blend together for his workload.

He kissed the top of Aggie's head and said, "Thanks for an amazing night. It was extra special."

Aggie said, "It was. Thanks for a great time Jack, and listening."

Jack smiled as he reached the door. "Keep me posted won't you. I'm there for you if you need me."

"Thanks. Bye."

The door closed and Aggie heard Jack clattering down the stairs. There were times, she had to admit, when having someone care for you was both appealing and comforting. She tried to dismiss the thought by owning to the possibility that she was showing signs of growing old. But, yes, sometimes it did feel good. She decided to go back to bed for an hour because there was still plenty of time before she had to meet with Maisie. She set the alarm and soon sank into a light doze.

An hour later, she climbed out of bed feeling thoroughly refreshed and in hardly any pain. She showered and dressed in readiness for her meeting with Maisie, a meeting that was not at the top of her happy to do list. She decided to dispense with the sling. While getting ready she had mentally covered the ground that she would venture across with Maisie.

She walked to the diner, taking in the light breeze and enjoying the hazy sunlight and ignoring the modest but noisy traffic Once inside the diner, she could see that she was the first to arrive and asked for a relatively secluded booth, saying that she was waiting for a friend. With something of a start, it occurred to her that Maisie was meeting her on a Sunday. Surely David was back. He probably did not work at the weekend, in which case she wondered how difficult it had been for Maisie to meet up with her. Anyway, Maisie had appeared in the doorway and so she would soon get the answer to that. Maisie was dressed in black jeans, black boots, black shirt and a leather jacket.

The black was relieved by a thick silver chain necklace. She smiled as she came over and hugged Aggie but her face looked tired and strained.

She said, "We finally made it then."

Aggie said, "We did. How are you holding up?"

"Oh, I've been better. But there it is."

A waiter in a white shirt and black vest came to the table and they ordered coffee with omelets and English muffins.

Aggie said, "Shall we wait to eat first before we talk?"

"No. I've been going crazy just thinking about all of this. I want to get it over with."

Aggie said, "This is a Sunday. Isn't David at home?"

"Yes, he is. I told him that I was meeting you."

Aggie looked askance.

"Really? Is that OK?"

"You know, Aggie, I don't care anymore. He can think what he likes."

Their coffees arrived and they both took some sips. Maisie looked at Aggie with wary eyes.

"Not good news is it?"

"I'm sorry, Maisie. No, it's not."

"Is there a good news, bad news scenario?"

Aggie felt very unhappy, "No. I'm afraid not."

"OK." Tears welled up and she quickly brushed them away. "Tell me then."

Aggie took a deep breath, "Well, I am almost positive that David has a second family."

Maisie put both hands up to her face and turned very pale. She said, "I thought you were going to say he's having an affair. You know, the usual. But a second…" Her voice tailed off and tears once again washed the edges of her eyes. "You said, almost. Does that mean that you are not absolutely sure?"

"Maisie, I would have liked to have done a little more because I like to be thorough. There is little doubt. Let me tell you what I have found out and you can be the judge."

Their omelets arrived but they ignored them. Aggie decided not to mention that David had threatened her because it would just add to her misery and achieve nothing.

She began by asking a question.

"Did David ever tell you why he left Turner and Bowden?"

"Why he left? No. He just said that he wanted to work for himself. He did not like the lack of freedom there. He said that Delaware had opportunities in his new line of work." Maisie reflected for a moment. "I wasn't interested in all of that. Maybe, I should have been. He has never shown the slightest interest in my books. People live that way, you know."

"Yes. I asked because the job at Turner and Bowden must have been lucrative and it is not easy to start up on your own."

Maisie sighed, "Yes, I suppose that I should have paid more attention to it."

Aggie said, "He didn't have to leave them, did he?"

Maisie looked puzzled. "I don't think so, why?"

"No reason. As you say, he probably wanted some kind of autonomy."

Maisie was silent so Aggie began, "OK. As you know, I checked on both his offices. The one in Queens has the name of his company on the window but the one in Delaware does not. He shares space there with some kind of talent agency and uses it on occasion. It seems like a pied-à-terre but he does go there and, of course, sharing keeps the costs down. I could not find any company apartment. The address that you gave me does exist but the apartments there are all residential with no evidence of David's company. That means that he has to stay somewhere else."

Maisie said, "Did you check all the names at that address? He may have used other names, mine for instance?"

"I did. I photographed all of them and went through the lot. I also spoke to a super who had never seen David."

"He also likes Days Inn hotels so that is a possibility."

Aggie realized that Maisie was looking at ways to avoid the truth. "It is. But I followed him after work one day and he eventually finished up at a suburban house. Parked in the drive."

Maisie looked distraught. Aggie said, "Do you want me to go on?"

"Yes."

"When he parked and got out of the car, a little girl came rushing out of the house to greet him. He carried her inside."

"How old do you think?"

"Maybe around two. That sort of age."

"That would correspond to David's change of occupation. Did you see a woman?"

"No. She remained out of sight."

Maisie said, "So, a child. It need not be his."

"True. I could not confirm that. But he parked in the drive for the night and knew the kid well. I was on my way there the other night to make sure of a couple of things but I had an accident and did not get there."

Maisie looked concerned. "But you are OK though."

"Yes. Just shaken up."

Maisie poked at the omelet, not eating any. "So, at the very least, he is having an affair. Doesn't seem as though he would be using a spare room or something."

"No. And there is one other thing Maisie."

Maisie said, "Oh no. What is that?"

"I looked up the owner of the house and it belongs to Elizabeth Sharkey."

Maisie was shocked. "Elizabeth?"

"I'm sorry."

Maisie said, "Oh my God. Elizabeth. I wonder how long this has been going on. I mean, I've known her for years—and so has David."

Aggie did not respond. She felt relentlessly sad.

There was a long period of silence as Maisie wrestled with her feelings.

Finally, Aggie said, "What will you do?"

The question felt silly but she had to say something.

"I don't know. Perhaps nothing."

Aggie wondered if she had misinterpreted the reply. "What do you mean?"

Maisie turned her tearful eyes up to the ceiling and then glanced around the diner. "It means status quo. I can live with it, I think."

This response was nowhere on Aggie's radar.

"Are you sure?"

"It's possible. We all know each other. Unless she wants more, like the whole package."

"You mean that you would share David?"

"Yes."

Aggie said, "I don't know what to say."

"It has sort of been at the back of my mind. You know, a way through it all where I still keep a piece."

"Would this plan be with or without David's knowledge? That you know about it?"

"That is a difficult one. Probably with. He must already know that I know, or suspect. He probably knows that you are checking him out."

Aggie thought more than probably. This was working out rather well for David.

"He still loves me you know. A lot depends on Elizabeth, I suppose."

There was an air of resignation about Maisie now. She went on, "When he is away, I can just forget about what is happening, do something interesting, not think about it." She smiled fleetingly. "Maybe there is some compensation out there."

Aggie said, "A guy you mean?"

"Yes. Who knows. This is a bit of a mess isn't it?"

She sighed and grimaced, "It's hard. We had good times and now it is mostly gone."

Aggie took her hands. "You need time to take all of this in. Give yourself some space. You need not let on just yet. Think it through. Your options are really going to be status quo or some variation of it or a clean break. You have to do what is best for you."

Maisie said, "You are right. I'll tell him we had a bite to eat to catch up and then I'll work my way through it. I've gone through bad things before and I'll do it again."

A positive gleam was beginning to germinate in Maisie's eyes. She had strength of character Aggie knew and she could see her getting on top of it all. David deserved comeuppance but that probably would not happen. Maisie gave a big sigh.

"Thanks for this Aggie. It could have gone on for years. I wanted to know. I'd like to meet up and buy you dinner in a week or two. Let you know what is going on."

Aggie said, "Great. I would like that."

"Right. I'll be off then. Oh, let me pay."

Aggie said, "No, I'll take care of it."

They both stood, briefly hugged and then Maisie was gone. Aggie sat down, feeling wiped out.

The waiter came over and gazed at the full plates as he placed the check on the table.

"Have you finished, ma'am?"
Aggie said, "Yes, thanks. Bad day."
She paid out front and then stepped into the fresh, afternoon air.

Chapter 36

Aggie walked briskly towards her apartment, again promising herself that she needed some cardio work at the gym. There was no room in her apartment for a treadmill or anything useful for the exercise that she needed. As she reached the last block of her walk, she was joined by someone else walking beside her. She turned briefly and saw that it was David. There was nothing about his demeanor that was threatening but she prepared herself for any kind of violence.

He said, "I want to speak to you."

Aggie responded, without slowing down, "You are speaking to me."

They were close to her apartment now. David said, "Can I come up?"

"No way."

They paused at the entrance to her walk up.

He said, "What did you talk about, with Maisie today?"

"None of your business, David."

"It is my business. You know it is."

He moved very slightly to impede her progress into the doorway.

"When I talk to a friend that is our business. I don't repeat any of our conversations to someone else. Especially if it is you."

He ignored her, "I have to know. Did you say anything about Delaware?" He looked drawn and now, vaguely belligerent.

"David, you are a bully. I never knew that about you. Leave me alone. In fact, why don't you fuck off."

David looked angry. He moved to block her entrance to the building.

Aggie said, "Like to push women around, do you?"

Anger and frustration flashed across his features.

Just then, a third presence made itself known when a lilting, deep voice was heard.

"Hi Aggie. Any trouble here?"

Cedric had arrived silently beside her, big and powerful, looking disarmingly at David.

David looked shocked and disoriented.

Aggie said, "No, Cedric. David was just leaving. Fucking off, as it were."

David gave her a quick, troubled glance, turned and scuttled away.

Aggie looked at Cedric and the huge smile on his face. "Thank you, Cedric. That was most timely."

"My pleasure Aggie. Have a good day."

He slipped effortlessly away along the sidewalk.

Aggie went through the building doorway and was soon in her apartment. Interesting. David had followed her to the diner. He was now really worried about his exposure. Serves him right. Let him worry. She wondered whether one ever fully knows another person. David still does not have an answer. Maisie could decide when that should be. Aggie thought a clean break was the way to go. She doubted that David would ever be a worthwhile partner again. Maisie would eventually be a happier person without him. All Aggie could do now was wait and see. She found herself considering whether David could have been the driver of the other car but she still could not see him having the mettle for that kind of behavior but, anything is possible. She felt that she just didn't know him well enough to have an informed opinion.

Chapter 37

Aggie spent the rest of the day reading and watching TV. She needed a break. She was supposed to have eaten out but that had not worked out too well. She had no real appetite so just dipped odd vegetables into a blue cheese dressing that she was trying out. Coupled with a glass of wine, it went down well.

The next day, Monday, she was surprised by an early telephone call. It turned out to be from Cat Jensen who said that Lisa Begu was ready to talk to her. The ground rules were that Cat Jensen had to be present and that, if at any time Lisa Begu felt uncomfortable, the meeting would be over. Aggie agreed enthusiastically with the limitations and, after putting the phone down, felt in a buoyant mood. Handled correctly, this meeting could lead to something good. They had chosen midday as a reasonable time to meet up.

After a light breakfast and some rather aimless pottering around, Aggie was ready to go to the gym. The morning had been defined by a light drizzle which had now stopped, leaving wet sidewalks and cloud filtered sunlight. She walked to the gym and upon entering, spotted Cat Jensen and another, small woman standing behind the counter. The other woman could be described as petite with pretty Eastern European features and long, dark hair fashioned into a pony tail. Cat Jensen introduced her as Lisa Begu and asked that they move away from the counter to a quieter place behind all of the machines, which were in use. They stood rather awkwardly in a small area by a window and Aggie introduced herself and said, without any preamble,

"It is my understanding that you were assaulted in some way in the recent past."

Lisa Begu's eyes widened a fraction and she spoke in a quiet voice with a faint accent.

"Oh. Where did you get that idea?"

Aggie said, "I was told by another woman who had a similar experience."

"Really? Who was that?"

"Sorry, but I can't release her name at this point."

Lisa Begu said, "You are saying that she knows me?"

"Well, more likely knows of you, I think, through this gym. She also knew that you had been through a similar experience to hers. By that, I mean an assault by a sexual predator."

Lisa Begu looked away and seemed to be pulling up old memories which, by her unhappy expression, were unpleasant.

"I was attacked, yes. What's all this in aid of?"

"I am investigating the guy who did it and, in fact, who attacked several women, including me."

"You were attacked by him?"

"Yes. In my apartment about three weeks ago."

"When you say investigating, what do you mean? You are not a cop."

Aggie sighed. She sensed that this was an important moment. "I am trying to get him into court. I want him put away where he belongs."

"Ah. You want my help. That's what you are doing here."

She looked at Cat Jensen. "I don't like this. I want to forget all of it."

Cat Jensen turned her attention to Aggie, "I think we are done here. Lisa has had enough."

Aggie smiled in what she hoped was a sympathetic way. "OK. But can I ask a couple of questions before I go?"

Lisa Begu looked doubtful but said, "Yes, if you like. Go ahead."

"When did your attack take place?"

"About fifteen months ago. It was in Central Park. I was walking home after a party."

"You didn't report it or try to get this guy caught?"

She closed her eyes momentarily. "I just wanted to forget it. It was very frightening. I wanted it gone, never wanted to think about it again."

Aggie paused for a few moments. When she had mentioned this woman's name to Jonathan, he had not heard of her. That did not preclude a fixer being involved. "Please do not be offended by this but did you receive any cash from anyone after the attack?"

"Cash? What for? I don't know what you mean."

"Well, there have been several attacks on women by this guy. Each of those women, as far as I can make out, was paid to be quiet. To go away, in fact."

"What? Nothing like that happened to me."

Aggie realized that Lisa Begu wanted to forget and consequently, turned out to be an easy target. She said, "OK. It was a question that I had to ask. Thank you." Clearly, this situation was delicate and, if she wanted to get anything out of it, she had to proceed with care. She continued, "Look, I know that this is really hard for you. Dragging up the past in a bad way. Let's leave it at that. Would you, at least, give some thought to helping me with this. That's all I ask. I want to see justice done."

Cat Jensen put her arm around her partner. "OK. We will give it some thought. That's enough for now."

Aggie took her leave and was soon on her way home.

As she walked, she ran her mind over the meeting. At least there had been a meeting. Nothing that new really, just the same pattern and the Toomeys had not even had to cover it up. There was a faint chance that Lisa Begu would help her and go to court but she thought that she wouldn't hold her breath. Lisa Begu was quiet, did not like the spotlight and was protected by a rather dominant Cat Jensen. One way to go in all of this was to visit or call Katherine Toomey and let her think that she was closing in on her son. Aggie knew that this was a tad vengeful but she wanted to rattle that cage, shake up that cloistered, self-satisfied, smug existence.

Yes, she thought, that would be on the agenda, and soon.

Chapter 38

Apart from writing up her notes on the Begu meeting, Aggie had a quiet day, reading and catching up on some politics on TV. She ate a fresh fruit and yogurt meal in the evening and decided to hit bottled water instead of wine.

The next morning, she contemplated her prospective call to Katherine Toomey. It still felt a little unwise and more than a trifle malicious but she felt compelled to do it. She called the number. The call was answered quickly. Clearly, she had not checked the ID.

"Katherine Toomey."

"This is Agnes Trout. You might remember me."

"I... I know who you are. What do you want?" Already, the voice radiated that 'I wish I hadn't answered the phone' quality.

"I want to talk about your son. You know, the pervert."

There was a sharp intake of breath. "What's this about. You after money or something?"

"No. I don't need your money. I just wanted you to know that he will be going to jail."

"What do you mean?"

"What I mean is that I have put a case together now. He will be put away without question."

"You have a case? What's the matter with you?"

"Nothing. I want him in prison where he belongs. Hopefully, a nasty one."

"You are crazy, do you know that?"

"It's your fault, your responsibility. Always protecting him."

Katherine Toomey sounded angry, "So what. Do you think I care?"

Aggie said, "I am sure that you don't. But you might enjoy the publicity."

There was an immediate response as Katherine Toomey raised her voice.

"Oh, I see. You are getting at me or, so you think. Some sort of stupid crusade. Makes you feel good does it? In your little world."

"It does. You are as bad as he is. You know what he's like and you still cover for him, just to protect yourself."

"Well, good for you. Have your fun. I don't give a damn." After a significant pause, she added, "Do your best, you bitch."

Aggie said, "There is no answer to that."

There was a protracted silence and then Katherine Toomey said, "Don't think that you won't pay for this. I'll see to it that you do."

The phone went dead.

Aggie allowed herself some sarcasm.

That went well. Stirred the shit up there.

Not quite what she had envisioned but she couldn't take it back. She had achieved something but she didn't know what. All in all, it felt a bit hollow.

She felt at a bit of a loss and decided to take another look at Parker, the dentist. There seemed to be plenty of evidence, with all his surreptitious comings and goings, that he was having an affair with Sandra Taylor and that had come to an end at some point, before she was murdered, although, it was not quite clear when it petered out. With some relatively easy Internet research, Aggie determined that Parker was married with a ten-year-old child which accounted for all of the secrecy.

That seemed to be it. Nothing very exciting, just a run of the mill affair and everyone moving on except the unfortunate Sandra Taylor. Aggie was no nearer to solving that one, except for the vague idea that the Toomeys somehow shut her up. She really wanted to see some justice there and resolved not to let it go. She wondered if it was worth talking to the cops who had looked into the killing. Maybe. She put it on the back burner for the time being. She thought that another call to Parker might give her some more insight. She could ask if he knew of any boyfriends. He might admit that he had been one of them and might know if Sandra Taylor was working on acquiring some more ready money. That began to sound promising. She would give it a shot in the next day or so.

Chapter 39

Dougal Toomey was feeling rather down. Not exactly depressed but he thought that nothing was going his way. The world was against him and he wondered where all the breaks were. Surely, things were meant to go one's way just once in a while. He had been discharged from the hospital and was in his familiar mode of downing several beers while watching Survivor and Wheel of Fortune on TV. If he felt like educating himself, the urge to do so coming upon him on occasion, he watched Swamp People or Mountain Men. He saw himself in a different life as living off the land, being self-sufficient, strong and resourceful. If only things had gone his way for once.

Anyway, his leg was still in a cast and still itched and even hurt when he put any weight on it. He was stuck with it for at least another month and had been given a pair of crutches to move about on. Stairs were immensely difficult to negotiate but he managed, although his armpits were feeling sore from the crutch tops supporting his weight. He had been advised to go to the hospital twice a week for some silly kind of therapy to do with muscle loss. Fuck that.

There were big changes coming in his life. His worthless mother, who had eventually covered his hospital bills, had informed him that he had to move. He had to leave his apartment, leave the city and, in fact, leave the country. Her telephone call had sounded especially cold and distant. Once again, he dwelt on the lack of motherly feelings coming his way. Couldn't she, at least, sound warm once in a while? He had no feelings for her, any that mattered anyway, so he supposed that it all cancelled out in the general scheme of things. She said that the private investigator, the one that hurt him unnecessarily, had a case against him. Apparently, she was not now the only woman trying to make his life a misery. There was, at least, one other vindictive woman who wanted to see his freedom taken away. What was wrong with these people? He was just having a bit of fun and now they wanted to turn his life upside down. There was a family lawyer that his mother had spoken to and he had said that the case probably would not stand up in court but he also said why take any risks? Ergo, he should skip the country to be on the safe side.

Nothing permanent, just a sort of extended vacation, maybe for two or three years until everyone had moved on. He did not like to give in like that. It was not in his nature, he knew. He had backbone. But his mother did not want the publicity. Even though he was entirely innocent, there would be a court appearance and people would draw the wrong conclusions his mother had said. She wanted none of it. For the sake of the family, i.e. her, he should take heed of the situation and do the right thing. The only good bit was that she would pay for everything or, as he well knew, his grandfather would pay for everything. Now, the only questions there seemed to be, choices really, were where would he go and when? These matters were just not easy. What would happen to all of his stuff? He had a comprehensive collection of beer mats and another of old sneakers. Where would they go? Would he take them with him? Yes, he would take everything. He would not be paying for it. At least his passport was in order and he would continue to receive an allowance, so no real worries. He would need to have his possessions put in storage at his destination and he would spend a bit of time in a hotel. As he finished another beer, he began to slide into an alcoholic doze, thinking of his future destination. Maybe Canada, Mexico, UK or even France. It began to feel like a good idea.

Chapter 40

Aggie decided to go to her gym in the afternoon. She went through a two-hour workout that included a half-hour of kick boxing. It felt especially good and had an almost cleansing effect on her body. She would, no doubt, feel it the next day but it was unquestionably worth the effort. She went home for her shower and, after a light meal of soup and buttered toast, spent the evening reading.

The next day, after an early orange juice and cereal, Aggie called Dr. Parker. To her surprise, he answered quickly. Not so busy this morning, then.

She said, "Hi Dr. Parker. This is Agnes Trout. I don't know if you remember me. I dropped by last week."

"Ah. Ms. Trout. Yes, I remember you, of course. How are things?"

"Good. I'm calling about Sandra Taylor. Just a couple of things."

There was a prolonged silence. "I thought we had been over all of that. What more is there to say?"

Aggie said, "Well, I remember you indicating that you thought that she was rather lonely."

"Did I?"

"I think so. I wondered if she ever gave you any indication of boyfriends."

"Boyfriends?"

"I mean, did she tell you about any of them, if she had any?"

Silence again. "I wasn't really party to her relationships. She may have mentioned someone now and again but I don't recall too much about that. Except, of course, the guy she took off with."

"So, no names. Nothing definite?"

"No, I don't think so. What are you looking for?"

Time for directness and to stir the pot.

"The person that killed her. I'm thinking that it might have been a boyfriend."

"Really?"

"Yes. There is another possibility though."

"And what is that?"

"She could have been short of cash. She could have been asking someone for money."

"What? You mean a shakedown? I can't imagine that."

"I don't know. I'm checking out anything I can think of. You said you didn't know about her finances I seem to remember."

"That is true. As I said, she seemed to be managing. A house and all that." He paused.

"The boyfriend thing. Why would a boyfriend kill her?"

"I don't know. I'm looking for answers. You said she was a good person."

"She was."

"It just seems sad that no one has been caught for her murder."

"It is sad but isn't it up to the cops to find whoever did it?"

"Yes, it is. You're right. I am just doing my own thing. You know, looking for justice."

"Well, good luck with that. Talk about a cold case." Parker paused. "But worth doing if you can get somewhere."

Aggie said, "I'll keep trying. Got a couple of people to talk to. Anyway, thanks for your time."

"OK. Bye".

They rang off.

Aggie thought not too productive. Dr. Parker had no intention of admitting to an affair, even though it must have been clear that Aggie was guessing there had been one. She supposed that it was not the sort of thing to admit to. In fact, Dr. Parker was careful about admitting to anything. She needed a quick shop and so walked to her local supermarket and picked up a few groceries. Never one of her favorite activities, she was glad to pay, get out quickly and go back to her apartment. Immediately, she noticed a message on her home phone. She clicked on messages and was surprised to hear Dr. Parker's voice. He said that he had checked through his Human Resources files and had some extra information about Sandra Taylor. He didn't know if it would be helpful but there was some financial information and a bit about mortgage guarantors and addresses. He also said that he could xerox and send the file to Aggie but, since it was a decent size, that would have to be a last resort. If necessary, though, he would do it. That was it.

Aggie mulled it over for a while and thought that she could combine a trip to read or get the files and try to talk to the original investigating officer of the Sandra Taylor murder. He might be forthcoming, or not. It was worth a try though. She called Jack and, after some initial chatting about his case with which he was finally done, he gave her the name of the cop that she wanted to talk to. He was George Millman who had since retired. She thanked Jack, saying that she intended tracking him down and seeing if he could give her any useful information.

She took less than fifteen minutes to find him and get an address and phone number in Point Pleasant at the Jersey shore. So, Parker's dental practice and George Millman were close enough for her to cover both in a single trip. All that she had to do, was drop by Dr. Parker for a look at the files and then go on to talk to the cop. She could probably get all of the information needed from a phone call to the cop but a face to face always trumped a phone call. She would take a chance that he was home because she liked the element of surprise. Next, she called Dr. Parker.

"Dr. Parker. Agnes Trout."

"Oh. Great. You got my message then."

"Yes. Do you think that the files will help me?"

"They might. I don't know what you are looking for but I thought anything is better than nothing."

"I would like to see them."

"Well, as I said, it would be a chore to xerox them all to you. Unless I was selective and just picked out a few details."

Aggie said, "No, that's OK. I can come by and take a look."

"Good. When would that be?"

Aggie paused.

"No time like the present. How about later today."

"Today? That's perfect. I have a couple of patients this afternoon. How about after office hours, say 6:00 or 6:30?"

Aggie said, "Great, I'll be there." They rang off.

So far, so good. Aggie would see Dr. Parker first and then drop by the cop's place and then drive back.

Suddenly, it dawned on her. Drive back. She had no car. Next step was to secure a rental. Suddenly, it was all go and she loved the heightened activity. Soon, she had a 24-hour rental Camry. She would pick it up at an agency about twenty blocks away. Walking distance. Around 4 pm would work. Over the last week, she had received two inquiries about taking on some new PI work. Not the kind that she liked. They were the inevitable infidelity bummers. But work was work and she needed it so, in the next week or so she would interview two new clients.

She grabbed a quick lunch of soup again and a chunk of French baguette from the supermarket and began to get ready for her trip. She called Jonathan to bring him up to date. He answered almost immediately.

"Aggie."

"Yes. How are you Jonathan?"

"Getting by. Nothing too exciting. I have had one or two things to take care of."

Aggie smiled, "Ever vague, of course. One day you really will tell me what you do all day."

"All very boring Aggie. Not as exciting as your lifestyle. That's for sure."

"Ha. Anyway, I'm calling to let you know what I am doing. I know you are dying to know."

"I am. What have you got lined up?"

"I am off to look at the ocean again."

"Vacation time?"

"No. You are not always funny you know. I am going to the Jersey shore to follow up on Sandra Taylor."

"Ah. Your praiseworthy pursuit of justice. I mean that in the best possible way."

"I know. Thank you. Yes, I want to interview the lead investigator in charge of her murder."

"You managed to arrange that?"

"Not really. He has retired and I am going to call on him."

Jonathan chuckled, "The old surprise tactic."

"I hope so. I don't know what to expect but it can only help."

"Well, have a safe trip."

"Oh, and I am going to see that dentist as well."

"What dentist?"

"The one that Sandra Taylor worked for. You know, Dr. Parker, the one I think was having an affair with her."

"Right. And what does he have to offer?"

"He told me that he has some files on Sandra Taylor. Personnel stuff but it sounded useful."

"Good, then. When do you see him?"

"At the end of office hours. Around 6:00/6:30. I thought I'd see him first and then the cop."

"OK Aggie. Thanks for calling. Take care and drive safely."

Of course, he was nudging her about 'the crash'.

"I will."

"And don't forget that dinner."

Then he was gone.

She spent an hour or so getting ready for her trip and after a brisk walk to the rental agency, was in the driver's seat of a black Toyota Camry and on her way to the shore in reasonable comfort. She stopped briefly at a Starbucks for a coffee and pound cake and arrived at the dental practice at just after 6 pm. Perfect timing. She parked her car next to the only car in the car park, Dr. Parker's black Highlander and walked around to the entrance. Once again, the old-fashioned doorbell clanged and she entered the reception area. There were no patients and the receptionist must have left for the day. The door to the surgery rooms opened and Dr. Parker emerged, looking cheerful and Aggie supposed, wearing his sympathetically earnest expression. He had on a white lab coat and, surprisingly, a dark blue shirt and a long light blue tie instead of an open neck.

"Ah. Ms. Trout. Do come into the back. I have an office back there."

Aggie followed him through into a spacious hallway with two surgical rooms on either side to an airy room at the back of the building with windows on two sides. She noticed a metal back door at the end of the hallway. Parker's office contained bookshelves on two walls, a large oak desk, two easy chairs and two hard chairs next to a coffee table. In the corner, was a coffee and cold-water machine with stacks of paper cups and some mugs, next to a filing cabinet. Aggie's first thought was that the filing cabinet looked rather small for a thriving dental practice, if it was thriving. He was the only dentist, it seemed, but he would bring in dental hygienists as needed and probably had dental assistants also. Dr. Parker indicated one of the easy chairs for Aggie to sit.

He said, "Well, now, I hope you had a pleasant trip."

Aggie said, "I did. It was a nice day for driving."

"Good. I've got some coffee ready, if you would like some."

"I just had some, thanks."

Parker looked disappointed.

"OK. I'll have a small one."

Parker came from the coffee machine and put down two mugs of coffee. The one next to Aggie was only half full.

Parker said, "Right, the file."

He went to the small filing cabinet and dug out a blue folder which was of average thickness and brought it over to Aggie, as she sipped her coffee. "Here it is. I don't know how helpful it will be but have a look anyway."

Aggie took the folder and opened it on her lap. There were several pages. Her first thought was why couldn't this guy have shown me this before? The first couple of pages had Sandra Taylor's resume, name and address. She had graduated college from Lafayette, as Georgia Kaplan with decent grades and had worked in a library, a clothing store, a medical practice and Dr. Parker's dental practice. She had volunteered at a local hospital and had even ridden with an ambulance crew. She had a mortgage with Wells Fargo for the small house in Seaside Heights and, as Aggie combed through the paperwork, she saw that the guarantor for the mortgage was Dr. Parker.

As she drained her coffee, Aggie thought that to be an interesting and curious development.

She looked up at him. "It states here that you were her guarantor for the mortgage. You might have told me."

Parker sat in the other easy chair watching her. "I might have but I didn't, my dear."

Aggie was not feeling right, a little woozy. Parker's voice sounded very loud. She did not like the 'my dear' bit. Patronizing, she thought. Suddenly, she flopped back in the chair, her cheeks felt flushed and her arms and legs felt very weak, almost floppy.

She wondered what was going on. She looked over at Dr. Parker who was gazing at her with mild disinterest.

He said, "Something wrong? A little dizzy perhaps?"

Aggie stared up at the ceiling, feeling helpless. Her lips tried to form words but could not. Her brain though, still felt active, unhindered.

Dr. Parker said, "Well now, Ms. Trout, you have been rather a nuisance to me. In fact, you have been a fucking pain in the neck. I really don't like people interfering in my affairs." He laughed, "That was good wasn't it? My affairs or, rather, one affair."

Aggie could barely move anything now.

Parker got up and leaned over her staring into her eyes.

"I've given you a little something to keep you quiet. You look a bit fit and I do not want to mess with that. You are very attractive too. I'm really tempted to enjoy myself but I have to be practical and deal with you. A pity, because you look worth the effort."

Aggie could only listen and make very small movements.

Parker said, "You might like to know, my dear, just so that you don't go off into that good night without full knowledge of the situation. I killed Sandra Taylor. Yes, I did it because she threatened to blackmail me. Good riddance. She served a purpose. Then you had to come along poking around in things that are none of your business. You should have left well alone but you are not put off so easily, are you?"

He leaned over her again. "Pretty eyes haven't you. What a waste. Anyway, I paid some idiot a lot of money to warn you off. Did not work, of course, and now he's gone. God knows where."

He straightened up and glanced out of the window into the distance, whistling softly. Then he turned his gaze back to Aggie. "You know, I tried to get rid of you last week and that was a failure too. Yes, you were lucky and you cost me a bomb for the damage to the van. But here we are, at last. I don't like you and, my dear, I want you gone."

He stood, looking down at her for a few moments. "You have a minute or two to contemplate your end."

He smiled smugly, "Not much of a future in that is there!" He shook his head. "Sometimes I am so funny."

He left the room abruptly for about five minutes and came back with a hypodermic. "This, my dear Ms. Trout, will put you to sleep nicely. If you wake up, which you won't, you will be in a lake."

He leaned further over Aggie and injected her forearm, slipping her into unconsciousness.

He left the room, went through the back door, checked the car park in the failing light, opened the back door of his car and came back. He had a large sheet which he wrapped around Aggie with some difficulty. He then pulled her up from the chair and carried her in a fireman's lift over his shoulder out to his car. He pushed her unceremoniously into the back seat and closed the door.

Glancing over at the Camry, he thought it needed to go. The sooner, the better.

He went back inside and picked up Aggie's purse, checked through it absent mindedly, took it out to his car and lobbed it in the back. Ready to go. He knew the best lake for the job. Secluded and deep. Just then, a car, another Highlander, came into the car park and drew up behind his car sideways on.

What the hell is this, he thought, as 'sorry we are closed' messages flashed through his mind.

The freshly arrived car door opened and a very large man with a big smile climbed out and walked over to him.

"Good evening. Dr. Parker, I presume. My name is Cedric."

Parker looked nonplussed. "That is correct. What do you want?"

The eyes fixed on Parker and bored into him.

"Looking for Agnes Trout. Where is she?"

Parker's eyes flicked to his car before he could stop them.

The big man reached out and grabbed Parker's tie and dragged him forwards as he reached out with the other hand and opened the back door of the car. He glanced inside, lifted the sheet, saw Aggie and felt her pulse; strong and OK.

He closed the door, glared angrily at Parker and lifted him up to his full height by means of his tie and then struck his right cheekbone with back of his hand, which made a loud crunching sound, and then followed that with a blow to the left cheekbone coming back the other way. Parker collapsed unconscious and the big man tossed him aside like a sack of rocks. He opened the car door again and very gently lifted Aggie out and put her in the back of the other Highlander. He made sure that she was comfortable, retrieved her purse from the other car and placed it next to her. He made sure that her head was supported and then used the safety belt to secure her. He then called the local police and gave them a brief rundown on what had happened. He gave them Jonathan's phone number and said that he would call first thing in the morning to give a full account of all the circumstances. Cedric turned to the limp figure on the paving and gave it three bad intention kicks that produced the sounds of a broken bone or two. He checked the Camry, took out the rental documents and locked it. He then climbed into the Highlander and pulled out of the car park.

Chapter 41

Cedric drove carefully, making sure that there were no sudden movements that would make Aggie uncomfortable. He called Jonathan and brought him up to date. Towards the end of the journey, she began to stir and make an occasional sighing sound and as he pulled into Jonathan's building car park, she was slowly regaining consciousness. Cedric parked and gently freed Aggie from the back seat and, with her purse, carried her to the service elevator and up to Jonathan's apartment. Jonathan met him at the door and Cedric carried her into the spare bedroom, depositing her tenderly on the bed. Jonathan covered her with a blanket, thanked Cedric warmly and as he left, settled in a chair next to the bed to wait for Aggie's full return to wakefulness.

About an hour later, she stirred positively and tried to sit up. Jonathan assisted her and lifted the pillows behind her.

"Well now, you have come to life at last."

Aggie felt disoriented and found it difficult to take everything in. "How did I get here?"

Jonathan smiled, "You came on the Cedric express. He took care of you."

"What time is it?"

"Around midnight. Let me get a drink. You must be parched."

He left briefly and returned with some orange juice. Aggie sipped it, enjoying the effect on her dry mouth.

"What happened exactly. I remember passing out with that creep hanging over me."

Jonathan looked angry. "As far as I know, he drugged you somehow and was carting you off to what I imagine, was an unpleasant fate. Probably going to bury you somewhere."

"Yes, I remember now. He told me that he killed Sandra Taylor and he was the one who forced me off the road. He must have waited outside my apartment until I showed up to go to Delaware. He had my car torched by that Peachy guy too, so Peachy must have lied to you."

"Yes, so it seems. Well, by now Parker is in custody I would think."

"How? Where were the cops?"

"Cedric left Parker taking a nap in his car park and called the local cops. I will talk to them in the morning."

"Wish I could have hurt him. He was actually going to kill me."

Jonathan smiled, "Cedric has ensured that he is in some reasonable discomfort. He will not feel too active for some time."

"I hope that he pays for Sandra Taylor's murder."

"I'll do what I can. At the very least, he is involved in kidnapping you and attempted murder, if intent can be shown. Would you like some coffee or a bite to eat?"

"Not coffee, I think. He drugged my coffee and injected me with something. More juice please."

Jonathan went off again and Aggie reflected on the past few hours. She thought life can be so tenuous. She could be gone now because of the whim of a killer. Just for his self-preservation. She vowed to get the most out of her existence, be useful, keep in touch with friends, her parents. All of that.

Jonathan returned with more juice and some buttered toast with a small pot of preserve. "Didn't know if you'd want this. Blackcurrant."

Aggie did and ate it all with gusto.

Chapter 42

Aggie slept soundly until nearly 10:00 am. She awoke without the headache that was starting just before she went to sleep. She got up, called to Jonathan, who was in the living room reading, that she was going to shower. After showering she put on her used clothing and joined Jonathan in the living room. She was happy now, to have morning coffee.

Jonathan said, "You will be glad to know, or at least, I hope you will, that I have cleared up a few things."

Aggie looked at him over the rim of her cup.

He said, "First, I have sent the rental keys to the agency. They will pick up the rental at the shore. They will charge you a fee though."

"Great. Thanks for that."

"Second, Parker is in the hospital. He sustained a concussion, a cracked orbital cheekbone and a couple of broken ribs. He works in a hazardous area, apparently."

Aggie said, "Good. I hope he suffers."

"I spoke to the cops and Parker will face a number of charges with respect to his treatment of you. You have to go down there again as soon as possible to make a full statement. They are going to reopen the Sandra Taylor case. The guy who worked with Millman is still active and he will follow up. Early days yet, but promising. They will only have your statement but the local press is on it which might help."

"I hope they get him."

"Well, whatever happens, Parker is due for plenty of jail time."

"Good."

Jonathan said, "When you are up for it, I'll run you down there. I think that you should avoid driving cars for a while, not that you have one yet."

Aggie smiled, "Not lucky, am I? Do you think that we should get it over with?"

"I do. How about this afternoon?"

"OK. I'll drop by my apartment and then I'll be set."

Aggie went back to her apartment to get a change of clothing and was soon ready for the trip to the shore. Jonathan picked her up and she spent over two hours with the cops, answering questions and making a comprehensive written statement about her interactions with Parker. She would be needed in court proceedings at a later date but his future looked suitably grim and unpleasant. As for the murder of Sandra Taylor, the lead investigator, Albert Hopper, was hopeful that they could get a conviction but they needed more than Aggie's statement. There was, if seemed, no chance of a confession but they did have the circumstantial evidence of the financial arrangement and Parker's relationship with Sandra Taylor.

They were back in the city by nightfall and, before being dropped off, Aggie promised dinner with Jonathan at her apartment the following evening. He elected to bring dessert and wine. She felt exhausted and, after a perfunctory bite to eat, was soon asleep again.

At mid-morning the next day, after coffee and cereal, Aggie heard from Lisa Begu. She half expected Cat Jensen to call on her behalf but her petite partner was calling herself. She said that she fully understood what Aggie was trying to do and, although she thought that it was an admirable pursuit, to put a predator away, she could not bring herself to relive it all again. She was sorry but that was the way it was. Aggie realized that she was going to find it difficult to make Toomey pay for his assaults but she would keep trying.

Jack called to see how things were going, having a bit more time than usual to keep up to date with Aggie's activities. He was shocked and upset when she told him about the attempt on her life. He was having deep misgivings about not being there for her at the right time. Each time that she had courted danger, he had somehow been absent or late on the scene. Aggie reassured him that she had not expected any problems from her trip to see Parker and that she was fortunate that Cedric, a friend and colleague of Jonathan's, had been asked by him to monitor her activities as a precaution. Jack had no way of doing that but it proved difficult to mollify him. At least, she would be in no further danger as her cases reached their conclusion. In spite of her natural resistance, she was more than beginning to appreciate having people care about her. She had always felt a strong streak of independence and self-sufficiency but now could see those feelings coexisting with an acceptance that others had a vested interest in her safety and wellbeing. In any case, there was little she could do about it.

She spent much of the rest of the day preparing the evening dinner. It was quite refreshing to plan a meal from scratch and do some cooking. She did have to pick up some groceries from Whole Foods but it had been fairly quiet there and she was soon back in her apartment, preparing a Stroganoff to kill for. She made a broccoli and cheese soup which also contained leeks and took quite a bit of time to prepare. She kept the quantity down so that dinner would not be too much of a blowout. Late in the afternoon, her cell rang and she saw that it was Maisie. She hoped that it was not some sort of crisis as she was feeling good about the evening to come.

"Hi Maisie. How's everything?"

Maisie said, "Hi Ag. Hope you are not too busy. I just wanted to update you."

"No, I'm OK. Getting a dinner ready. I can talk."

Maisie did not show the usual interest in Aggie's evening.

"I've made a decision. I hope it's the right one."

Aggie put down the spatula with which she was stirring cream into the Stroganoff. "OK Maisie. What are you going to do?"

"Well, I've agreed to share."

"Share what? David you mean?"

"Yes."

Aggie had half expected something like this but hearing it first hand was a bit jarring.

"Wow. Are you sure? You have talked the whole thing through?"

"Yes. David came clean. The kid is his. He has been seeing Elizabeth for a while now."

Aggie thought that to be pretty obvious.

"Is Elizabeth going along with all of this?"

"Yes. She has a nuclear family after all."

"Well, yes. Part of the time anyway."

Maisie said, "You don't approve, do you?"

Aggie said, "Oh Maisie, my approval has nothing to do with it. I want you to be happy, that's all. If this works for you, that's good."

"We decided to do a trial run to see if it works. All above board."

Aggie thought that it was nice for David. He does have to support two families, though. She could see money being an issue, although Maisie had a good income from her books. Time would tell. "Well, at least you can give it a shot. If it doesn't work you can still start over. There is plenty of time. Please call me if you need to talk."

"I will. Thanks for doing this for me. It is much better now that I know what is going on. I don't have to worry all the time. I'll let you know how it goes."

"OK. Take care Maisie."

And she was gone.

Aggie let Maisie's news sink in. Her view was that this was some kind of interim measure on Maisie's part. An unusual one but, perhaps, a respite or refuge for her while she gathered her feelings and found a place for them. There was no denying the stark fact that David had betrayed her in a spectacular way and, although Maisie might bury that betrayal in some corner of her mind, she would pull it out at some point, confront it and, Aggie hoped, move on. If David and Elizabeth were half way decent human beings, Aggie imagined that they would always feel pangs of guilt during their lifetimes but, maybe not.

Enough, she thought. Status quo, it will be.

She would always be there for Maisie. Time to get ready for the evening ahead.

Chapter 43

By 7 pm Aggie had everything ready for dinner. She wore jeans, a white tee shirt and a brown vest and had bare feet. She had the soup and Stroganoff ready for the hot plates in the kitchen and had put out place settings on the coffee table next to the couch, along with wine glasses and napkins. She had never had need for a dining table and chairs; there was no room for them anyway. It came down to self-service in the kitchen followed by consumption on the couch. Take it or leave it. The smells in the kitchen were awesome and she began to look forward to a decent self cooked meal. She rarely, if ever, suffered from chef's remorse—don't fancy it once it's been cooked.

Jonathan arrived at about 7:15 pm, replete with two bottles of Shiraz and a pound cake of prodigious proportions. Under his usual black coat, he too sported jeans but with a cream tee shirt and a black sweater. They had a momentary, slightly awkward hug in the doorway before he took his bounty to the kitchen.

"Took a chance on the red," he said. "Hope it's OK."

Aggie said, "Perfect. Looking forward to it."

Jonathan said, "Smells amazing in here. Stroganoff?"

Aggie said, "You've got it. Let's have some wine."

Jonathan opened the first bottle and took it to the couch, pouring out two generous glasses. He said, "Here's to more investigations. But less dangerous ones."

Aggie responded, "Sounds good. I'm all for that. I've got a couple coming up soon. Harmless and perfectly safe, I think."

"And, of course, you will need to make a foray into the car market," he said, with a smile.

Aggie said, "Yes, sometime soon but not yet. The check for my dead Beamer is about to be cut, I think."

They sipped in agreeable silence for a few moments.

Aggie said, "Let's get started."

They stood side by side in the kitchen ladling out the soup and then returned to the couch.

"Delicious," said Jonathan. "I have a bit of information for you."

Aggie paused with her spoon in the air. "Good, I hope."

"Not especially. It seems that our predator has seen fit to depart the country."

"He's gone?"

"So it appears."

"What made him do that I wonder?"

"I understand that his mother gave him a push."

Aggie immediately knew why. She said, "That was me, I'm afraid. I called her and told her that he would be in prison soon. Said I was close, which was a bit of a stretch. She must have believed me though."

"Indeed."

"Do you know where he has gone?"

"I do. He has taken his talents to London."

They finished up the soup. Aggie said, "If he comes back, I'll still try to nail him. I won't forget."

"Of course you won't. I don't blame you."

They returned to the kitchen and put the bowls in the sink. Aggie had not invested in a dish washer yet. Maybe that would be on the horizon now. They heaped their plates with Stroganoff and saffron rice and returned to the couch.

Aggie laughed and said, " It has just dawned on me – you could have been a no-red-meat guy. I didn't think to ask."

"But then I would have missed this excellent meal. There you go."

She said, "You know, I would like to keep tabs on Toomey, if that is possible. He is not going to stay away for good."

Jonathan said, "We'll do our best. Chances are that he will not, in fact, be back."

Aggie searched Jonathan's face but detected only an air of mild innocence.

"Pity," she said.

"Indeed it is."

They finished dinner, ate only a small portion of the pound cake and Jonathan helped to clean up and wash the dishes, by which time they had started the second bottle of wine.

Aggie said, "How do you feel about a couple of personal questions? Not about your boring days but other stuff?"

"Ah. You would like to know more about me. Ask away."

"Well, here goes."

Aggie looked into the blue eyes. "Jonathan Groom, Alexander Kowolski, Henry Penn. How are you?"

Jonathan smiled approvingly, "Ah. The investigative mind is at work."

"It is. Which one are you?"

Jonathan laughed, "I am, and here comes a wonderful cliché, many people."

Aggie laughed too, "That was absolutely dreadful. You should know better. Are all of those characters friendly, good, honest people?"

"I certainly hope so."

"Enigmatic! Why would I expect anything less? We will find out, I suppose."

"Indeed, we will."

Chapter 44

After some hasty planning and a host of practical situations to sort out, Dougal Toomey eventually found himself on the way to London. In fact, the whole exercise had been completed fairly quickly. He spent less than a week in a small hotel and was finally ensconced in a decent flat, or apartment, in a place called Fulham. The apartment had a large living room, a long, narrow kitchen and, down a few steps, a bedroom and bathroom; all basically in a row. The kitchen was well equipped but he only needed a microwave and a saucepan. The apartment was on the ground floor of a Victorian building that had been renovated and was on a quiet street with a few old trees jutting out of a sidewalk that consisted of uneven flagstones with tufts of grass protruding between them. Both sides of the street were packed with parked cars with no vacant parking spaces in sight. Not that he cared. Driving was too difficult in a city and even worse in a crazy drive on the left one. The local take outs were good, especially the Indian curry houses and there were two pubs within shouting distance, The Frog and Bucket and The Royal Oak. He spent a lot of time at both, drinking IPA or Guinness and he had discovered a bottled beer called Bass, which went down very well in the apartment he now called home. Women, even British women, didn't seem to find him attractive. Hard to figure that with an American accent and all. Maybe, that would improve. The urge to engage in his normal method of communication with the opposite sex was quite strong but he did not seem to have the energy for it at present. Women needed to understand him but they never seemed to realize that just a little effort on their part could be so rewarding. He was what was known as a good catch.

Anyway, life was not too bad. His leg had finally healed and he was away from that nasty private investigator. She couldn't touch him now. Serves her right, wasting all that time on trying to spoil his lifestyle. New beginnings. Maybe, permanent new beginnings. He liked it here.

At the end of his second week of the new life, he ordered out for his weekend Indian and, soon, the delivery guy showed up with his order. Chicken curry, naan and Indian pickles. Very tasty. He had just sat down on his couch when the door buzzer went off. Without really thinking, he answered the door and was confronted with a giant of a man with a big smile.

He said, "Good evening, my name is Cedric. We met once, very briefly. I think we should have a little chat. We are about to discuss, in some depth, how you will comport yourself in the future."